MINECRAFT™

WITHER WITHOUT YOU

3

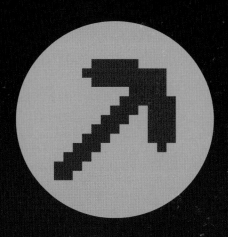

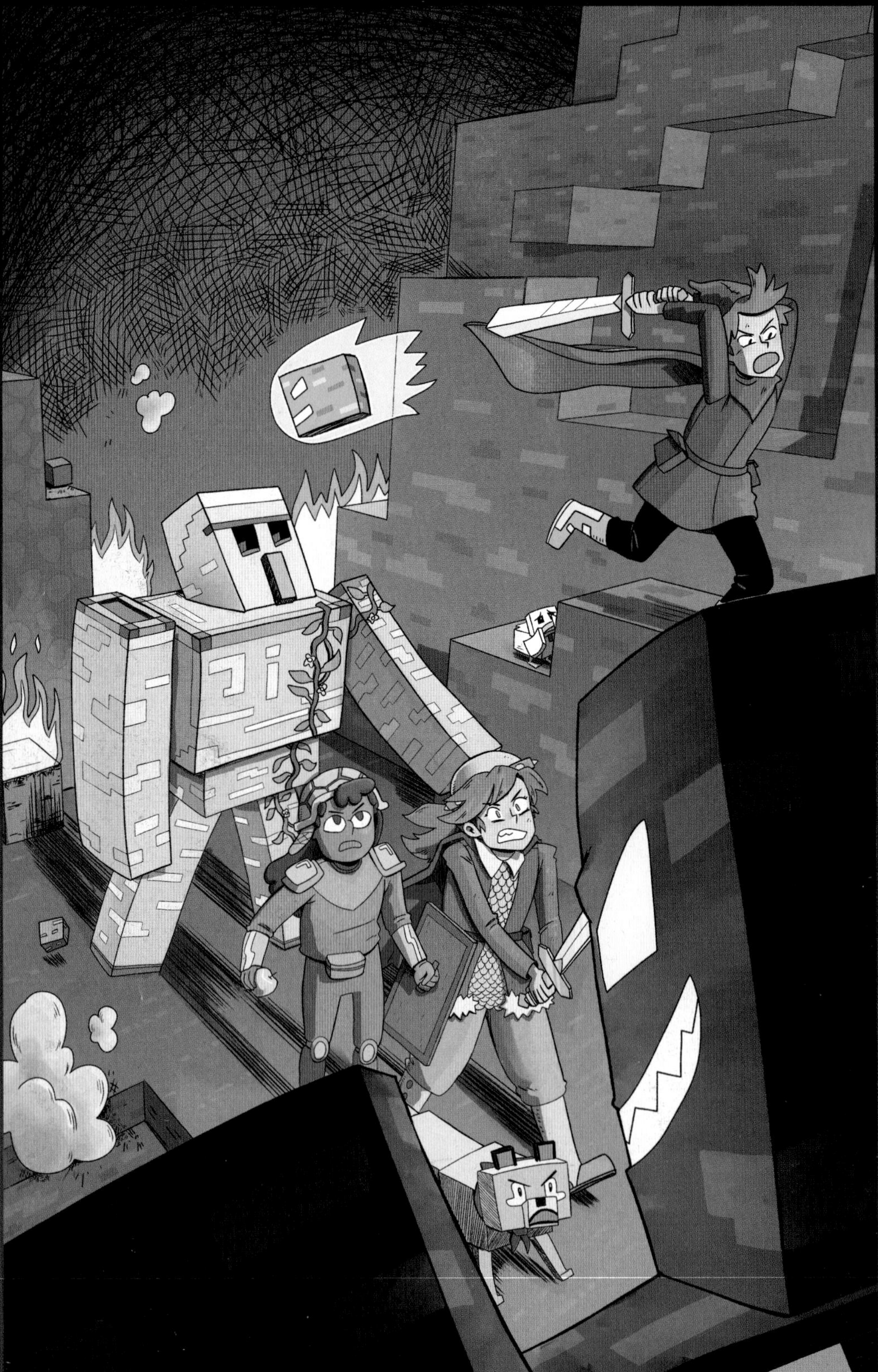

MINECRAFT
WITHER WITHOUT YOU
3

BY
KRISTEN GUDSNUK

COLOR ASSISTANT
KNACK WHITTLE

MOJ ANG STUDIOS

DARK HORSE BOOKS

PRESIDENT & PUBLISHER
MIKE RICHARDSON

EDITOR
SHANTEL LAROCQUE

ASSOCIATE EDITOR
BRETT ISRAEL

ASSISTANT EDITOR
SANJAY DHARAWAT

DESIGNER
KEITH WOOD

DIGITAL ART TECHNICIAN
SAMANTHA HUMMER

SPECIAL THANKS TO
**ALEX WILTSHIRE,
KELSEY HOWARD,** AND
SHERIN KWAN

Published by Dark Horse Books
A division of Dark Horse Comics LLC
10956 SE Main Street
Milwaukie, OR 97222

MINECRAFT.NET
DARKHORSE.COM

To find a comics shop in your area, visit ComicShopLocator.com.

First edition: May 2022
Ebook ISBN 978-1-50671-890-3
Trade paperback ISBN 978-1-50671-887-3

10 9 8 7 6 5 4 3 2 1

Printed in China

NEIL HANKERSON
Executive Vice President

TOM WEDDLE
Chief Financial Officer

DALE LAFOUNTAIN
Chief Information Officer

TIM WIESCH
Vice President of Licensing

MATT PARKINSON
Vice President of Marketing

VANESSA TODD-HOLMES
Vice President of Production and Scheduling

MARK BERNARDI
Vice President of Book Trade and Digital Sales

RANDY LAHRMAN
Vice President of Product Development

KEN LIZZI
General Counsel

DAVE MARSHALL
Editor in Chief

DAVEY ESTRADA
Editorial Director

CHRIS WARNER
Senior Books Editor

CARY GRAZZINI
Director of Specialty Projects

LIA RIBACCHI
Art Director

MATT DRYER
Director of Digital Art and Prepress

MICHAEL GOMBOS
Senior Director of Licensed Publications

KARI YADRO
Director of Custom Programs

KARI TORSON
Director of International Licensing

Library of Congress Cataloging-in-Publication Data

Names: Gudsnuk, Kristen, artist, author.
Title: Minecraft : wither without you / by Kristen Gudsnuk.
Other titles: Wither without you
Description: First edition. | Milwaukie, OR : Dark Horse Books, 2020. |
Series: Minecraft ; v. 1 | Audience: Ages 8+ | Summary: Cahira and Orion
are twin monster hunters who go on a mission to get their mentor back,
and meet Atria, a girl cursed as a monster lure, whom they convince to
join their rescue mission to use her monster-attracting abilities to
find the enchanted wither.
Identifiers: LCCN 2019053733 | ISBN 9781506708355 (trade paperback) |
ISBN 9781506708645 (epub)
Subjects: LCSH: Graphic novels.
Classification: LCC PZ7.7.G83 Min 2020 | DDC 741.5/973--dc23
LC record available at https://lccn.loc.gov/2019053733

MINECRAFT™

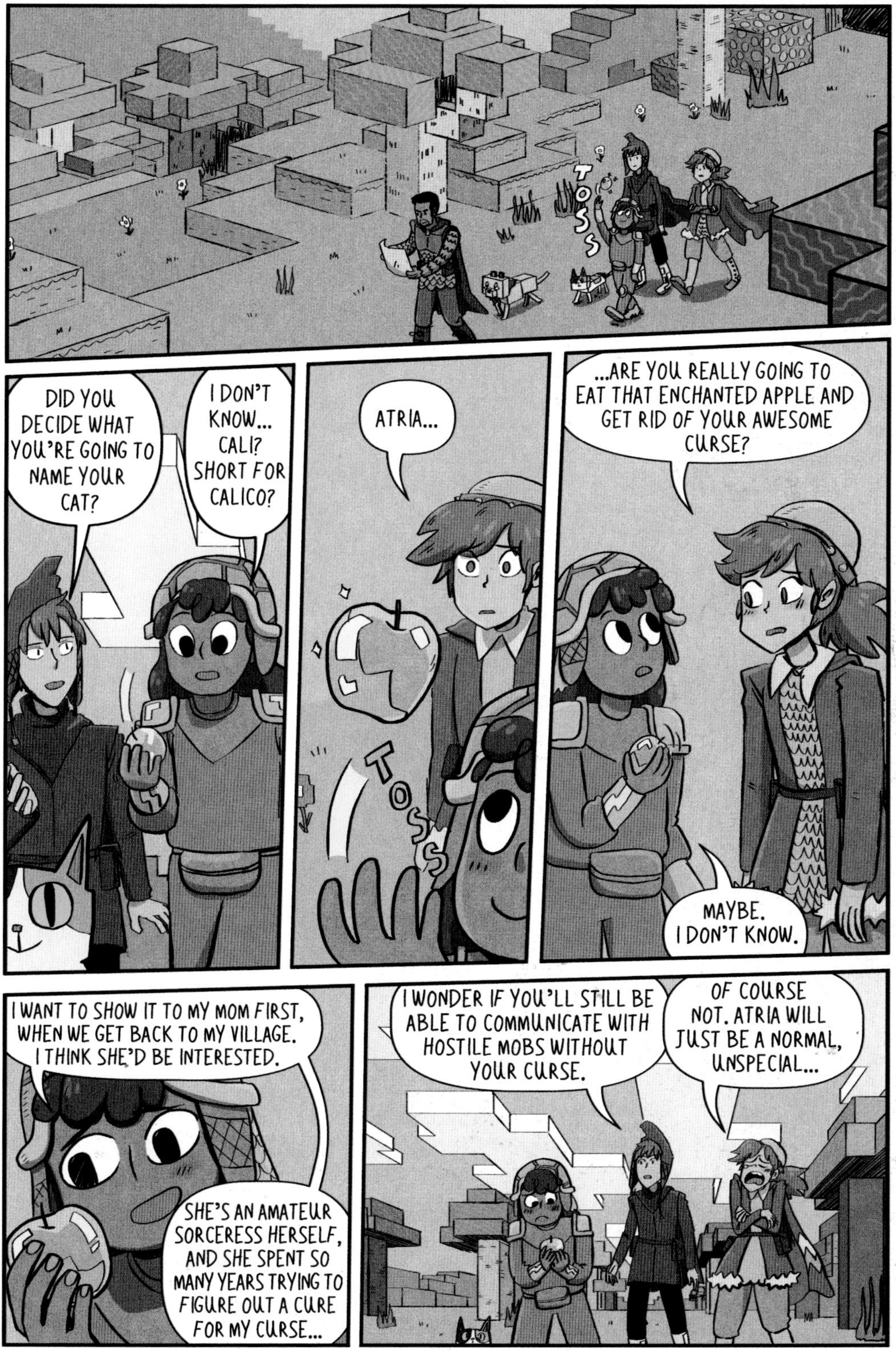
TOSS
DID YOU DECIDE WHAT YOU'RE GOING TO NAME YOUR CAT?
I DON'T KNOW... CALI? SHORT FOR CALICO?
ATRIA...
TOSS
...ARE YOU REALLY GOING TO EAT THAT ENCHANTED APPLE AND GET RID OF YOUR AWESOME CURSE?
MAYBE. I DON'T KNOW.
I WANT TO SHOW IT TO MY MOM FIRST, WHEN WE GET BACK TO MY VILLAGE. I THINK SHE'D BE INTERESTED.
SHE'S AN AMATEUR SORCERESS HERSELF, AND SHE SPENT SO MANY YEARS TRYING TO FIGURE OUT A CURE FOR MY CURSE...
I WONDER IF YOU'LL STILL BE ABLE TO COMMUNICATE WITH HOSTILE MOBS WITHOUT YOUR CURSE.
OF COURSE NOT. ATRIA WILL JUST BE A NORMAL, UNSPECIAL...

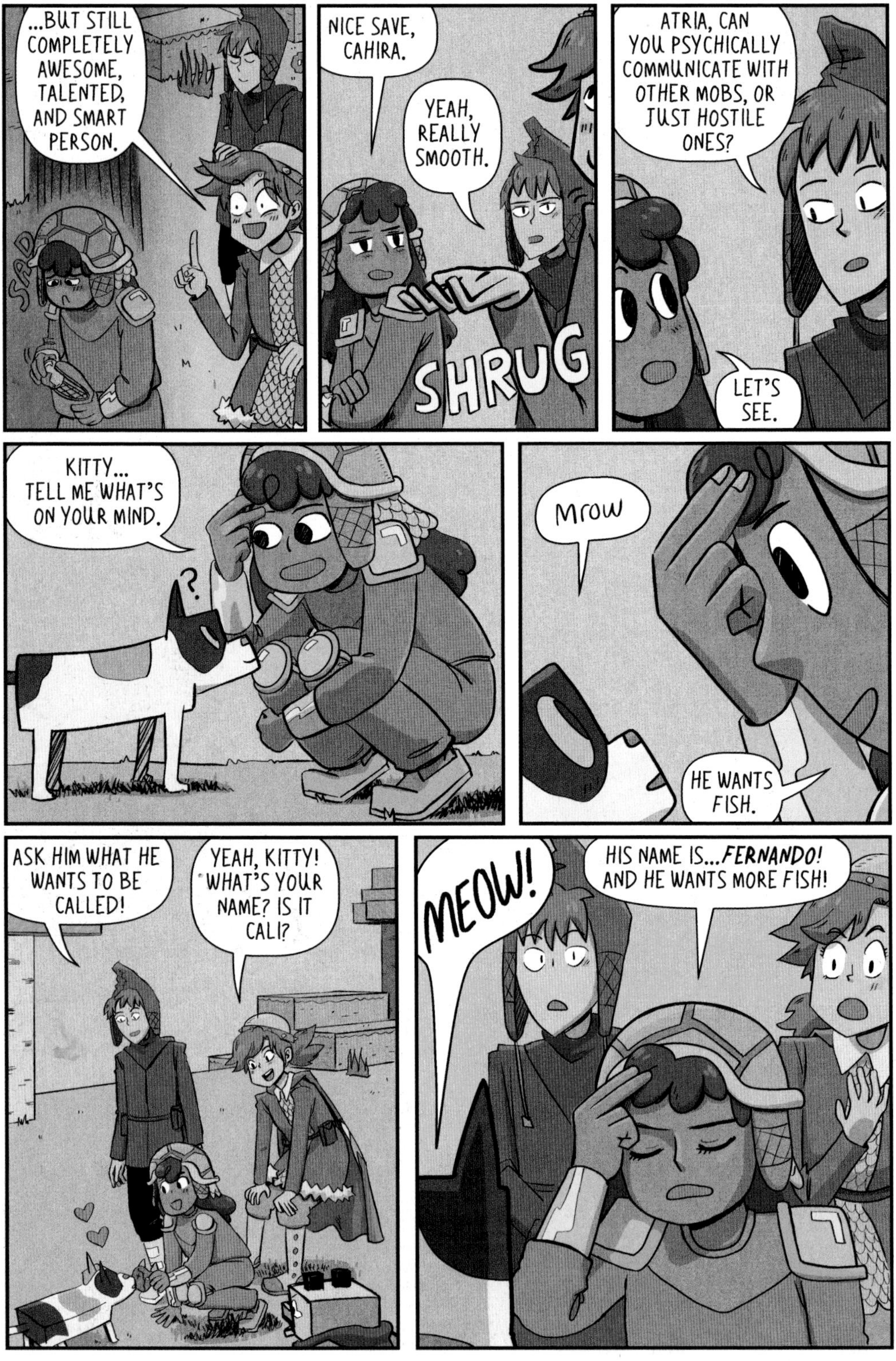
...BUT STILL COMPLETELY AWESOME, TALENTED, AND SMART PERSON.
SAD
NICE SAVE, CAHIRA.
YEAH, REALLY SMOOTH.
SHRUG
ATRIA, CAN YOU PSYCHICALLY COMMUNICATE WITH OTHER MOBS, OR JUST HOSTILE ONES?
LET'S SEE.
KITTY... TELL ME WHAT'S ON YOUR MIND.
?
Mrow
HE WANTS FISH.
ASK HIM WHAT HE WANTS TO BE CALLED!
YEAH, KITTY! WHAT'S YOUR NAME? IS IT CALI?
MEOW!
HIS NAME IS...FERNANDO! AND HE WANTS MORE FISH!

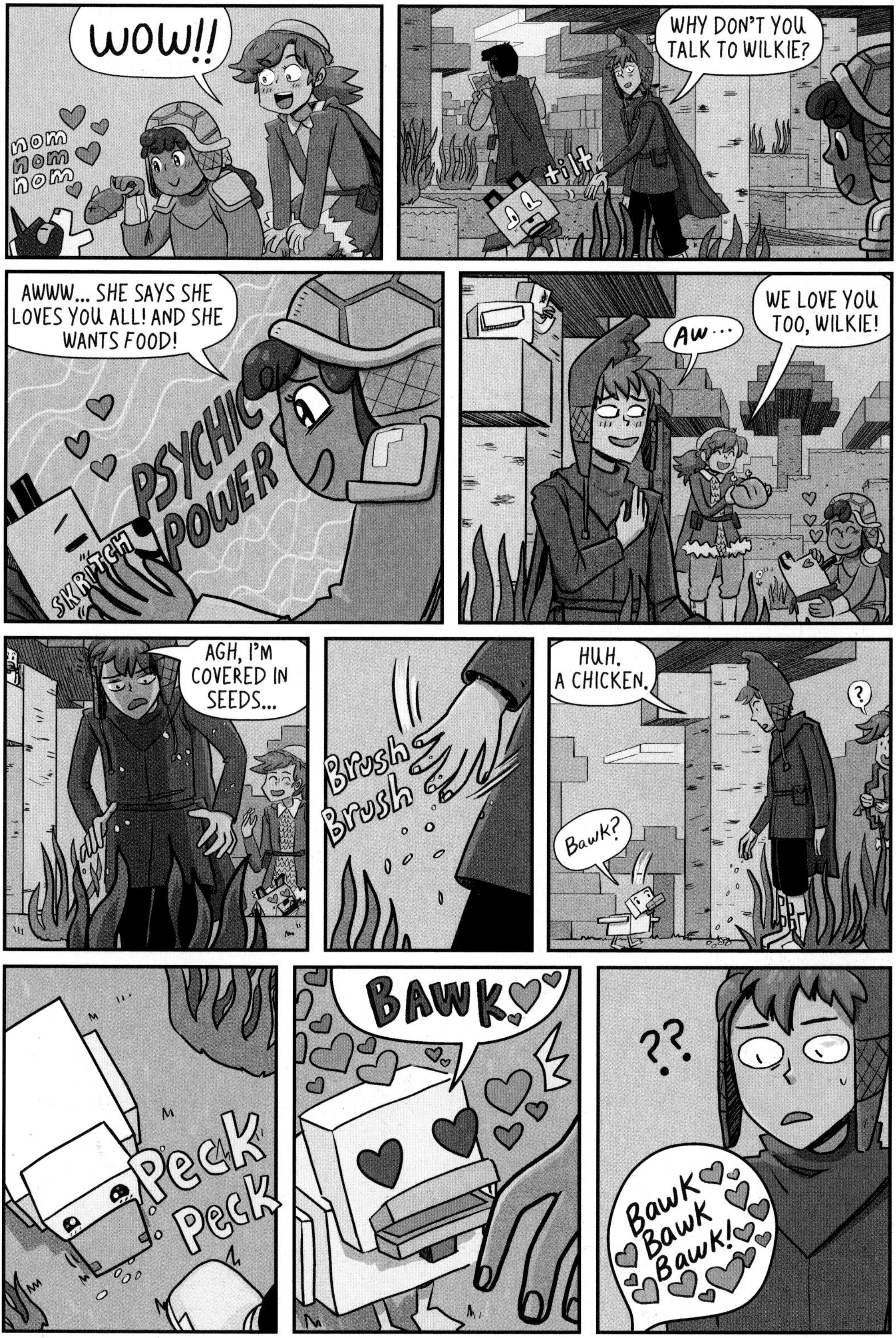

WOW!!
nom nom nom
WHY DON'T YOU TALK TO WILKIE?
tilt
AWWW... SHE SAYS SHE LOVES YOU ALL! AND SHE WANTS FOOD!
PSYCHIC POWER
SKRITCH
Aw...
WE LOVE YOU TOO, WILKIE!
AGH, I'M COVERED IN SEEDS...
Brush Brush
HUH. A CHICKEN.
?
Bawk?
Peck Peck
BAWK
??
Bawk Bawk Bawk!

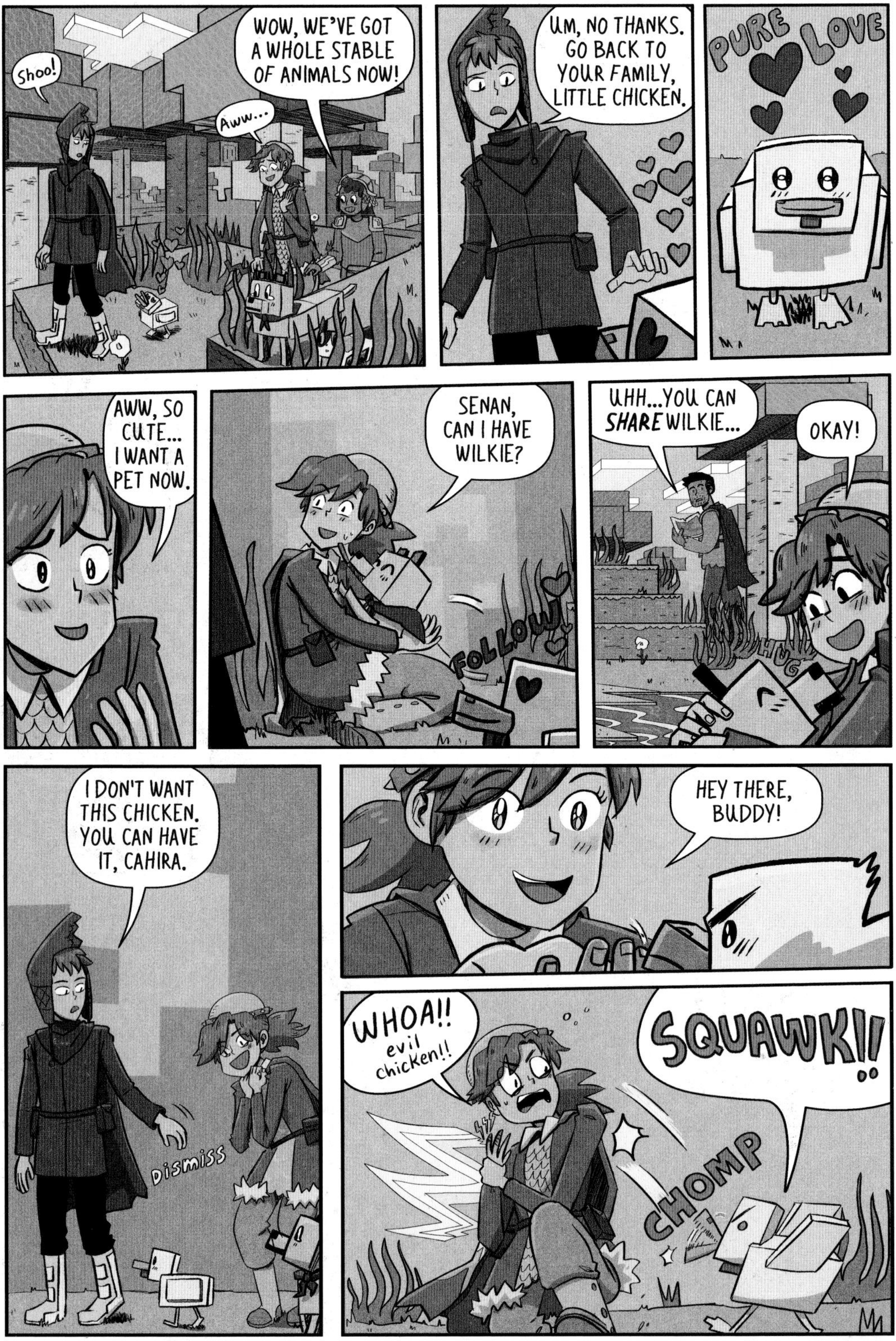
Shoo!
Aww...
WOW, WE'VE GOT A WHOLE STABLE OF ANIMALS NOW!
UM, NO THANKS. GO BACK TO YOUR FAMILY, LITTLE CHICKEN.
PURE LOVE
AWW, SO CUTE... I WANT A PET NOW.
SENAN, CAN I HAVE WILKIE?
FOLLOW
UHH...YOU CAN SHARE WILKIE...
OKAY!
HUG
I DON'T WANT THIS CHICKEN. YOU CAN HAVE IT, CAHIRA.
DISMISS
HEY THERE, BUDDY!
WHOA!! evil chicken!!
SQUAWK!!
CHOMP

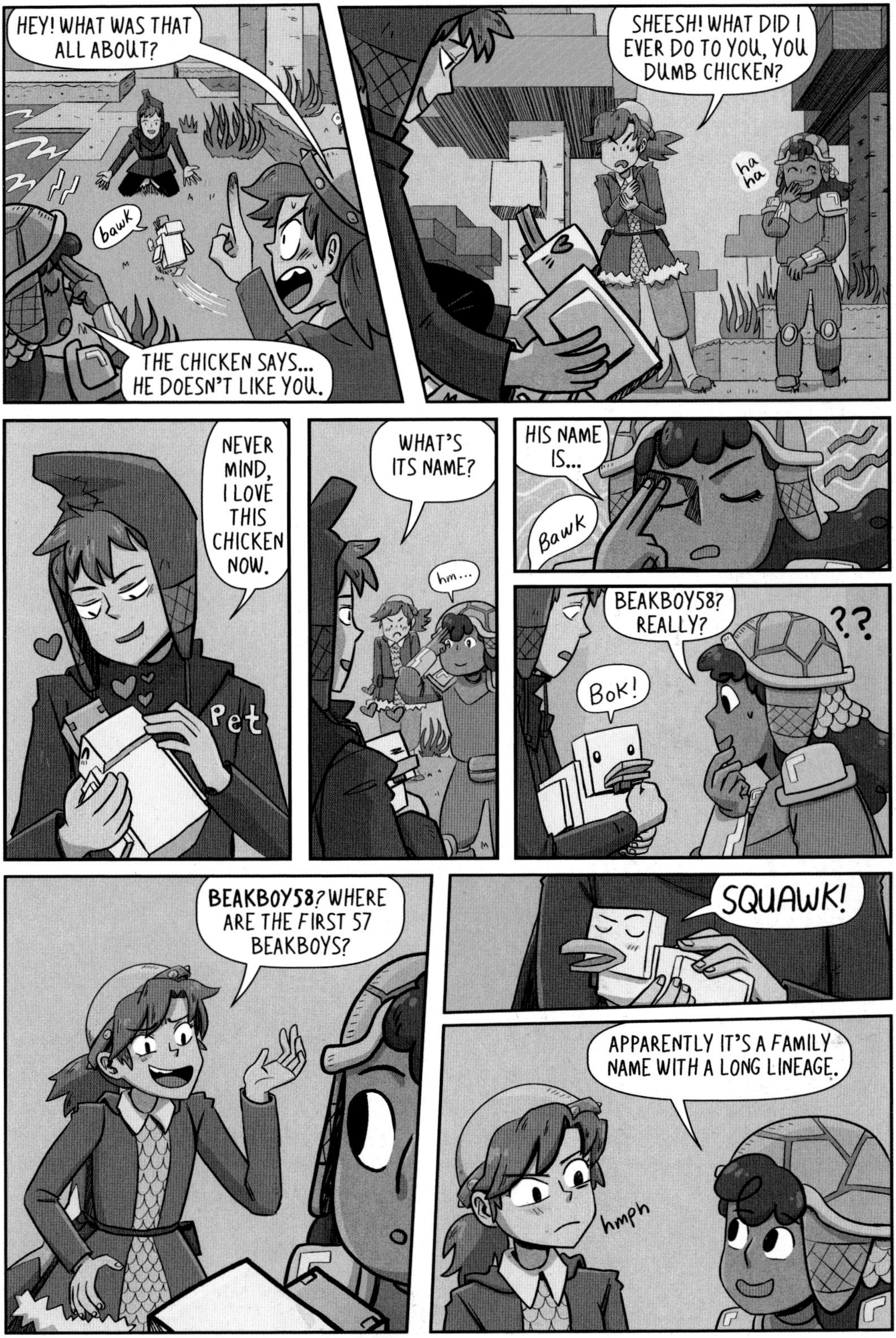
HEY! WHAT WAS THAT ALL ABOUT?
bawk
THE CHICKEN SAYS... HE DOESN'T LIKE YOU.
SHEESH! WHAT DID I EVER DO TO YOU, YOU DUMB CHICKEN?
ha ha
NEVER MIND, I LOVE THIS CHICKEN NOW.
Pet
WHAT'S ITS NAME?
hm...
HIS NAME IS...
Bawk
BEAKBOY58? REALLY?
Bok!
??
BEAKBOY58? WHERE ARE THE FIRST 57 BEAKBOYS?
SQUAWK!
APPARENTLY IT'S A FAMILY NAME WITH A LONG LINEAGE.
hmph

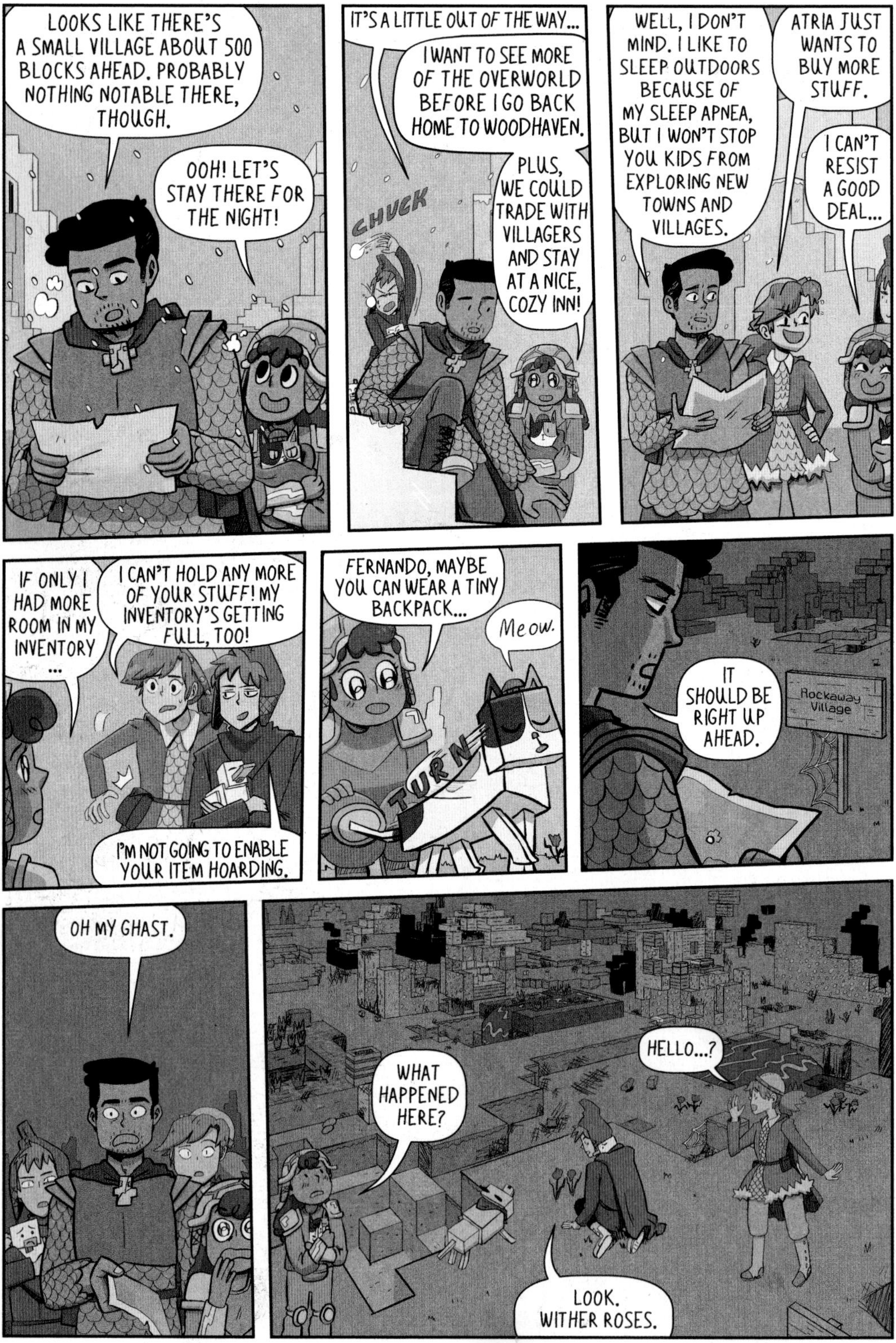
LOOKS LIKE THERE'S A SMALL VILLAGE ABOUT 500 BLOCKS AHEAD. PROBABLY NOTHING NOTABLE THERE, THOUGH.
OOH! LET'S STAY THERE FOR THE NIGHT!
IT'S A LITTLE OUT OF THE WAY...
I WANT TO SEE MORE OF THE OVERWORLD BEFORE I GO BACK HOME TO WOODHAVEN.
CHUCK
PLUS, WE COULD TRADE WITH VILLAGERS AND STAY AT A NICE, COZY INN!
WELL, I DON'T MIND. I LIKE TO SLEEP OUTDOORS BECAUSE OF MY SLEEP APNEA, BUT I WON'T STOP YOU KIDS FROM EXPLORING NEW TOWNS AND VILLAGES.
ATRIA JUST WANTS TO BUY MORE STUFF.
I CAN'T RESIST A GOOD DEAL...
IF ONLY I HAD MORE ROOM IN MY INVENTORY...
I CAN'T HOLD ANY MORE OF YOUR STUFF! MY INVENTORY'S GETTING FULL, TOO!
I'M NOT GOING TO ENABLE YOUR ITEM HOARDING.
FERNANDO, MAYBE YOU CAN WEAR A TINY BACKPACK...
Meow.
TURN
IT SHOULD BE RIGHT UP AHEAD.
Rockaway Village
OH MY GHAST.
HELLO...?
WHAT HAPPENED HERE?
LOOK. WITHER ROSES.

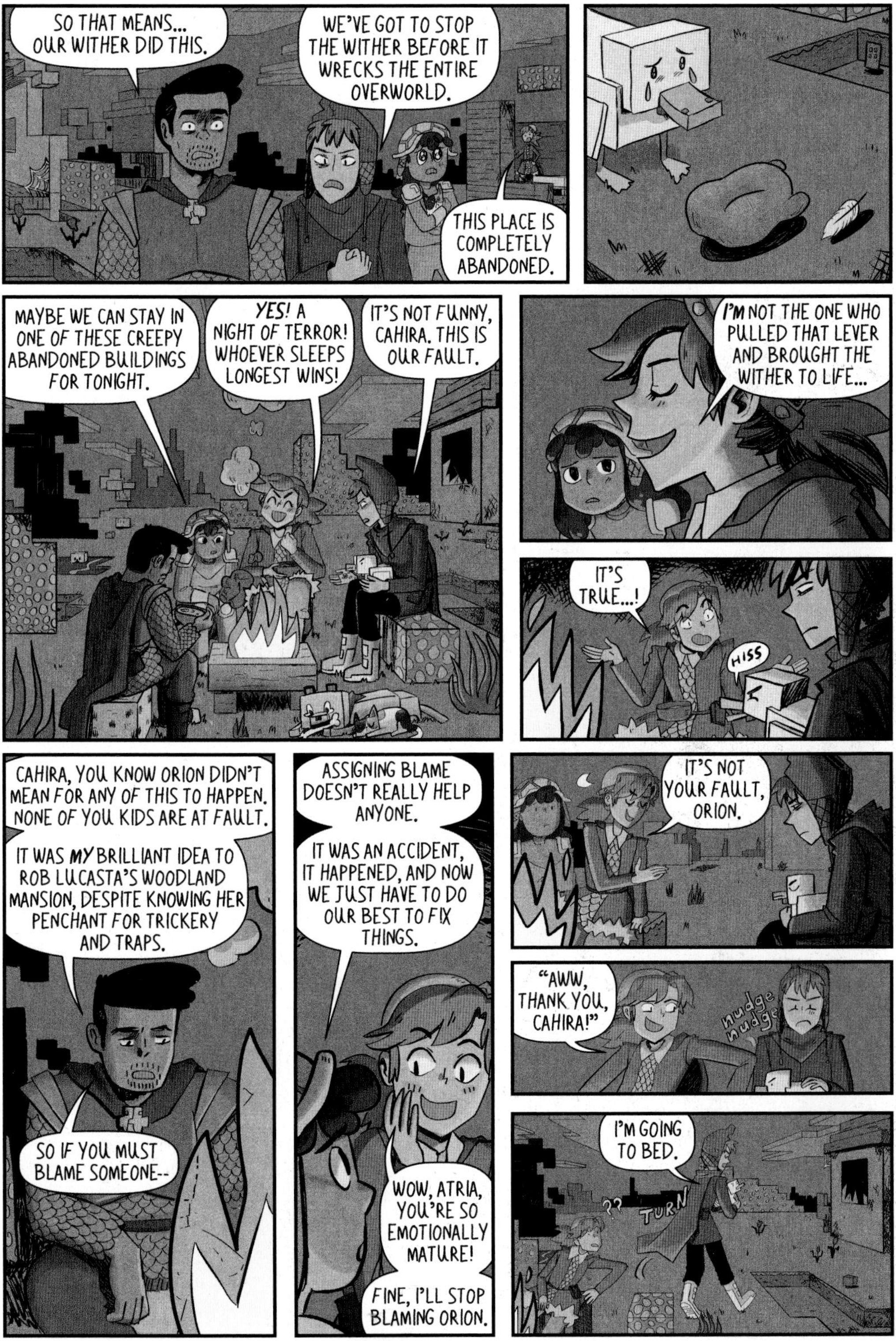
SO THAT MEANS... OUR WITHER DID THIS.
WE'VE GOT TO STOP THE WITHER BEFORE IT WRECKS THE ENTIRE OVERWORLD.
THIS PLACE IS COMPLETELY ABANDONED.
MAYBE WE CAN STAY IN ONE OF THESE CREEPY ABANDONED BUILDINGS FOR TONIGHT.
YES! A NIGHT OF TERROR! WHOEVER SLEEPS LONGEST WINS!
IT'S NOT FUNNY, CAHIRA. THIS IS OUR FAULT.
I'M NOT THE ONE WHO PULLED THAT LEVER AND BROUGHT THE WITHER TO LIFE...
IT'S TRUE...!
HISS
CAHIRA, YOU KNOW ORION DIDN'T MEAN FOR ANY OF THIS TO HAPPEN. NONE OF YOU KIDS ARE AT FAULT.
IT WAS MY BRILLIANT IDEA TO ROB LUCASTA'S WOODLAND MANSION, DESPITE KNOWING HER PENCHANT FOR TRICKERY AND TRAPS.
SO IF YOU MUST BLAME SOMEONE--
ASSIGNING BLAME DOESN'T REALLY HELP ANYONE.
IT WAS AN ACCIDENT, IT HAPPENED, AND NOW WE JUST HAVE TO DO OUR BEST TO FIX THINGS.
WOW, ATRIA, YOU'RE SO EMOTIONALLY MATURE!
FINE, I'LL STOP BLAMING ORION.
IT'S NOT YOUR FAULT, ORION.
"AWW, THANK YOU, CAHIRA!"
nudge nudge
I'M GOING TO BED.
??
TURN

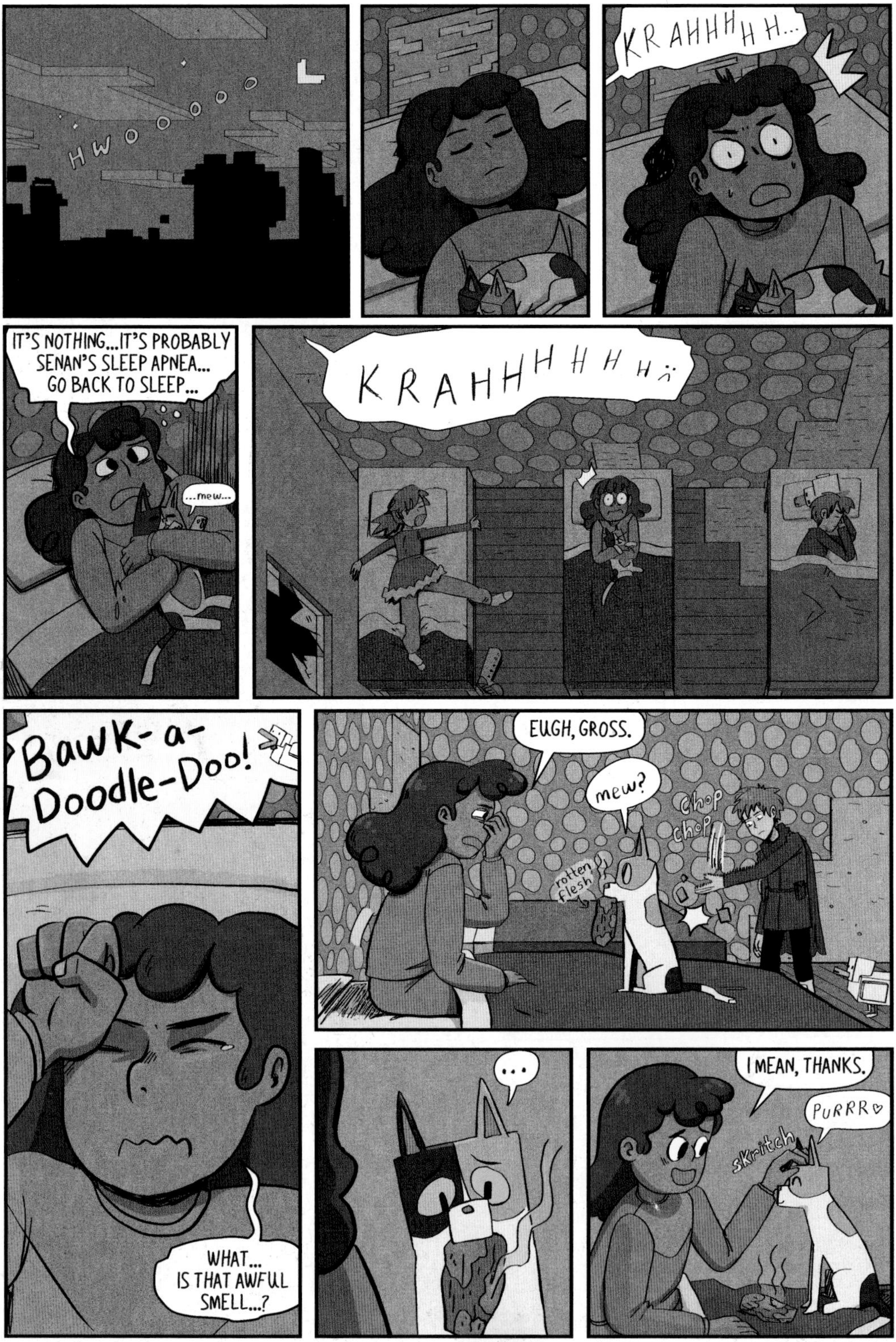
HWOOOOOOO
KRAHHHHH...
IT'S NOTHING...IT'S PROBABLY SENAN'S SLEEP APNEA... GO BACK TO SLEEP...
...mew...
KRAHHHHHHH
Bawk-a-Doodle-Doo!
WHAT... IS THAT AWFUL SMELL...?
EUGH, GROSS.
mew?
Chop chop
rotten flesh
...
I MEAN, THANKS.
PURRR♡
skritch

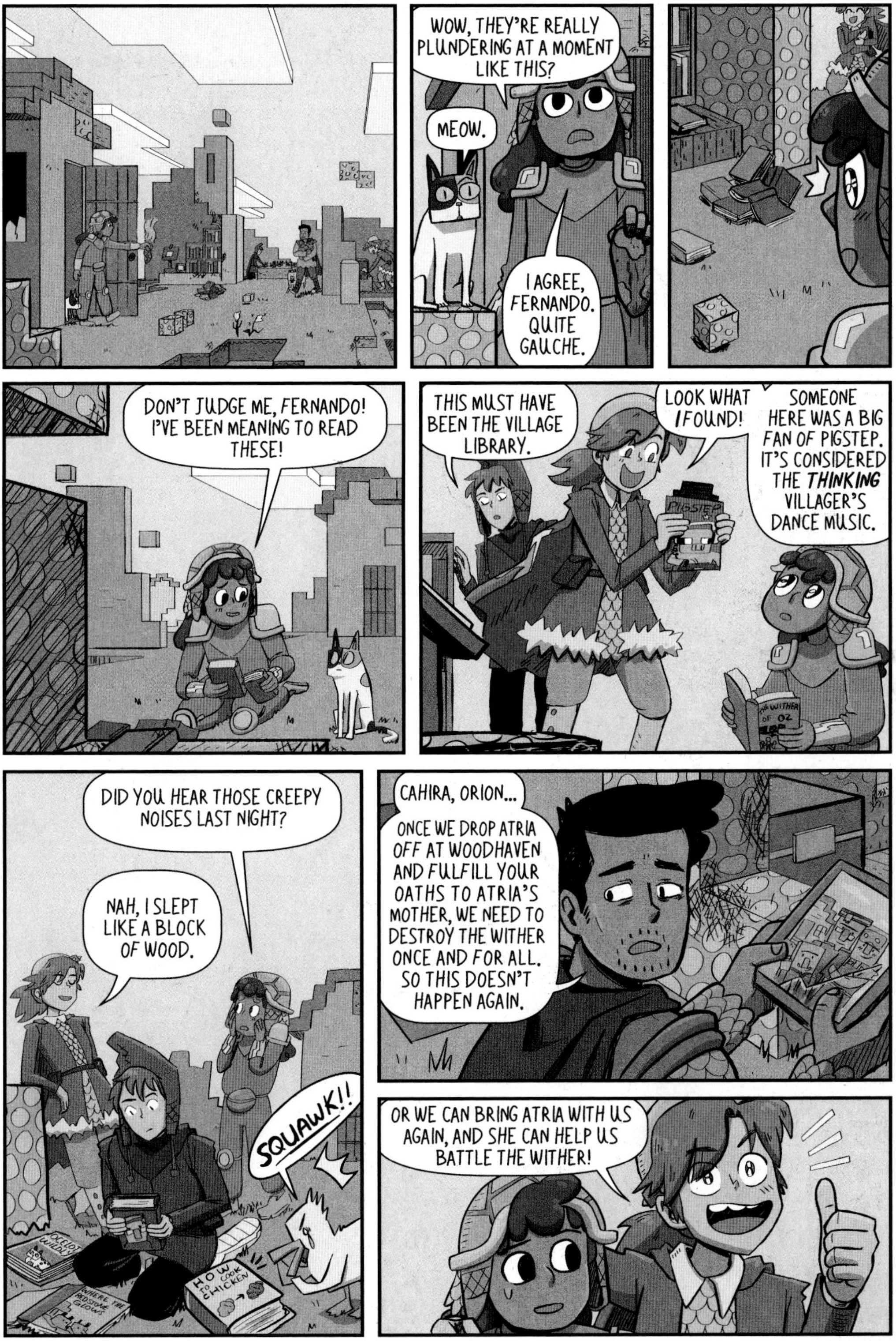
WOW, THEY'RE REALLY PLUNDERING AT A MOMENT LIKE THIS?
MEOW.
I AGREE, FERNANDO. QUITE GAUCHE.
DON'T JUDGE ME, FERNANDO! I'VE BEEN MEANING TO READ THESE!
THIS MUST HAVE BEEN THE VILLAGE LIBRARY.
LOOK WHAT I FOUND!
PIGSTEP
SOMEONE HERE WAS A BIG FAN OF PIGSTEP. IT'S CONSIDERED THE *THINKING* VILLAGER'S DANCE MUSIC.
THE WITHER OF OZ
DID YOU HEAR THOSE CREEPY NOISES LAST NIGHT?
NAH, I SLEPT LIKE A BLOCK OF WOOD.
SQUAWK!!
HOW TO COOK CHICKEN
WHERE THE REDSTONE GLOWS
CAHIRA, ORION...
ONCE WE DROP ATRIA OFF AT WOODHAVEN AND FULFILL YOUR OATHS TO ATRIA'S MOTHER, WE NEED TO DESTROY THE WITHER ONCE AND FOR ALL. SO THIS DOESN'T HAPPEN AGAIN.
OR WE CAN BRING ATRIA WITH US AGAIN, AND SHE CAN HELP US BATTLE THE WITHER!

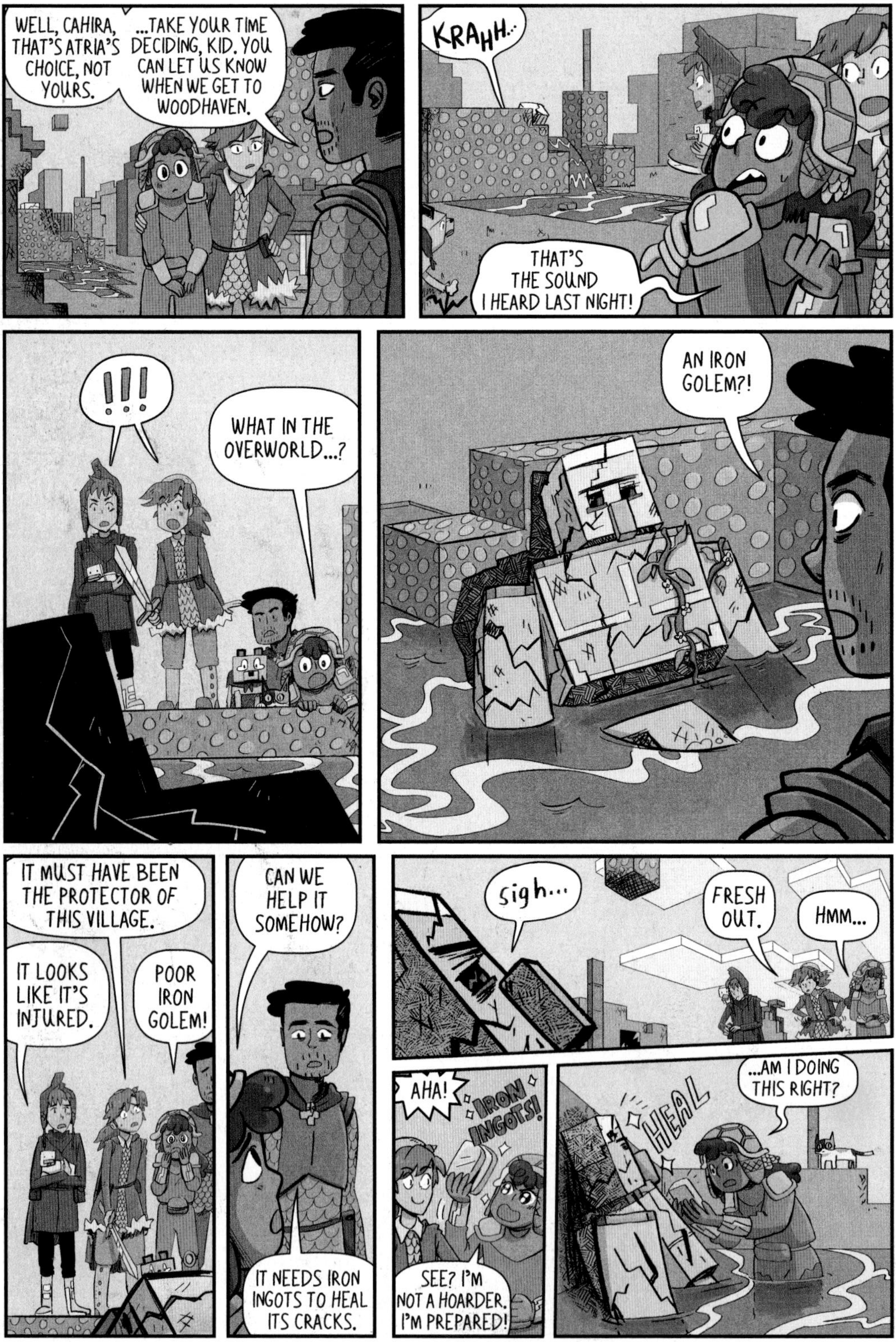

WELL, CAHIRA, THAT'S ATRIA'S CHOICE, NOT YOURS.
...TAKE YOUR TIME DECIDING, KID. YOU CAN LET US KNOW WHEN WE GET TO WOODHAVEN.
KRAHH...
THAT'S THE SOUND I HEARD LAST NIGHT!
!!!
WHAT IN THE OVERWORLD...?
AN IRON GOLEM?!
IT MUST HAVE BEEN THE PROTECTOR OF THIS VILLAGE.
IT LOOKS LIKE IT'S INJURED.
POOR IRON GOLEM!
CAN WE HELP IT SOMEHOW?
IT NEEDS IRON INGOTS TO HEAL ITS CRACKS.
sigh...
FRESH OUT.
HMM...
AHA!
IRON INGOTS!
SEE? I'M NOT A HOARDER. I'M PREPARED!
HEAL
...AM I DOING THIS RIGHT?

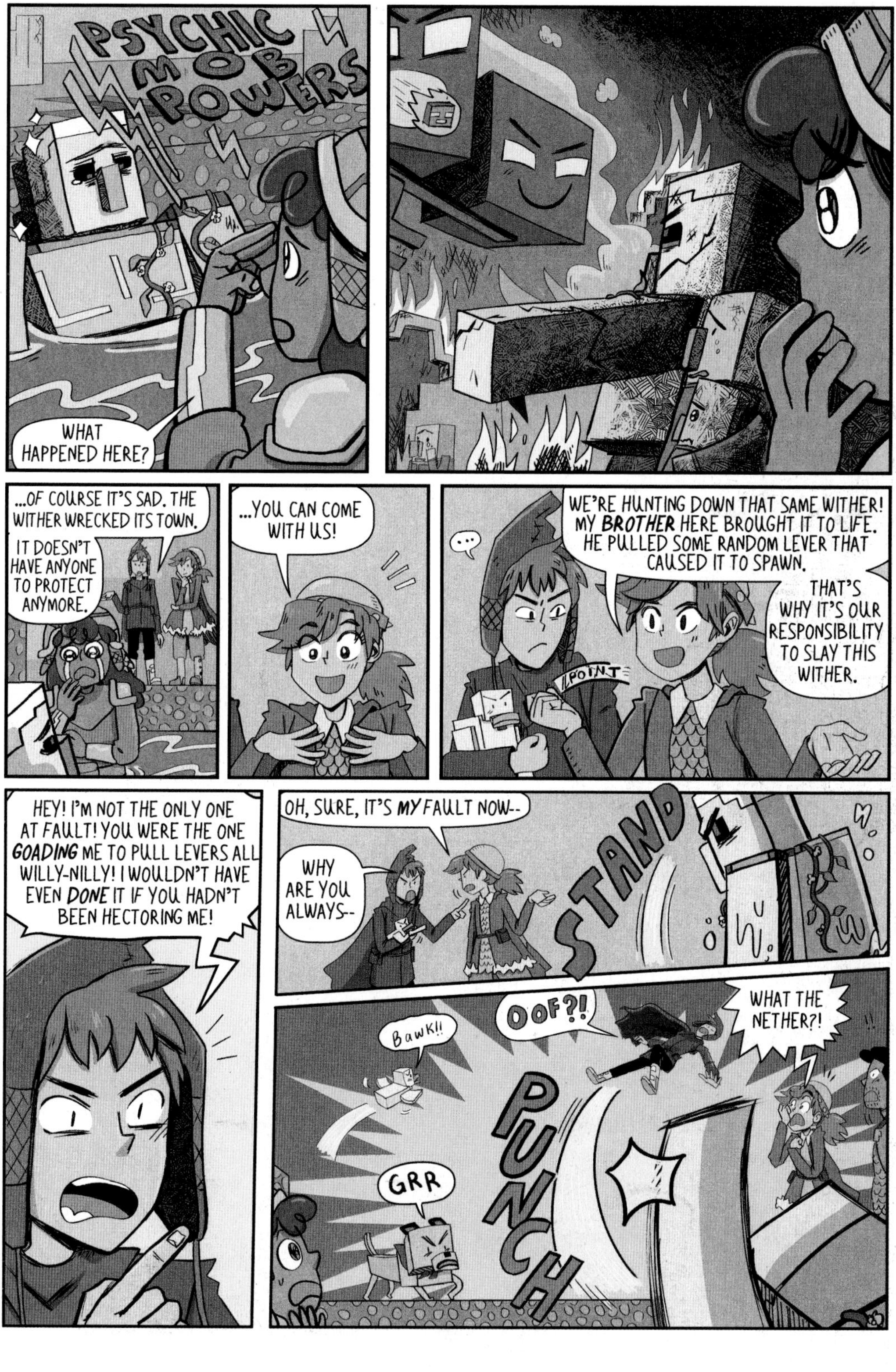
PSYCHIC MOB POWERS
WHAT HAPPENED HERE?
...OF COURSE IT'S SAD. THE WITHER WRECKED ITS TOWN.
IT DOESN'T HAVE ANYONE TO PROTECT ANYMORE.
...YOU CAN COME WITH US!
...
WE'RE HUNTING DOWN THAT SAME WITHER! MY BROTHER HERE BROUGHT IT TO LIFE. HE PULLED SOME RANDOM LEVER THAT CAUSED IT TO SPAWN.
THAT'S WHY IT'S OUR RESPONSIBILITY TO SLAY THIS WITHER.
POINT
HEY! I'M NOT THE ONLY ONE AT FAULT! YOU WERE THE ONE GOADING ME TO PULL LEVERS ALL WILLY-NILLY! I WOULDN'T HAVE EVEN DONE IT IF YOU HADN'T BEEN HECTORING ME!
OH, SURE, IT'S MY FAULT NOW--
WHY ARE YOU ALWAYS--
STAND
OOF?!
WHAT THE NETHER?!
BAWK!!
PUNCH
GRR

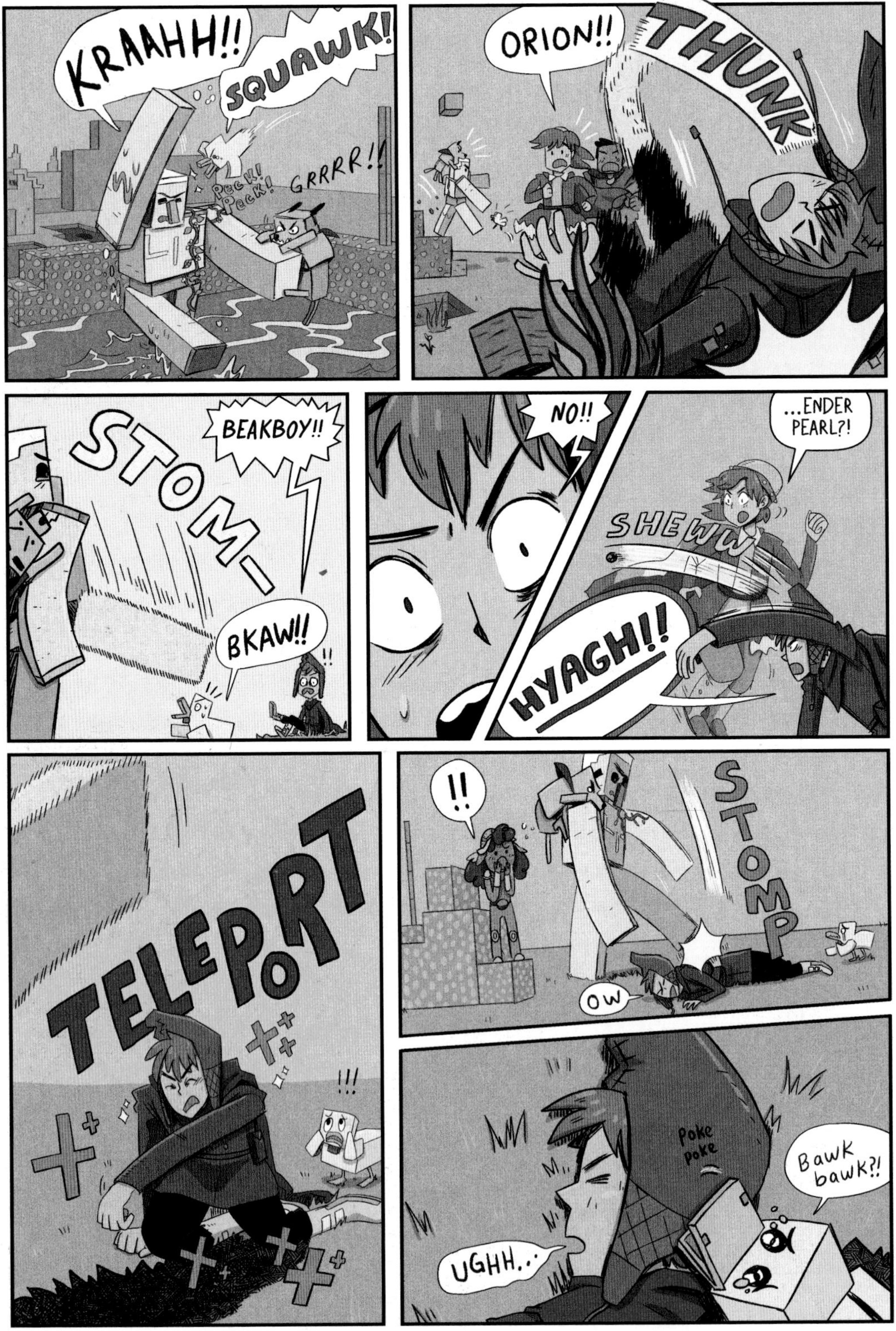
KRAAHH!!
SQUAWK!
Peck! Peck!
GRRRR!!
ORION!!
THUNK
STOM-
BEAKBOY!!
BKAW!!
!!
NO!!
...ENDER PEARL?!
SHEWW
HYAGH!!
TELEPORT
!!!
!!
STOMP
OW
Poke poke
Bawk bawk?!
UGHH...

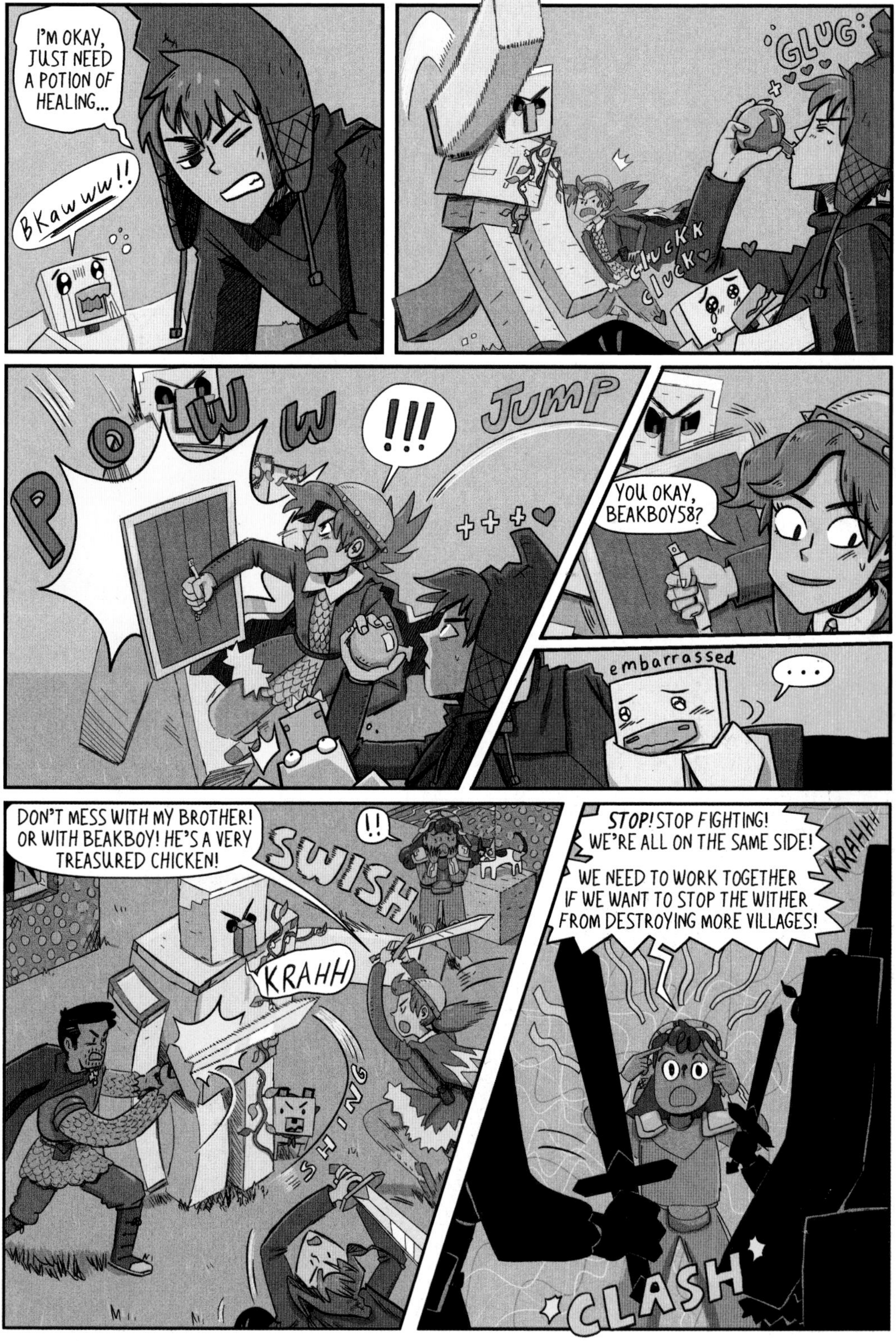
I'M OKAY, JUST NEED A POTION OF HEALING...
BKawww!!
GLUG
CLUCKK
CLUCK
POWW
!!!
JUMP
YOU OKAY, BEAKBOY58?
embarrassed
...
DON'T MESS WITH MY BROTHER! OR WITH BEAKBOY! HE'S A VERY TREASURED CHICKEN!
!!
SWISH
KRAHH
SHING
STOP! STOP FIGHTING! WE'RE ALL ON THE SAME SIDE!
WE NEED TO WORK TOGETHER IF WE WANT TO STOP THE WITHER FROM DESTROYING MORE VILLAGES!
KRAHHH
CLASH

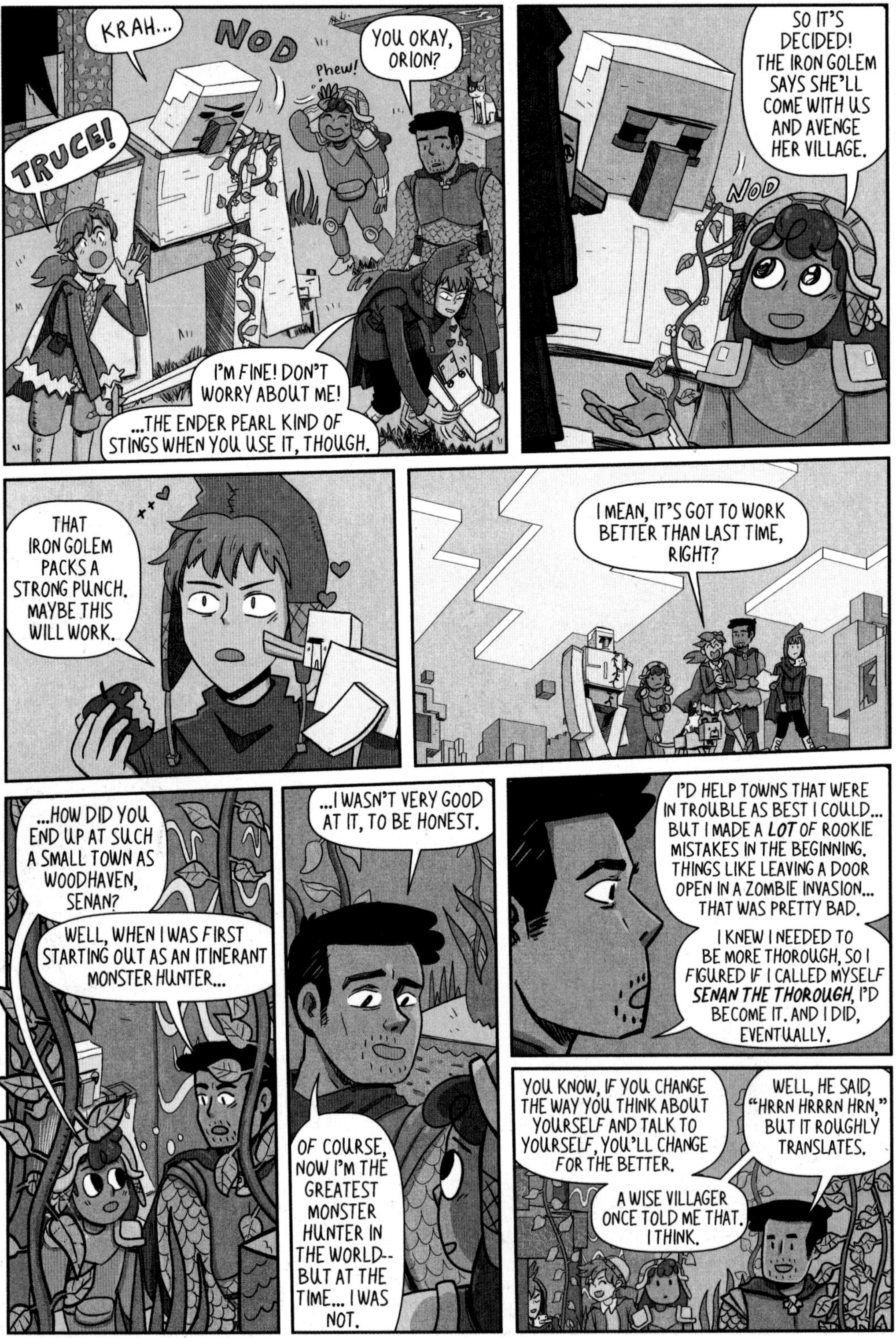
KRAH...
NOD
TRUCE!
Phew!
YOU OKAY, ORION?
I'M FINE! DON'T WORRY ABOUT ME!
...THE ENDER PEARL KIND OF STINGS WHEN YOU USE IT, THOUGH.
SO IT'S DECIDED! THE IRON GOLEM SAYS SHE'LL COME WITH US AND AVENGE HER VILLAGE.
NOD
THAT IRON GOLEM PACKS A STRONG PUNCH. MAYBE THIS WILL WORK.
I MEAN, IT'S GOT TO WORK BETTER THAN LAST TIME, RIGHT?
...HOW DID YOU END UP AT SUCH A SMALL TOWN AS WOODHAVEN, SENAN?
WELL, WHEN I WAS FIRST STARTING OUT AS AN ITINERANT MONSTER HUNTER...
...I WASN'T VERY GOOD AT IT, TO BE HONEST.
OF COURSE, NOW I'M THE GREATEST MONSTER HUNTER IN THE WORLD-- BUT AT THE TIME... I WAS NOT.
I'D HELP TOWNS THAT WERE IN TROUBLE AS BEST I COULD... BUT I MADE A LOT OF ROOKIE MISTAKES IN THE BEGINNING. THINGS LIKE LEAVING A DOOR OPEN IN A ZOMBIE INVASION... THAT WAS PRETTY BAD.
I KNEW I NEEDED TO BE MORE THOROUGH, SO I FIGURED IF I CALLED MYSELF SENAN THE THOROUGH, I'D BECOME IT. AND I DID, EVENTUALLY.
YOU KNOW, IF YOU CHANGE THE WAY YOU THINK ABOUT YOURSELF AND TALK TO YOURSELF, YOU'LL CHANGE FOR THE BETTER.
A WISE VILLAGER ONCE TOLD ME THAT. I THINK.
WELL, HE SAID, "HRRN HRRRN HRN," BUT IT ROUGHLY TRANSLATES.

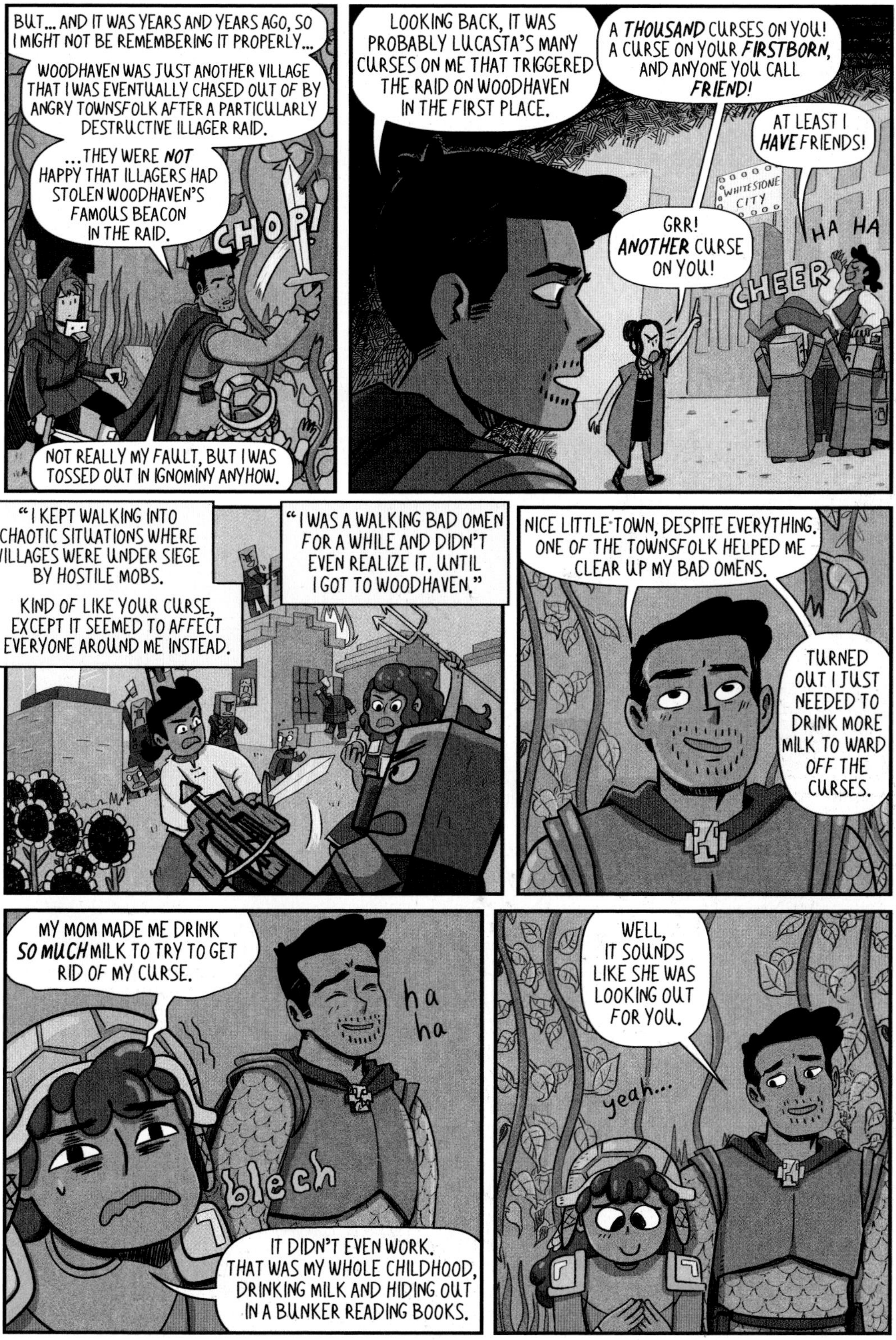
BUT... AND IT WAS YEARS AND YEARS AGO, SO I MIGHT NOT BE REMEMBERING IT PROPERLY...
WOODHAVEN WAS JUST ANOTHER VILLAGE THAT I WAS EVENTUALLY CHASED OUT OF BY ANGRY TOWNSFOLK AFTER A PARTICULARLY DESTRUCTIVE ILLAGER RAID.
...THEY WERE **NOT** HAPPY THAT ILLAGERS HAD STOLEN WOODHAVEN'S FAMOUS BEACON IN THE RAID.
CHOP!
NOT REALLY MY FAULT, BUT I WAS TOSSED OUT IN IGNOMINY ANYHOW.
LOOKING BACK, IT WAS PROBABLY LUCASTA'S MANY CURSES ON ME THAT TRIGGERED THE RAID ON WOODHAVEN IN THE FIRST PLACE.
A ***THOUSAND*** CURSES ON YOU! A CURSE ON YOUR ***FIRSTBORN***, AND ANYONE YOU CALL ***FRIEND***!
AT LEAST I ***HAVE*** FRIENDS!
WHITESTONE CITY
GRR! ***ANOTHER*** CURSE ON YOU!
HA HA
CHEER
"I KEPT WALKING INTO CHAOTIC SITUATIONS WHERE VILLAGES WERE UNDER SIEGE BY HOSTILE MOBS.
KIND OF LIKE YOUR CURSE, EXCEPT IT SEEMED TO AFFECT EVERYONE AROUND ME INSTEAD.
"I WAS A WALKING BAD OMEN FOR A WHILE AND DIDN'T EVEN REALIZE IT. UNTIL I GOT TO WOODHAVEN."
NICE LITTLE TOWN, DESPITE EVERYTHING. ONE OF THE TOWNSFOLK HELPED ME CLEAR UP MY BAD OMENS.
TURNED OUT I JUST NEEDED TO DRINK MORE MILK TO WARD OFF THE CURSES.
MY MOM MADE ME DRINK ***SO MUCH*** MILK TO TRY TO GET RID OF MY CURSE.
ha ha
blech
IT DIDN'T EVEN WORK. THAT WAS MY WHOLE CHILDHOOD, DRINKING MILK AND HIDING OUT IN A BUNKER READING BOOKS.
WELL, IT SOUNDS LIKE SHE WAS LOOKING OUT FOR YOU.
yeah...

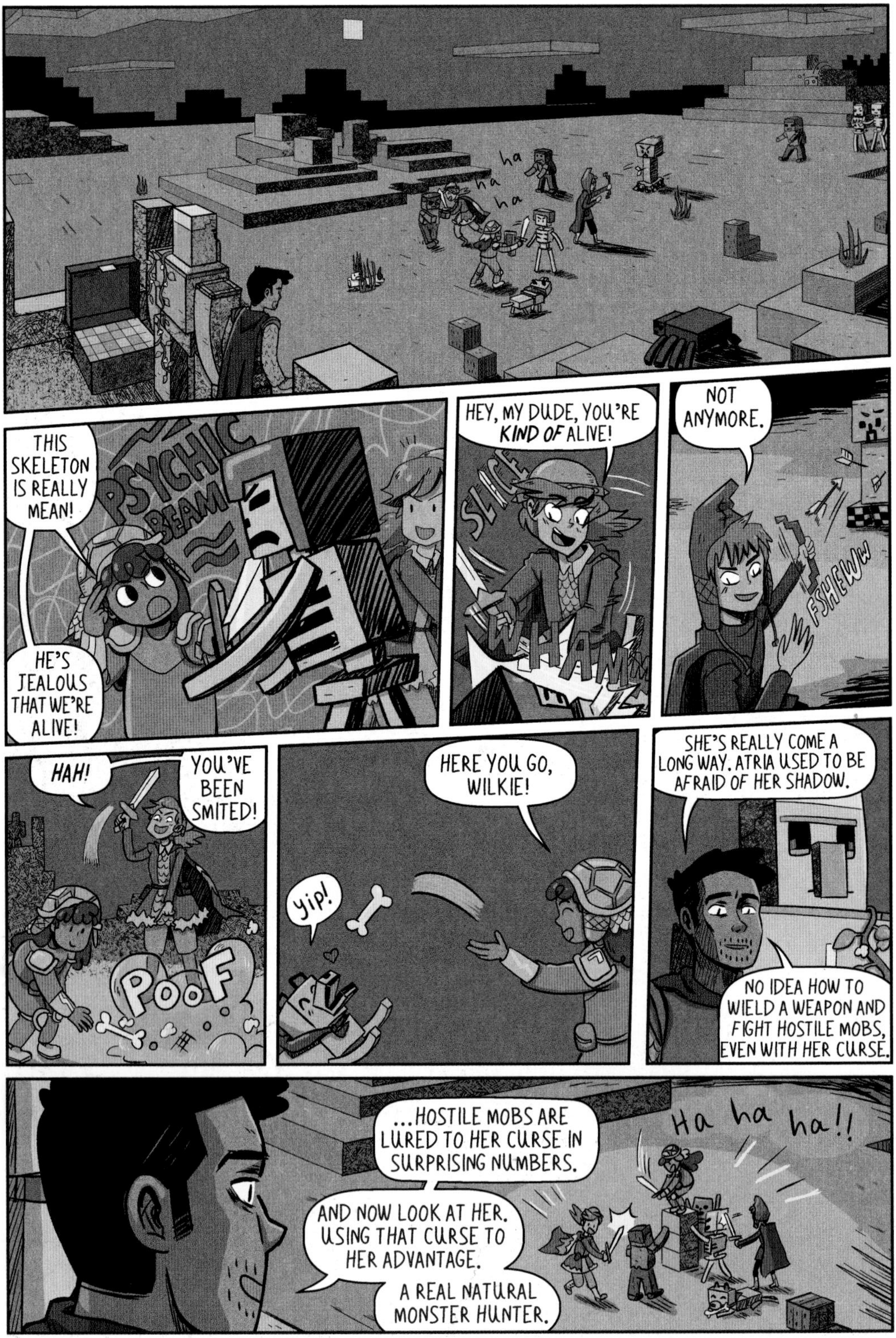

ha
ha
ha
THIS SKELETON IS REALLY MEAN!
PSYCHIC BEAM
HE'S JEALOUS THAT WE'RE ALIVE!
HEY, MY DUDE, YOU'RE KIND OF ALIVE!
SLICE
WHAM
NOT ANYMORE.
FSHEWW
HAH!
YOU'VE BEEN SMITED!
POOF
HERE YOU GO, WILKIE!
yip!
SHE'S REALLY COME A LONG WAY. ATRIA USED TO BE AFRAID OF HER SHADOW.
NO IDEA HOW TO WIELD A WEAPON AND FIGHT HOSTILE MOBS, EVEN WITH HER CURSE.
...HOSTILE MOBS ARE LURED TO HER CURSE IN SURPRISING NUMBERS.
Ha ha ha!!
AND NOW LOOK AT HER. USING THAT CURSE TO HER ADVANTAGE.
A REAL NATURAL MONSTER HUNTER.

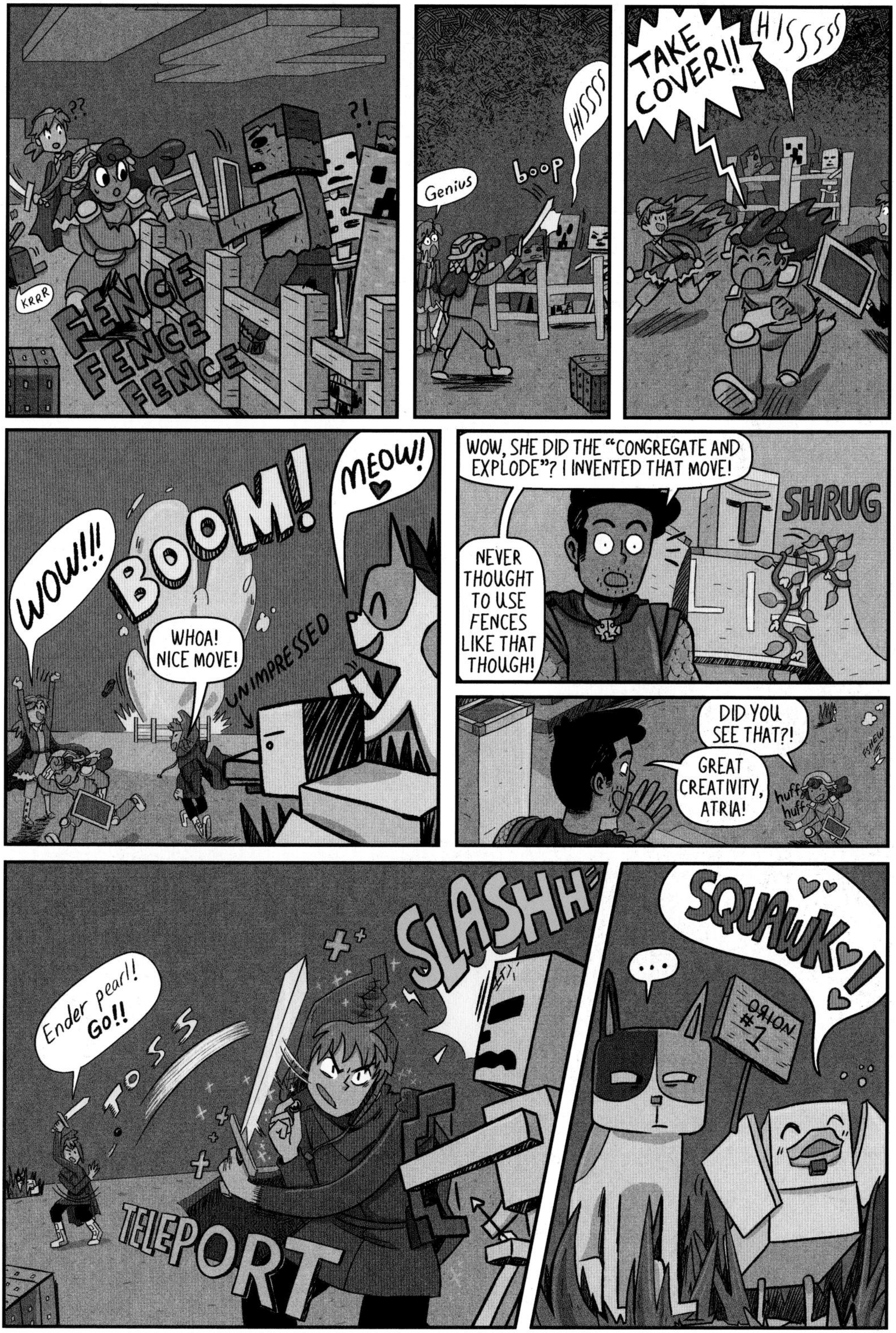
??
?!
KRRR
FENCE
FENCE
FENCE
Genius
boop
HISSSS
TAKE COVER!!
HISSSSS
WOW!!!
BOOM!
MEOW!
WHOA! NICE MOVE!
UNIMPRESSED
WOW, SHE DID THE "CONGREGATE AND EXPLODE"? I INVENTED THAT MOVE!
NEVER THOUGHT TO USE FENCES LIKE THAT THOUGH!
SHRUG
DID YOU SEE THAT?!
GREAT CREATIVITY, ATRIA!
huff huff
Ender pearl!! Go!!
TOSS
SLASHH
TELEPORT
SQUAWK!
...
ORION #1

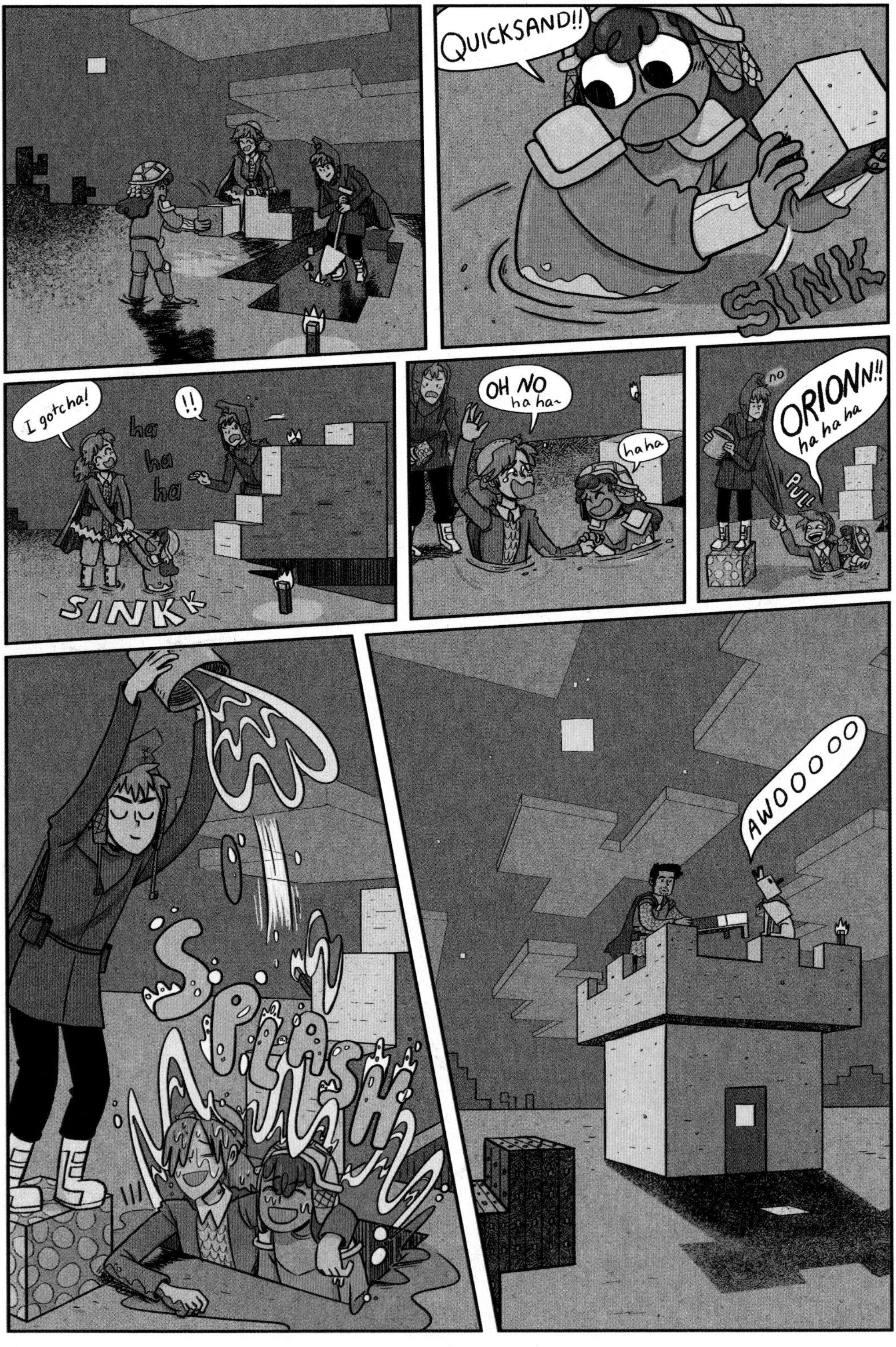
QUICKSAND!!
SINK
I gotcha!
!!
ha
ha
ha
SINKK
OH NO
ha ha~
haha
no
ORIONN!!
ha ha ha
PULL
SPLASH
AWOOOOO

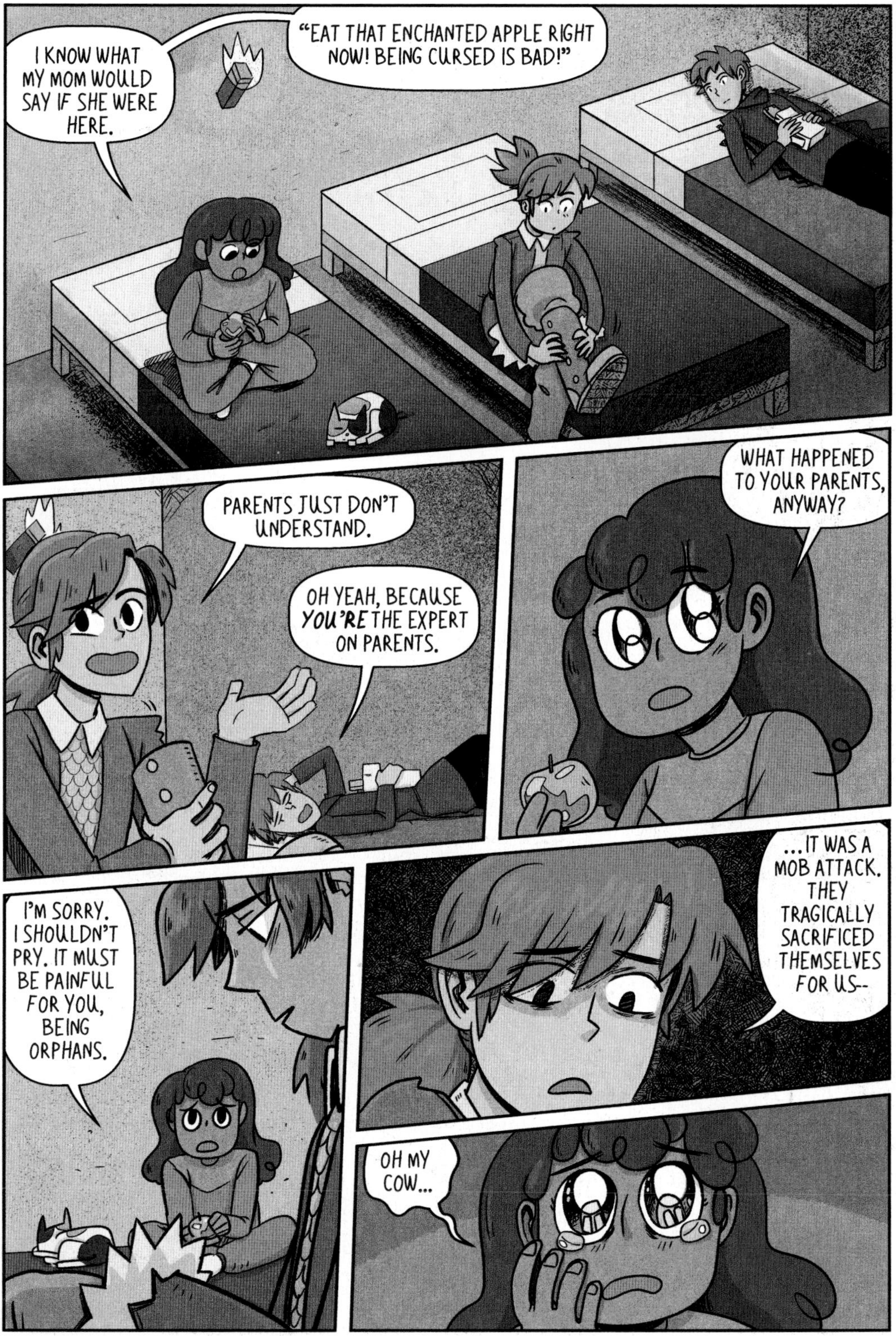
I KNOW WHAT MY MOM WOULD SAY IF SHE WERE HERE.
"EAT THAT ENCHANTED APPLE RIGHT NOW! BEING CURSED IS BAD!"
PARENTS JUST DON'T UNDERSTAND.
OH YEAH, BECAUSE *YOU'RE* THE EXPERT ON PARENTS.
WHAT HAPPENED TO YOUR PARENTS, ANYWAY?
I'M SORRY. I SHOULDN'T PRY. IT MUST BE PAINFUL FOR YOU, BEING ORPHANS.
...IT WAS A MOB ATTACK. THEY TRAGICALLY SACRIFICED THEMSELVES FOR US--
OH MY COW...

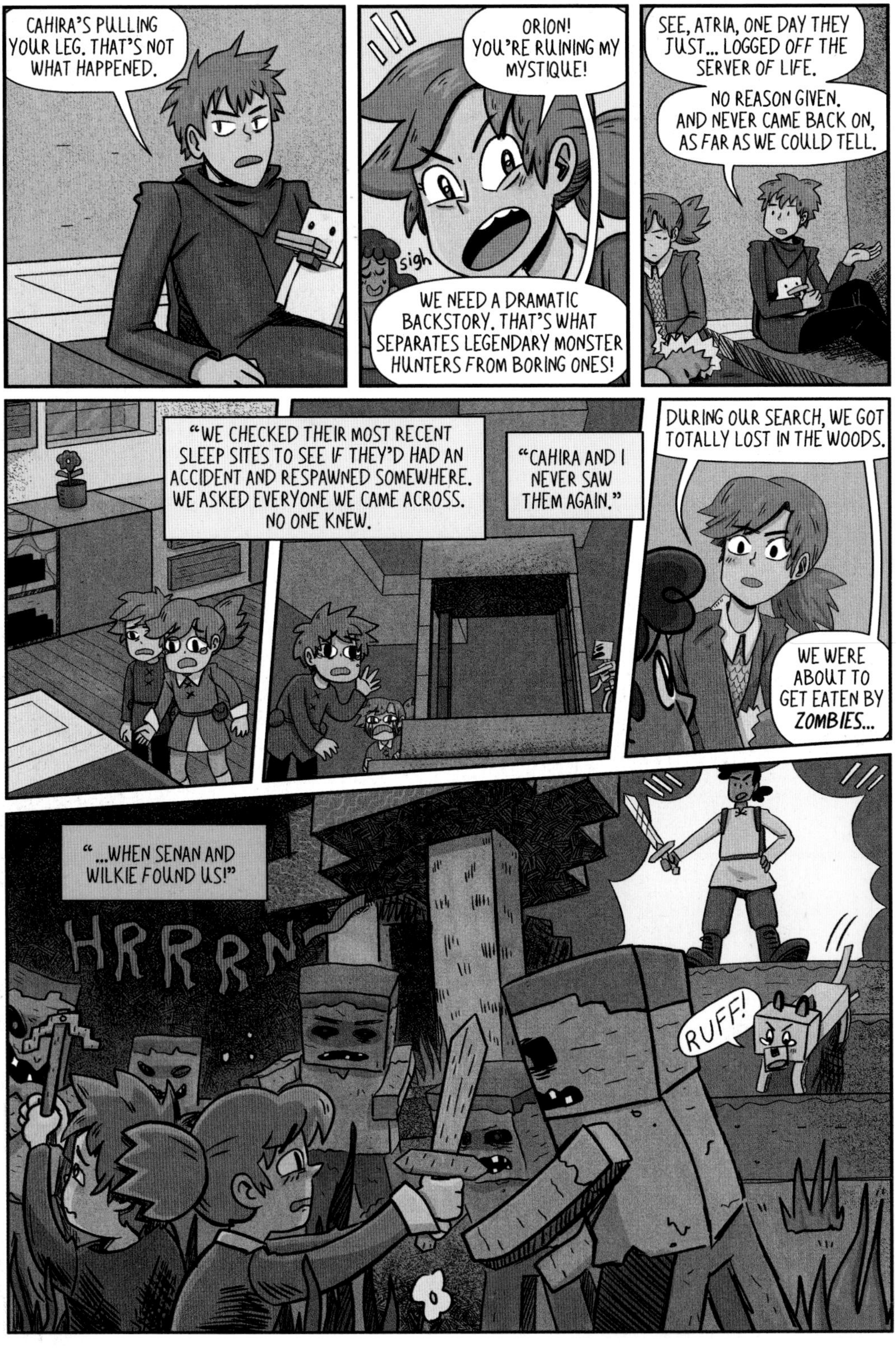
CAHIRA'S PULLING YOUR LEG. THAT'S NOT WHAT HAPPENED.
ORION! YOU'RE RUINING MY MYSTIQUE!
sigh
WE NEED A DRAMATIC BACKSTORY. THAT'S WHAT SEPARATES LEGENDARY MONSTER HUNTERS FROM BORING ONES!
SEE, ATRIA, ONE DAY THEY JUST... LOGGED OFF THE SERVER OF LIFE.
NO REASON GIVEN. AND NEVER CAME BACK ON, AS FAR AS WE COULD TELL.
"WE CHECKED THEIR MOST RECENT SLEEP SITES TO SEE IF THEY'D HAD AN ACCIDENT AND RESPAWNED SOMEWHERE. WE ASKED EVERYONE WE CAME ACROSS. NO ONE KNEW.
"CAHIRA AND I NEVER SAW THEM AGAIN."
DURING OUR SEARCH, WE GOT TOTALLY LOST IN THE WOODS.
WE WERE ABOUT TO GET EATEN BY ZOMBIES...
"...WHEN SENAN AND WILKIE FOUND US!"
HRRRN
RUFF!

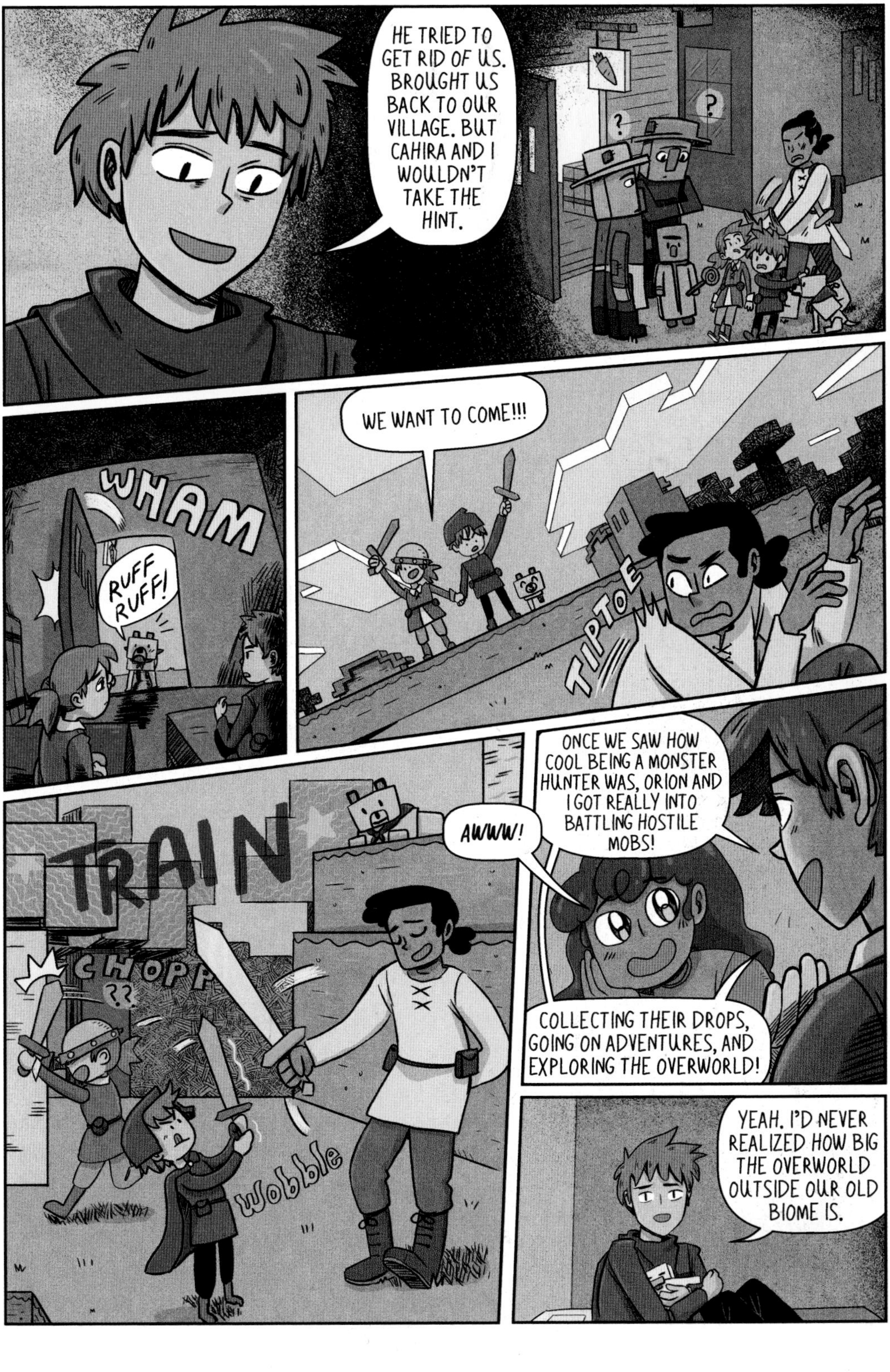
HE TRIED TO GET RID OF US. BROUGHT US BACK TO OUR VILLAGE. BUT CAHIRA AND I WOULDN'T TAKE THE HINT.
?
?
WHAM
RUFF RUFF!
WE WANT TO COME!!!
TIPTOE
TRAIN
CHOPP
??
wobble
AWWW!
ONCE WE SAW HOW COOL BEING A MONSTER HUNTER WAS, ORION AND I GOT REALLY INTO BATTLING HOSTILE MOBS!
COLLECTING THEIR DROPS, GOING ON ADVENTURES, AND EXPLORING THE OVERWORLD!
YEAH. I'D NEVER REALIZED HOW BIG THE OVERWORLD OUTSIDE OUR OLD BIOME IS.

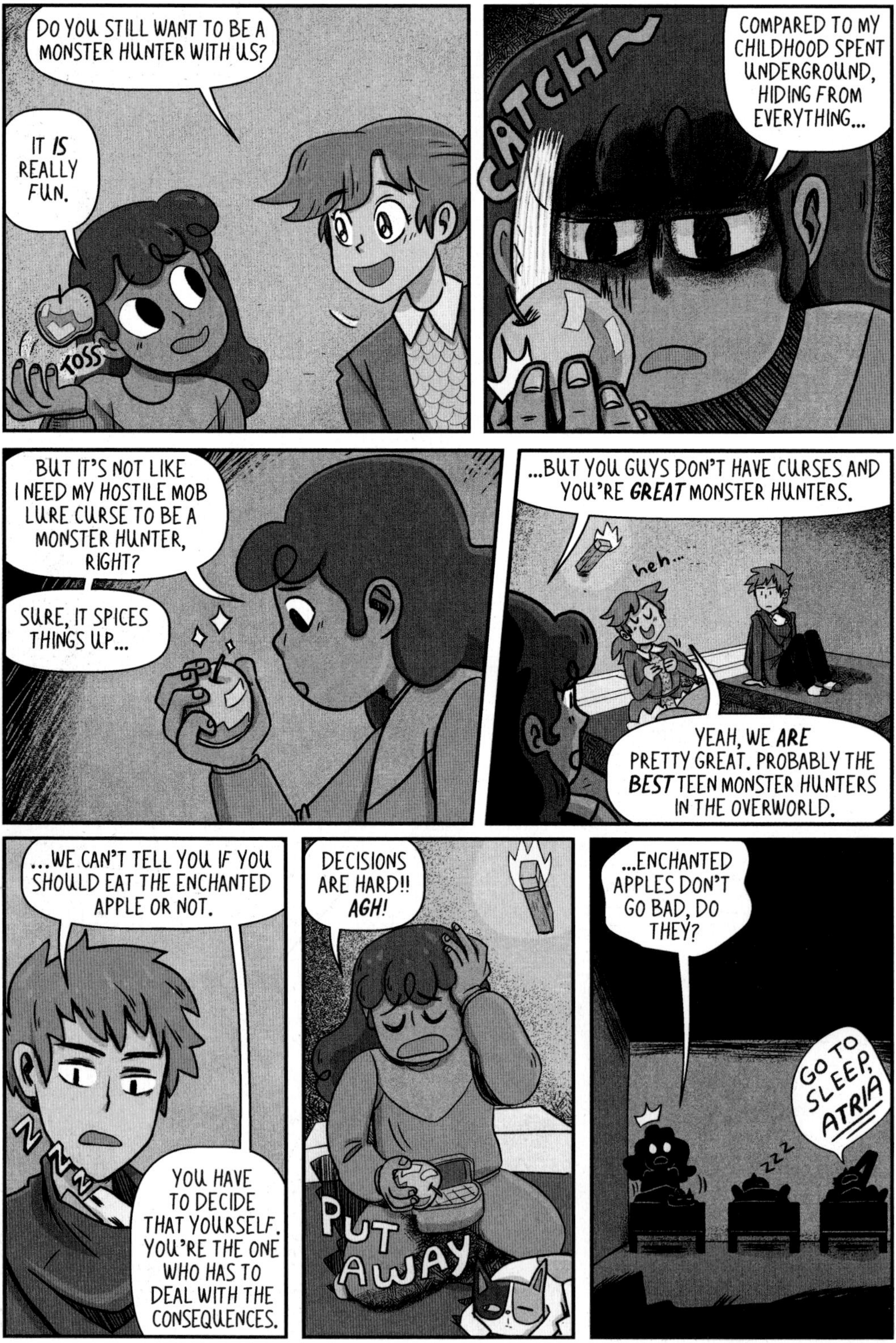
DO YOU STILL WANT TO BE A MONSTER HUNTER WITH US?
IT *IS* REALLY FUN.
TOSS
CATCH~
COMPARED TO MY CHILDHOOD SPENT UNDERGROUND, HIDING FROM EVERYTHING...
BUT IT'S NOT LIKE I NEED MY HOSTILE MOB LURE CURSE TO BE A MONSTER HUNTER, RIGHT?
SURE, IT SPICES THINGS UP...
...BUT YOU GUYS DON'T HAVE CURSES AND YOU'RE *GREAT* MONSTER HUNTERS.
heh...
YEAH, WE *ARE* PRETTY GREAT. PROBABLY THE *BEST* TEEN MONSTER HUNTERS IN THE OVERWORLD.
...WE CAN'T TELL YOU IF YOU SHOULD EAT THE ENCHANTED APPLE OR NOT.
YOU HAVE TO DECIDE THAT YOURSELF. YOU'RE THE ONE WHO HAS TO DEAL WITH THE CONSEQUENCES.
DECISIONS ARE HARD!! *AGH!*
PUT AWAY
...ENCHANTED APPLES DON'T GO BAD, DO THEY?
ZZZ
GO TO SLEEP, ATRIA

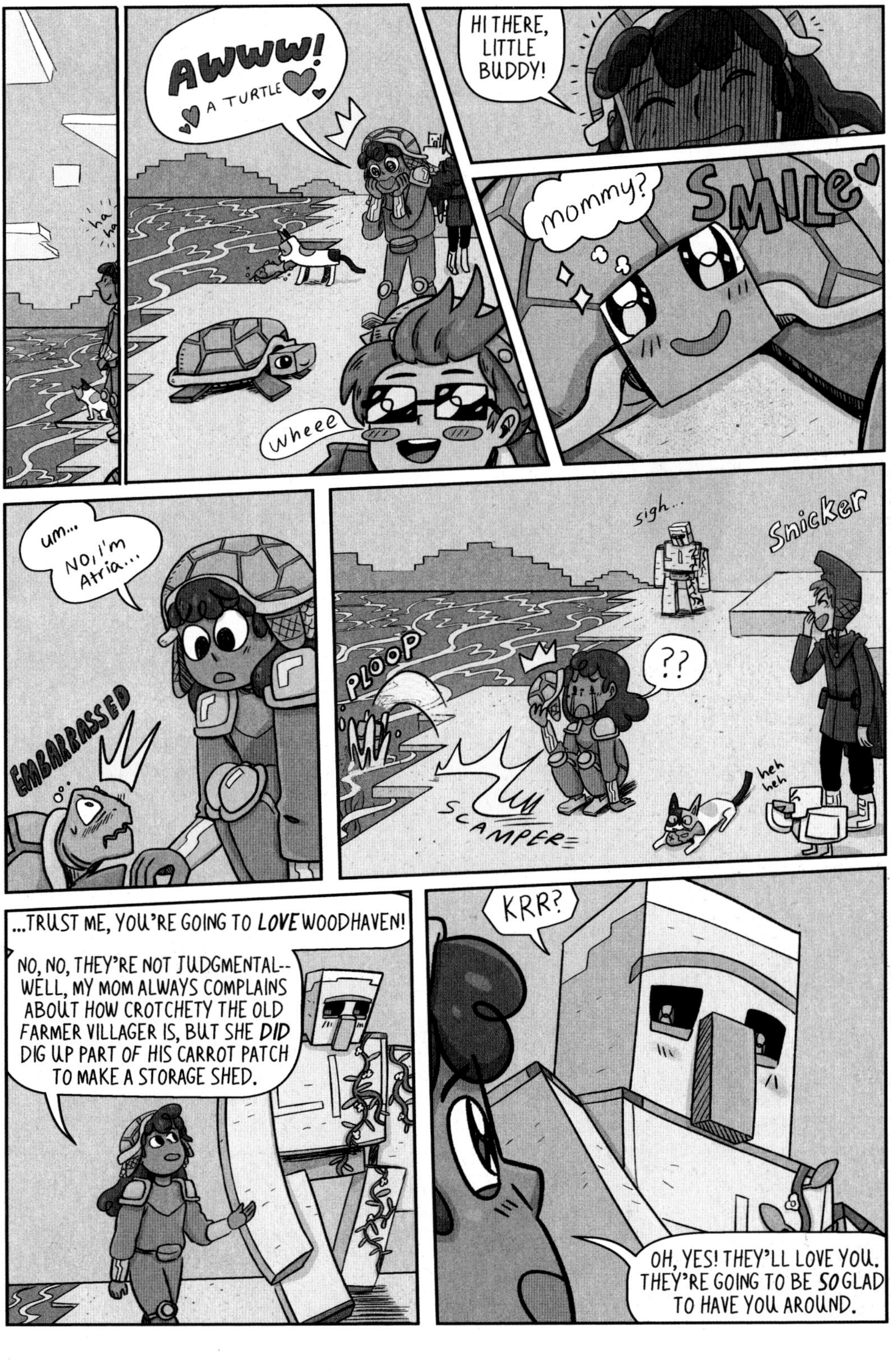
ha ha
AWWW! A TURTLE
HI THERE, LITTLE BUDDY!
wheee
mommy?
SMILE
um... No, I'm Atria...
EMBARRASSED
sigh...
Snicker
PLOOP
??
SCAMPER
heh heh
...TRUST ME, YOU'RE GOING TO LOVE WOODHAVEN!
NO, NO, THEY'RE NOT JUDGMENTAL-- WELL, MY MOM ALWAYS COMPLAINS ABOUT HOW CROTCHETY THE OLD FARMER VILLAGER IS, BUT SHE DID DIG UP PART OF HIS CARROT PATCH TO MAKE A STORAGE SHED.
KRR?
OH, YES! THEY'LL LOVE YOU. THEY'RE GOING TO BE SO GLAD TO HAVE YOU AROUND.

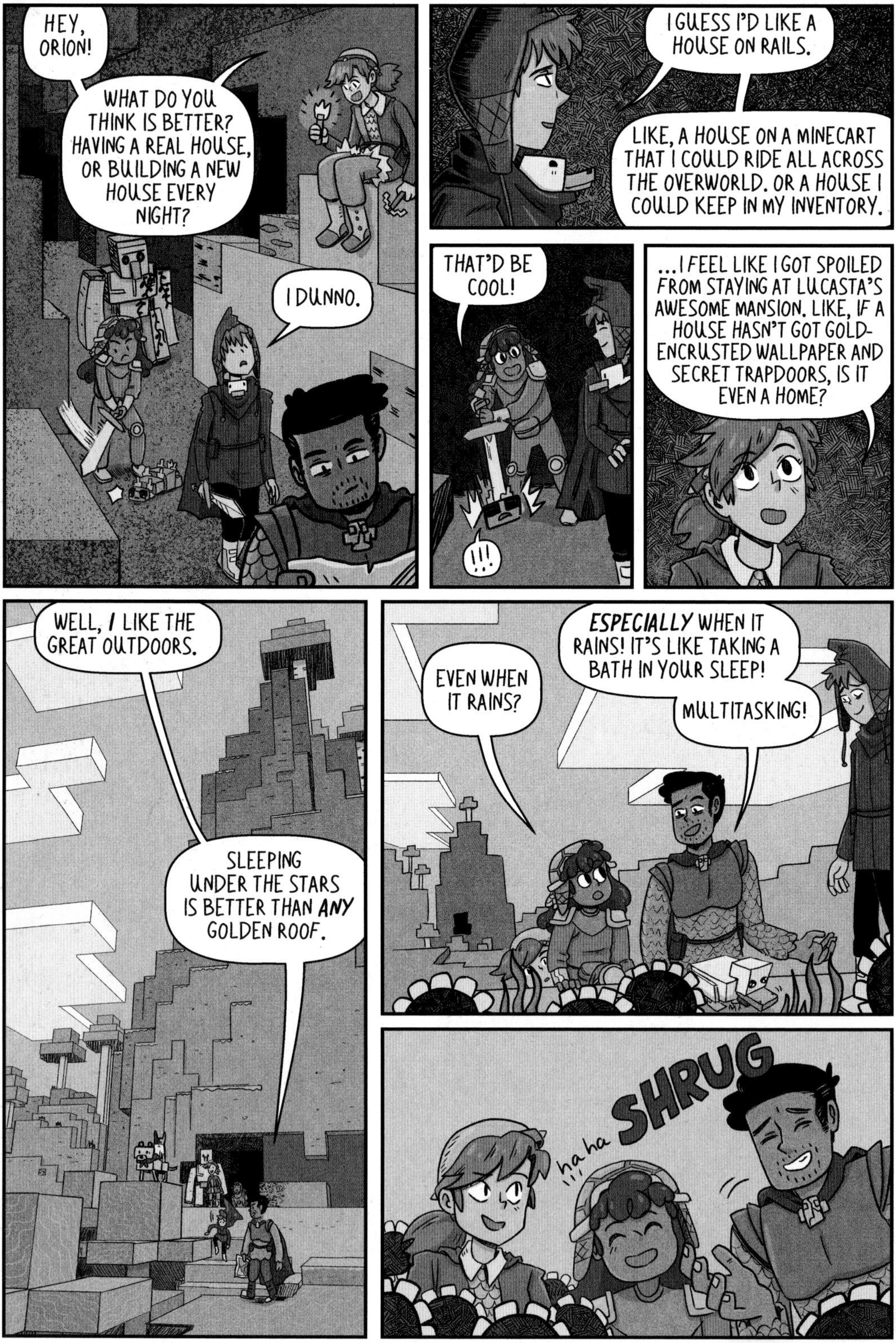
HEY, ORION!
WHAT DO YOU THINK IS BETTER? HAVING A REAL HOUSE, OR BUILDING A NEW HOUSE EVERY NIGHT?
I DUNNO.
I GUESS I'D LIKE A HOUSE ON RAILS.
LIKE, A HOUSE ON A MINECART THAT I COULD RIDE ALL ACROSS THE OVERWORLD. OR A HOUSE I COULD KEEP IN MY INVENTORY.
THAT'D BE COOL!
!!!
...I FEEL LIKE I GOT SPOILED FROM STAYING AT LUCASTA'S AWESOME MANSION. LIKE, IF A HOUSE HASN'T GOT GOLD-ENCRUSTED WALLPAPER AND SECRET TRAPDOORS, IS IT EVEN A HOME?
WELL, *I* LIKE THE GREAT OUTDOORS.
SLEEPING UNDER THE STARS IS BETTER THAN *ANY* GOLDEN ROOF.
EVEN WHEN IT RAINS?
ESPECIALLY WHEN IT RAINS! IT'S LIKE TAKING A BATH IN YOUR SLEEP!
MULTITASKING!
SHRUG
ha ha

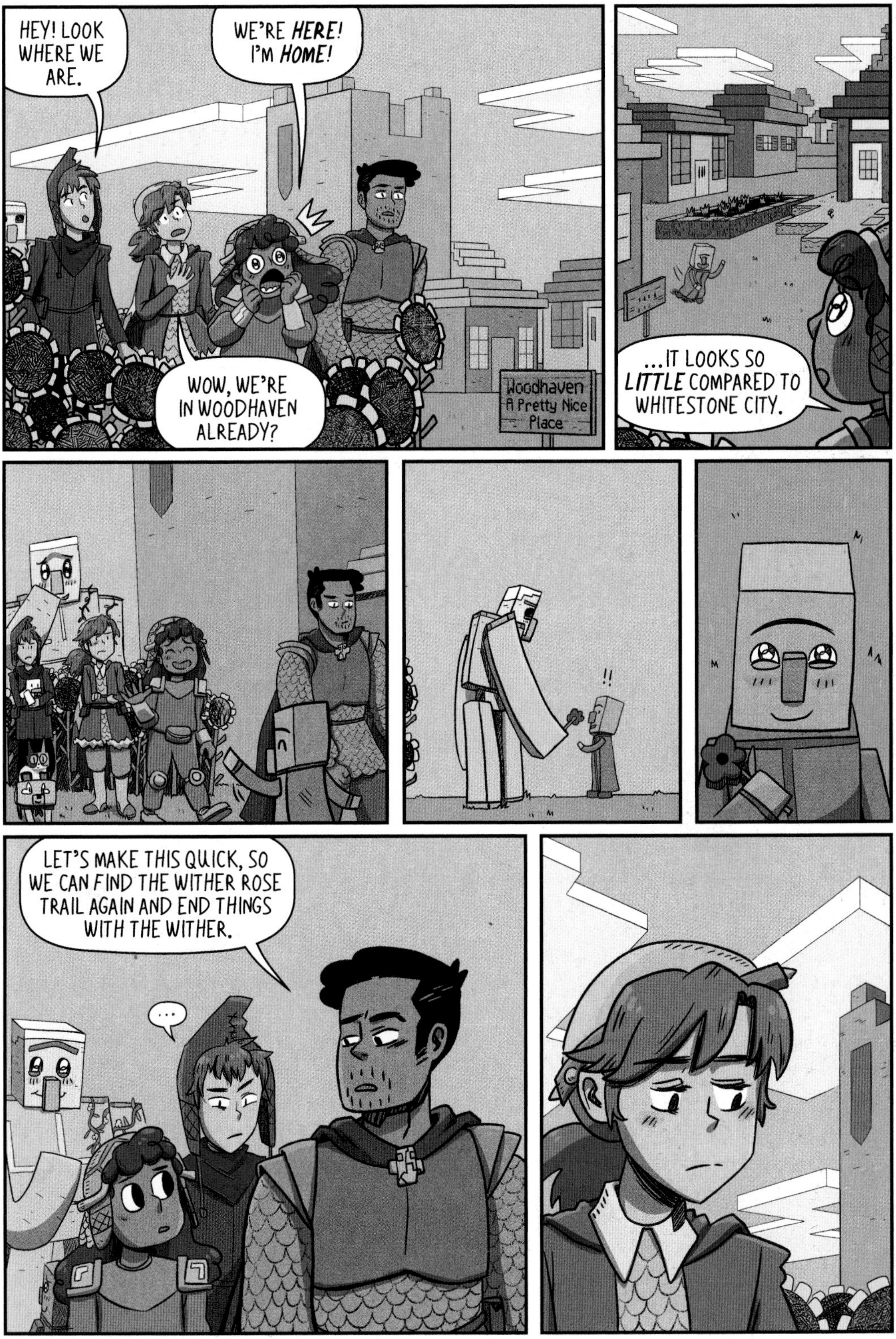
HEY! LOOK WHERE WE ARE.
WE'RE HERE! I'M HOME!
WOW, WE'RE IN WOODHAVEN ALREADY?
Woodhaven A Pretty Nice Place
...IT LOOKS SO LITTLE COMPARED TO WHITESTONE CITY.
!!
LET'S MAKE THIS QUICK, SO WE CAN FIND THE WITHER ROSE TRAIL AGAIN AND END THINGS WITH THE WITHER.
...

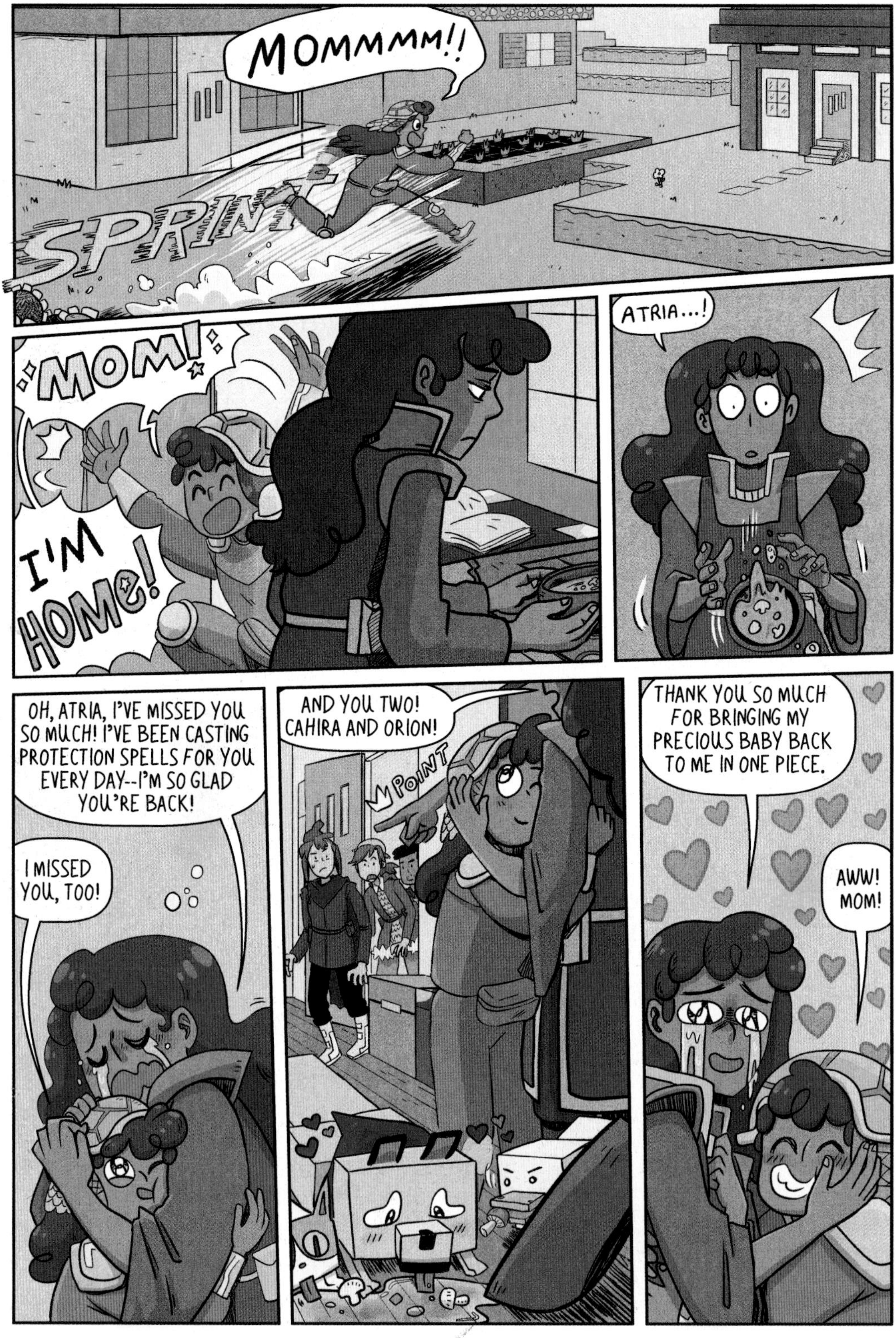
MOMMMM!!
SPRINT
MOM!
I'M HOME!
ATRIA...!
OH, ATRIA, I'VE MISSED YOU SO MUCH! I'VE BEEN CASTING PROTECTION SPELLS FOR YOU EVERY DAY--I'M SO GLAD YOU'RE BACK!
I MISSED YOU, TOO!
AND YOU TWO! CAHIRA AND ORION!
POINT
THANK YOU SO MUCH FOR BRINGING MY PRECIOUS BABY BACK TO ME IN ONE PIECE.
AWW! MOM!

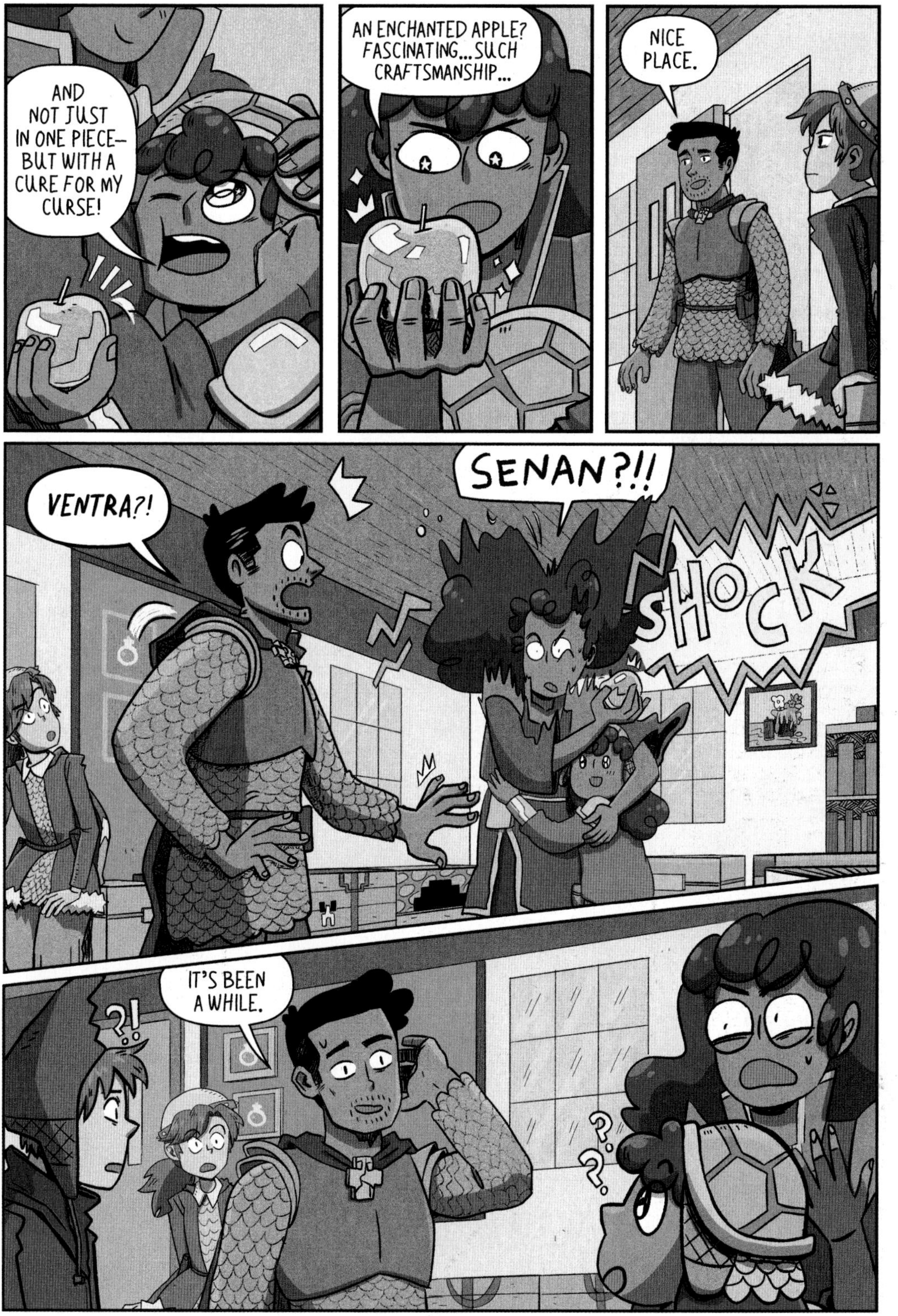
AND NOT JUST IN ONE PIECE— BUT WITH A CURE FOR MY CURSE!
AN ENCHANTED APPLE? FASCINATING... SUCH CRAFTSMANSHIP...
NICE PLACE.
VENTRA?!
SENAN?!!
SHOCK
IT'S BEEN A WHILE.
?!
??

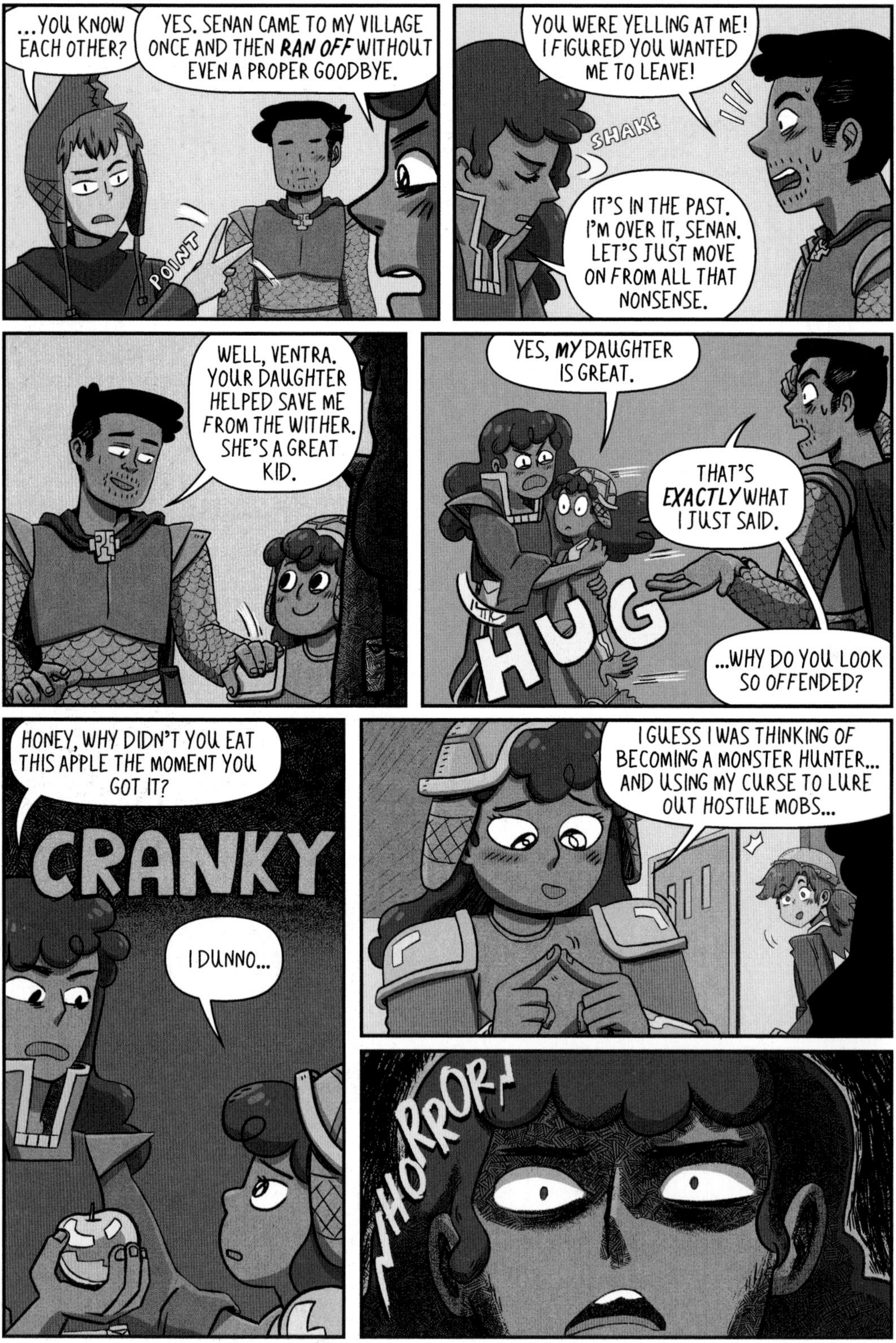
...YOU KNOW EACH OTHER?
YES. SENAN CAME TO MY VILLAGE ONCE AND THEN **RAN OFF** WITHOUT EVEN A PROPER GOODBYE.
POINT
YOU WERE YELLING AT ME! I FIGURED YOU WANTED ME TO LEAVE!
SHAKE
IT'S IN THE PAST. I'M OVER IT, SENAN. LET'S JUST MOVE ON FROM ALL THAT NONSENSE.
WELL, VENTRA. YOUR DAUGHTER HELPED SAVE ME FROM THE WITHER. SHE'S A GREAT KID.
YES, **MY** DAUGHTER IS GREAT.
THAT'S **EXACTLY** WHAT I JUST SAID.
HUG
...WHY DO YOU LOOK SO OFFENDED?
HONEY, WHY DIDN'T YOU EAT THIS APPLE THE MOMENT YOU GOT IT?
CRANKY
I DUNNO...
I GUESS I WAS THINKING OF BECOMING A MONSTER HUNTER... AND USING MY CURSE TO LURE OUT HOSTILE MOBS...
HORROR

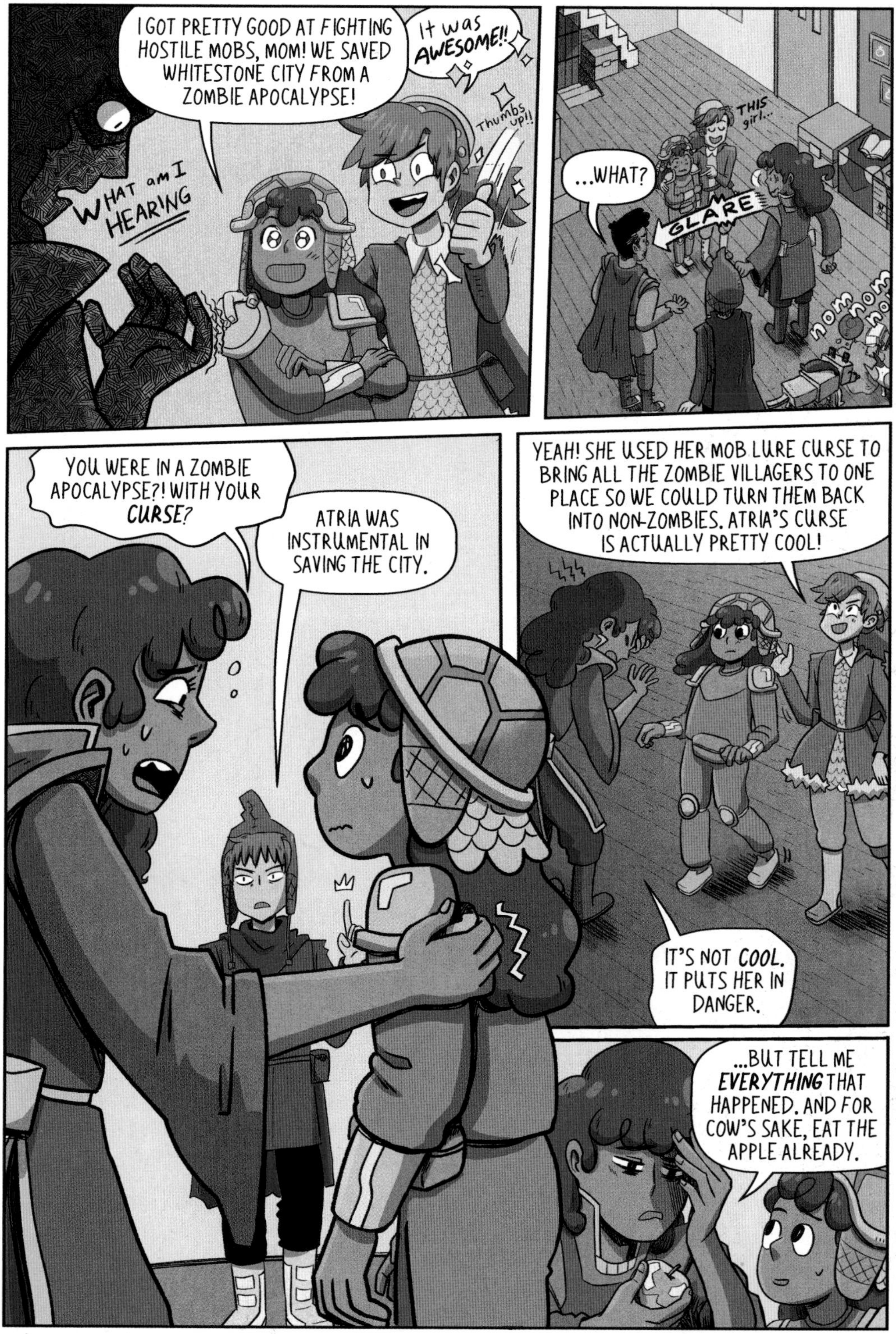
I GOT PRETTY GOOD AT FIGHTING HOSTILE MOBS, MOM! WE SAVED WHITESTONE CITY FROM A ZOMBIE APOCALYPSE!
It was AWESOME!!
Thumbs up!!
WHAT am I HEARING
THIS girl...
...WHAT?
GLARE
nom nom no
YOU WERE IN A ZOMBIE APOCALYPSE?! WITH YOUR CURSE?
ATRIA WAS INSTRUMENTAL IN SAVING THE CITY.
YEAH! SHE USED HER MOB LURE CURSE TO BRING ALL THE ZOMBIE VILLAGERS TO ONE PLACE SO WE COULD TURN THEM BACK INTO NON-ZOMBIES. ATRIA'S CURSE IS ACTUALLY PRETTY COOL!
IT'S NOT COOL. IT PUTS HER IN DANGER.
...BUT TELL ME EVERYTHING THAT HAPPENED. AND FOR COW'S SAKE, EAT THE APPLE ALREADY.

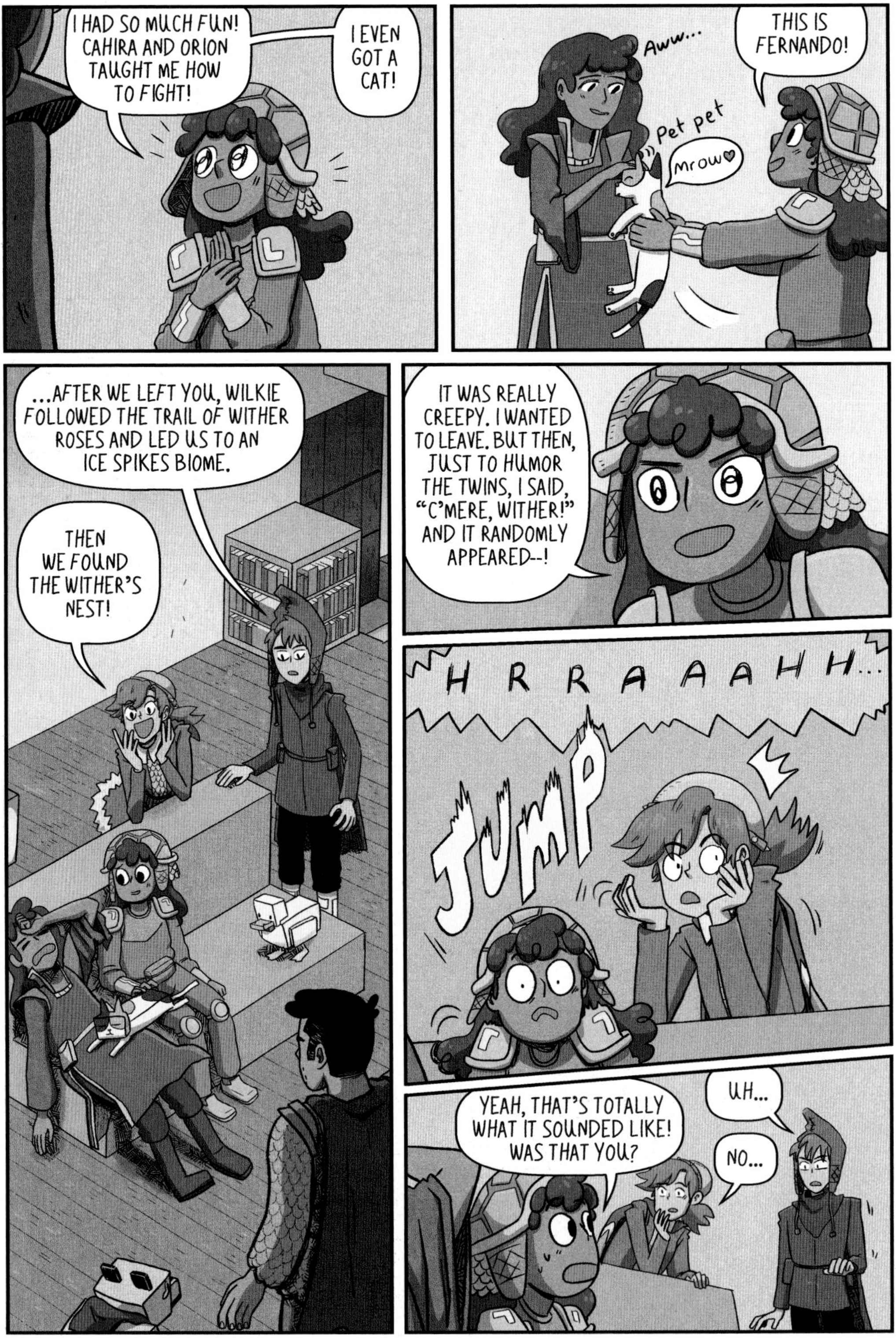
I HAD SO MUCH FUN! CAHIRA AND ORION TAUGHT ME HOW TO FIGHT!
I EVEN GOT A CAT!
Aww...
THIS IS FERNANDO!
Pet pet
Mrow♥
...AFTER WE LEFT YOU, WILKIE FOLLOWED THE TRAIL OF WITHER ROSES AND LED US TO AN ICE SPIKES BIOME.
THEN WE FOUND THE WITHER'S NEST!
IT WAS REALLY CREEPY. I WANTED TO LEAVE. BUT THEN, JUST TO HUMOR THE TWINS, I SAID, "C'MERE, WITHER!" AND IT RANDOMLY APPEARED--!
HRRAAAHH...
JUMP
YEAH, THAT'S TOTALLY WHAT IT SOUNDED LIKE! WAS THAT YOU?
UH...
NO...

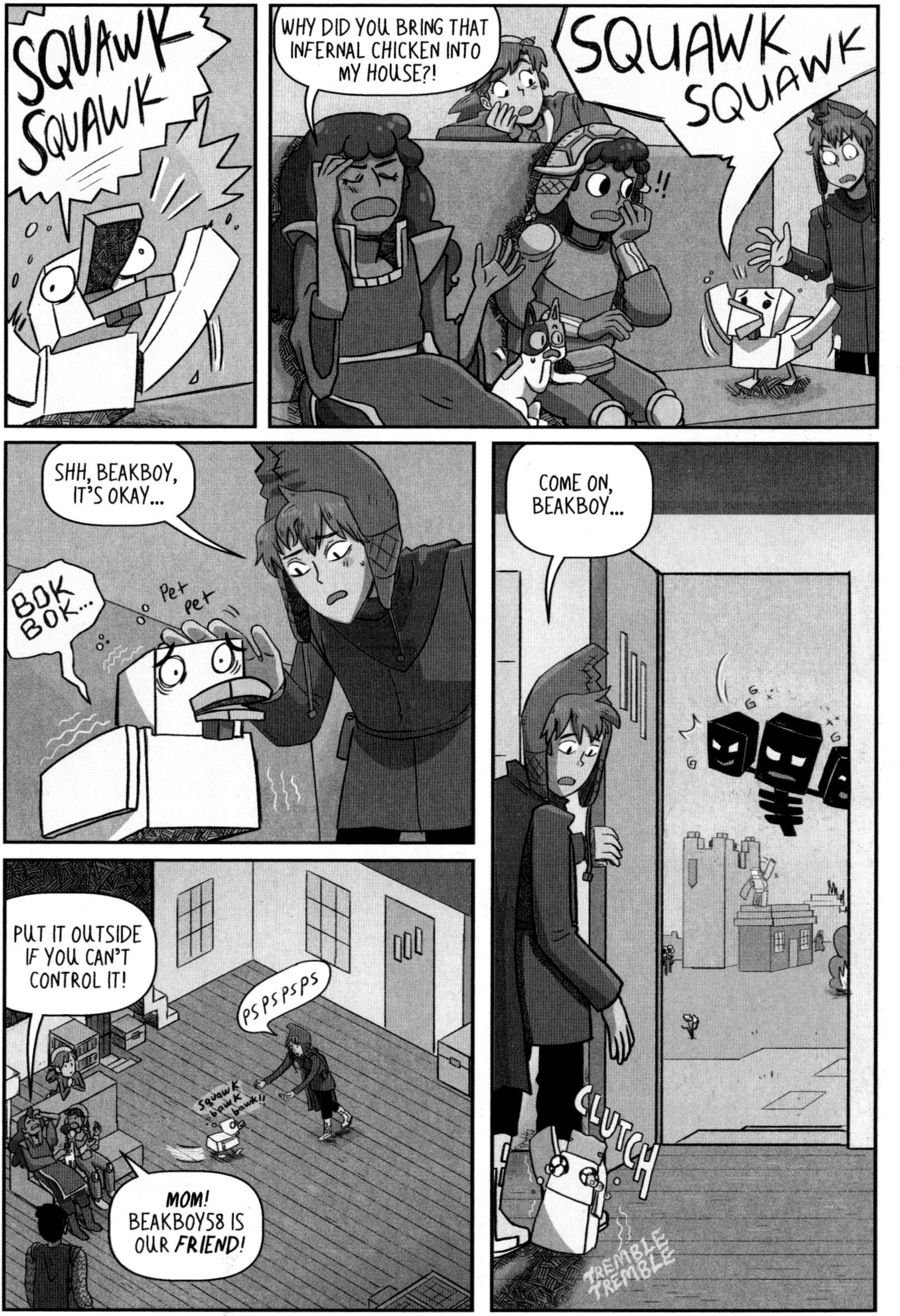
SQUAWK
SQUAWK
WHY DID YOU BRING THAT INFERNAL CHICKEN INTO MY HOUSE?!
SQUAWK
SQUAWK
SHH, BEAKBOY, IT'S OKAY...
BOK BOK...
Pet pet
COME ON, BEAKBOY...
PUT IT OUTSIDE IF YOU CAN'T CONTROL IT!
PSPSPSPS
SQUAWK BAWK BAWK!!
MOM! BEAKBOY58 IS OUR *FRIEND*!
CLUTCH
TREMBLE TREMBLE

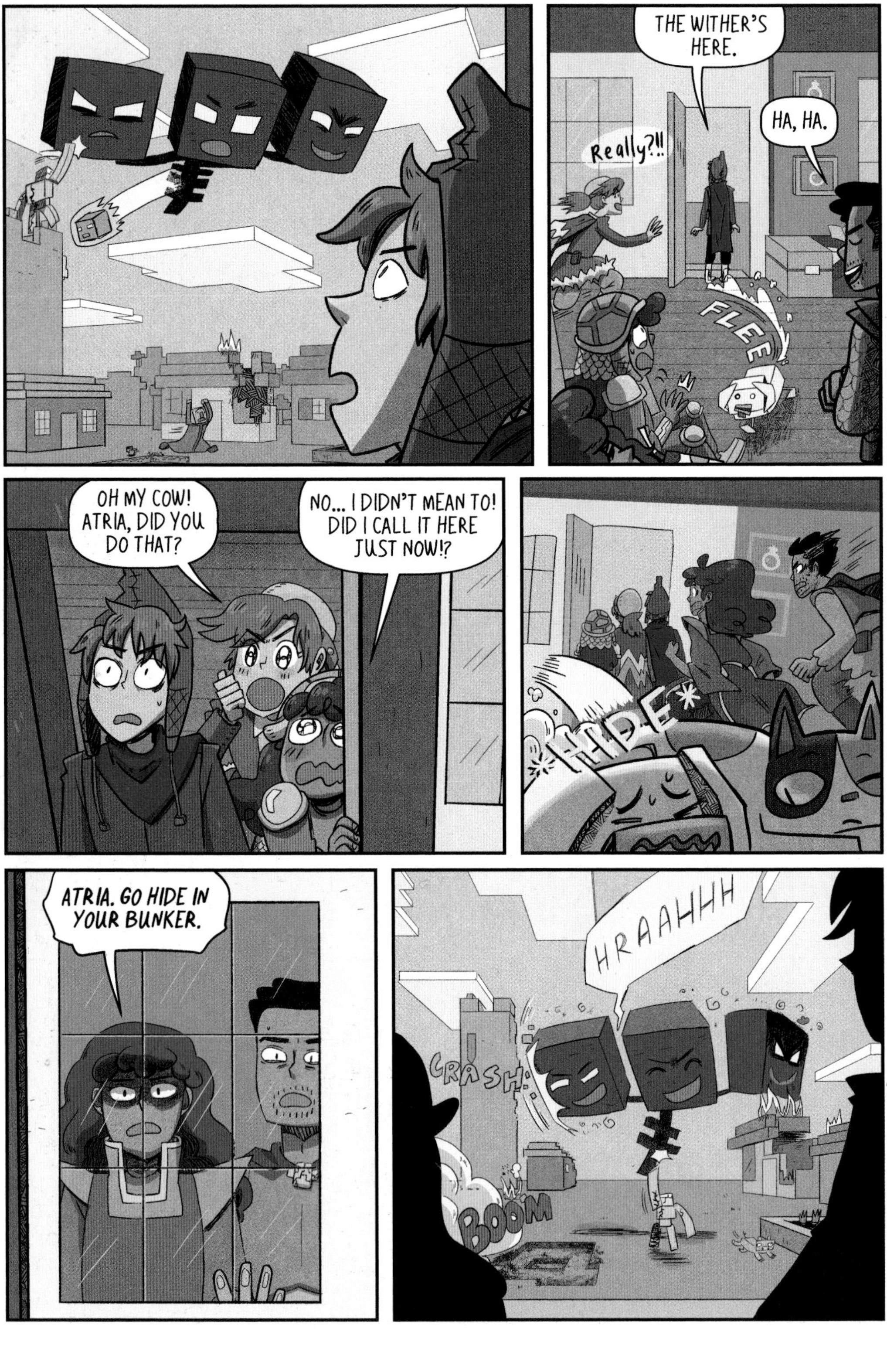
THE WITHER'S HERE.
Really?!!
HA, HA.
FLEE
OH MY COW! ATRIA, DID YOU DO THAT?
NO... I DIDN'T MEAN TO! DID I CALL IT HERE JUST NOW!?
HIDE*
ATRIA. GO HIDE IN YOUR BUNKER.
HRAAHHH
CRASH
BOOM

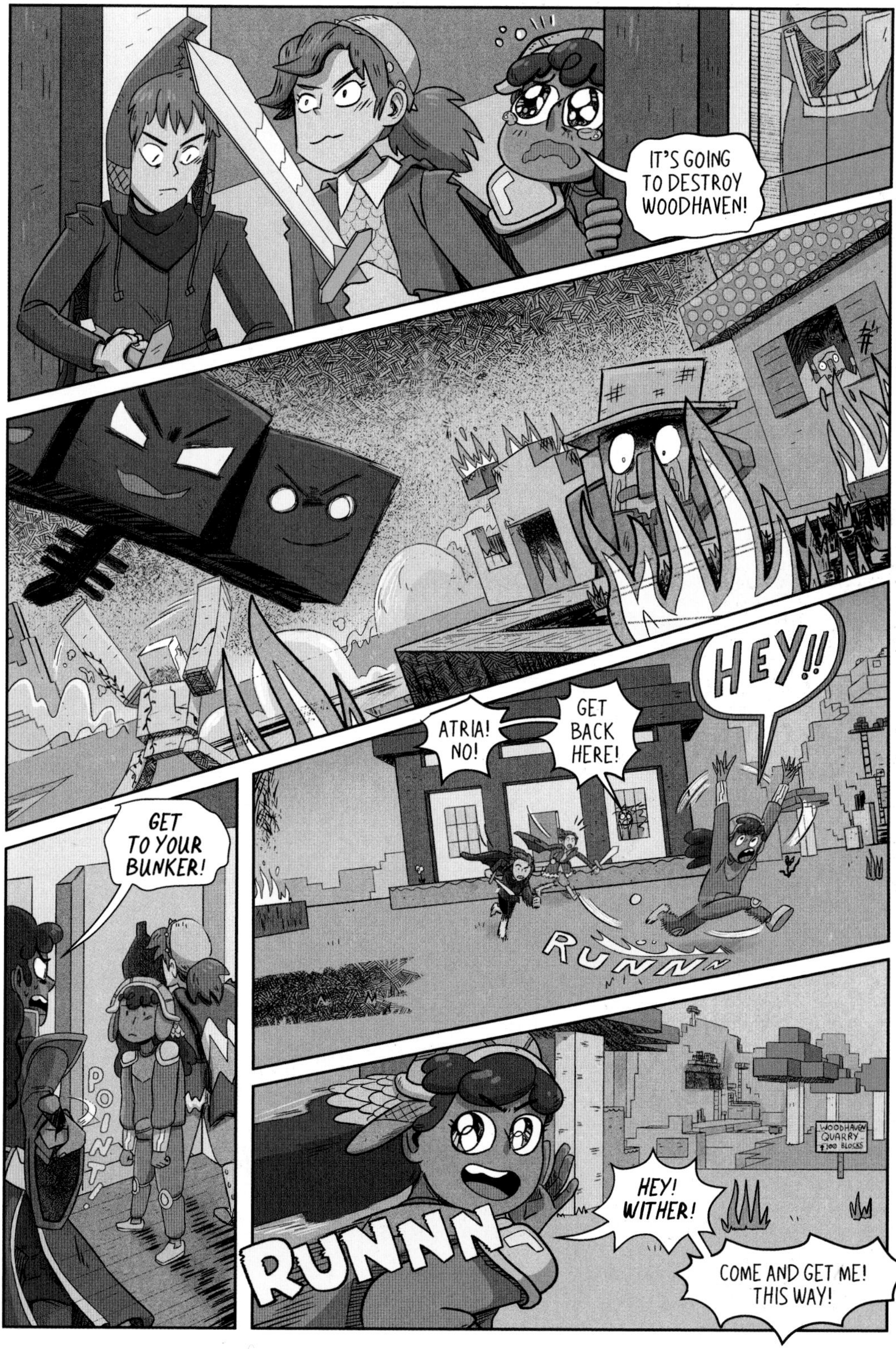

IT'S GOING TO DESTROY WOODHAVEN!
HEY!!
ATRIA! NO!
GET BACK HERE!
RUNNN
GET TO YOUR BUNKER!
POINT!
WOODHAVEN QUARRY 100 BLOCKS
RUNNN
HEY! WITHER!
COME AND GET ME! THIS WAY!

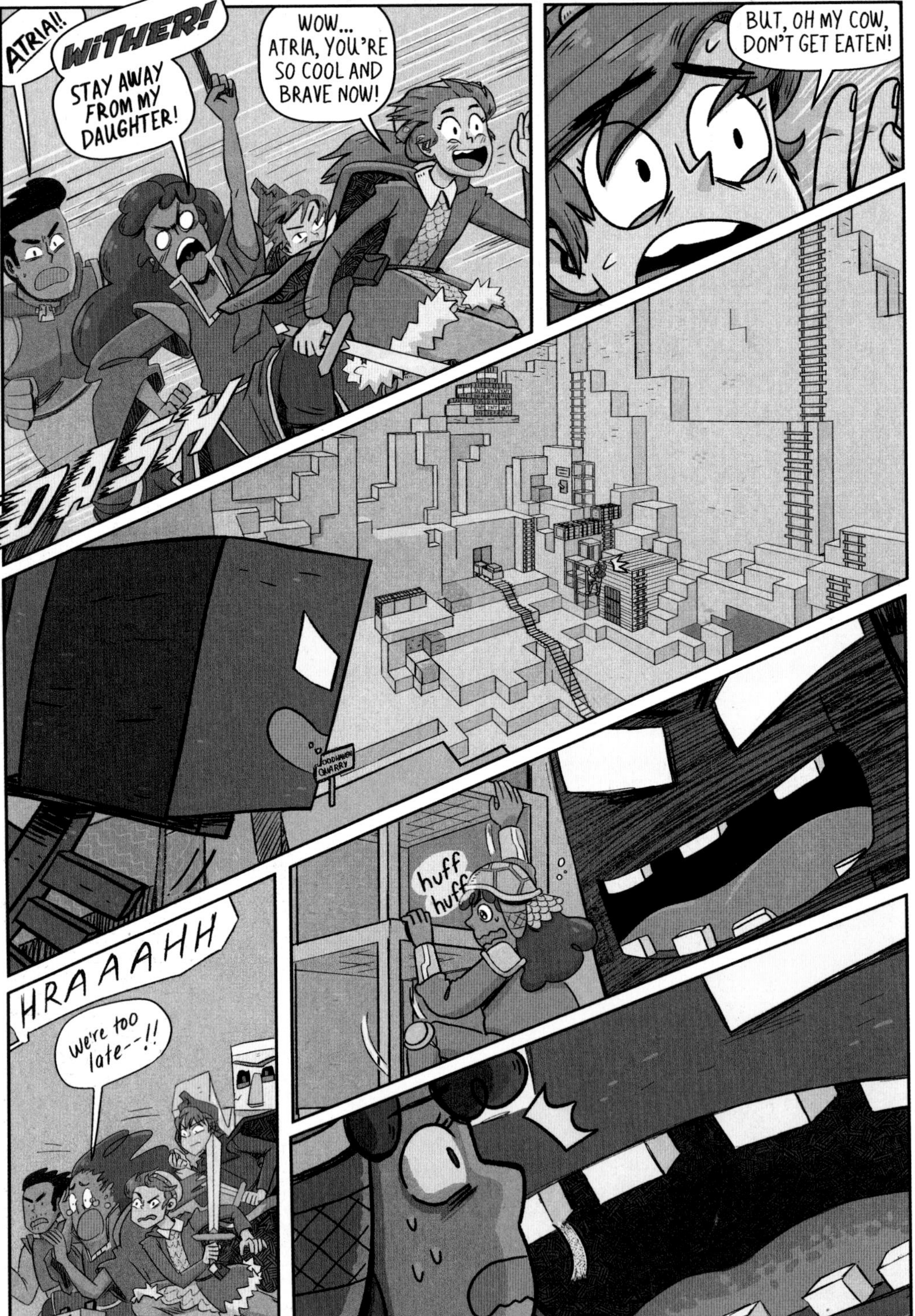
ATRIA!!
WITHER!
STAY AWAY FROM MY DAUGHTER!
WOW... ATRIA, YOU'RE SO COOL AND BRAVE NOW!
DASH
BUT, OH MY COW, DON'T GET EATEN!
QUARRY
huff huff
HRAAAHH
we're too late--!!

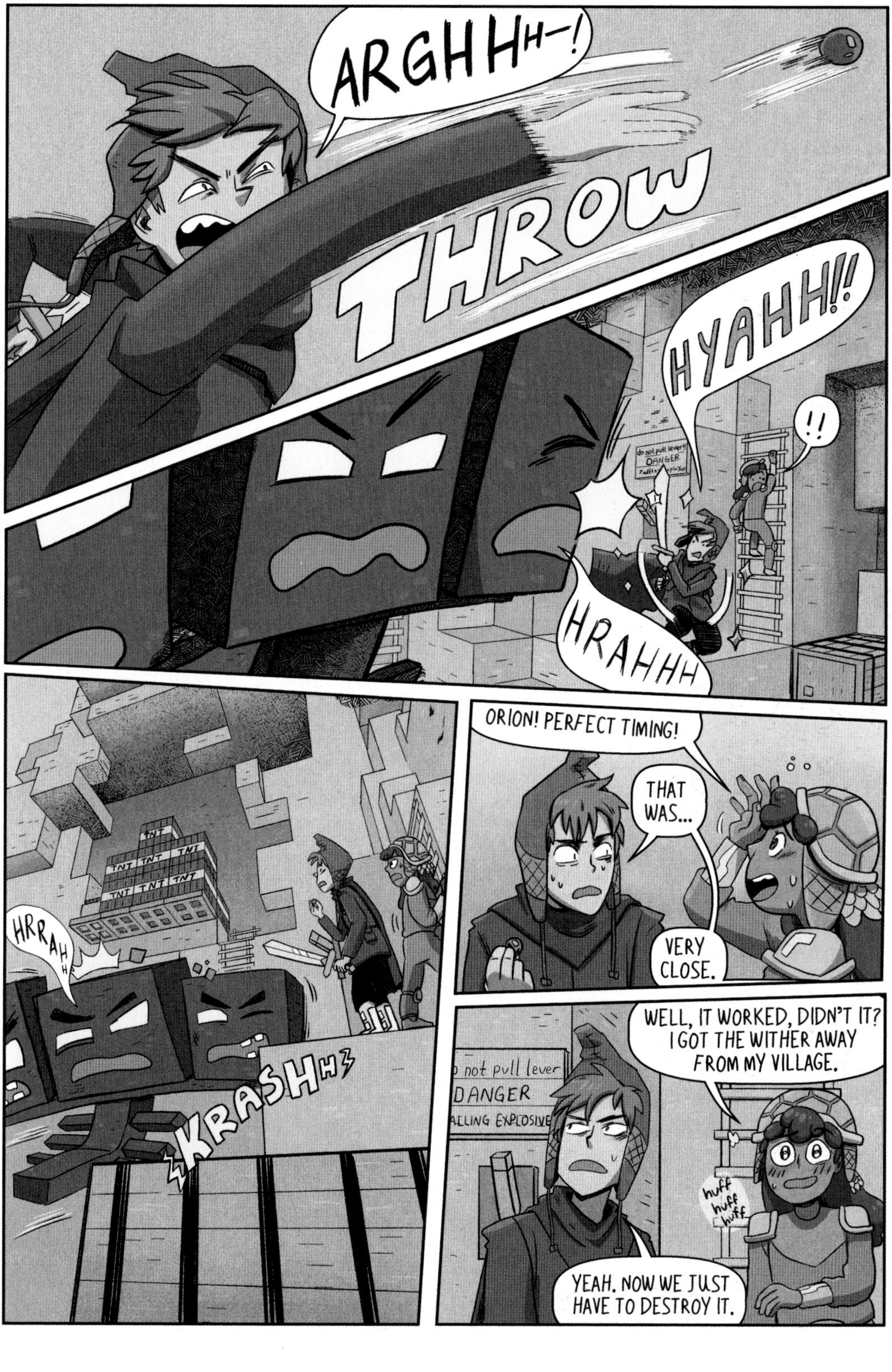
ARGHHH-!
THROW
HYAHH!!
!!
HRAHHH
HRRAHH
KRASHHH
ORION! PERFECT TIMING!
THAT WAS...
VERY CLOSE.
WELL, IT WORKED, DIDN'T IT? I GOT THE WITHER AWAY FROM MY VILLAGE.
o not pull lever
DANGER
ALLING EXPLOSIVE
huff huff huff
YEAH. NOW WE JUST HAVE TO DESTROY IT.

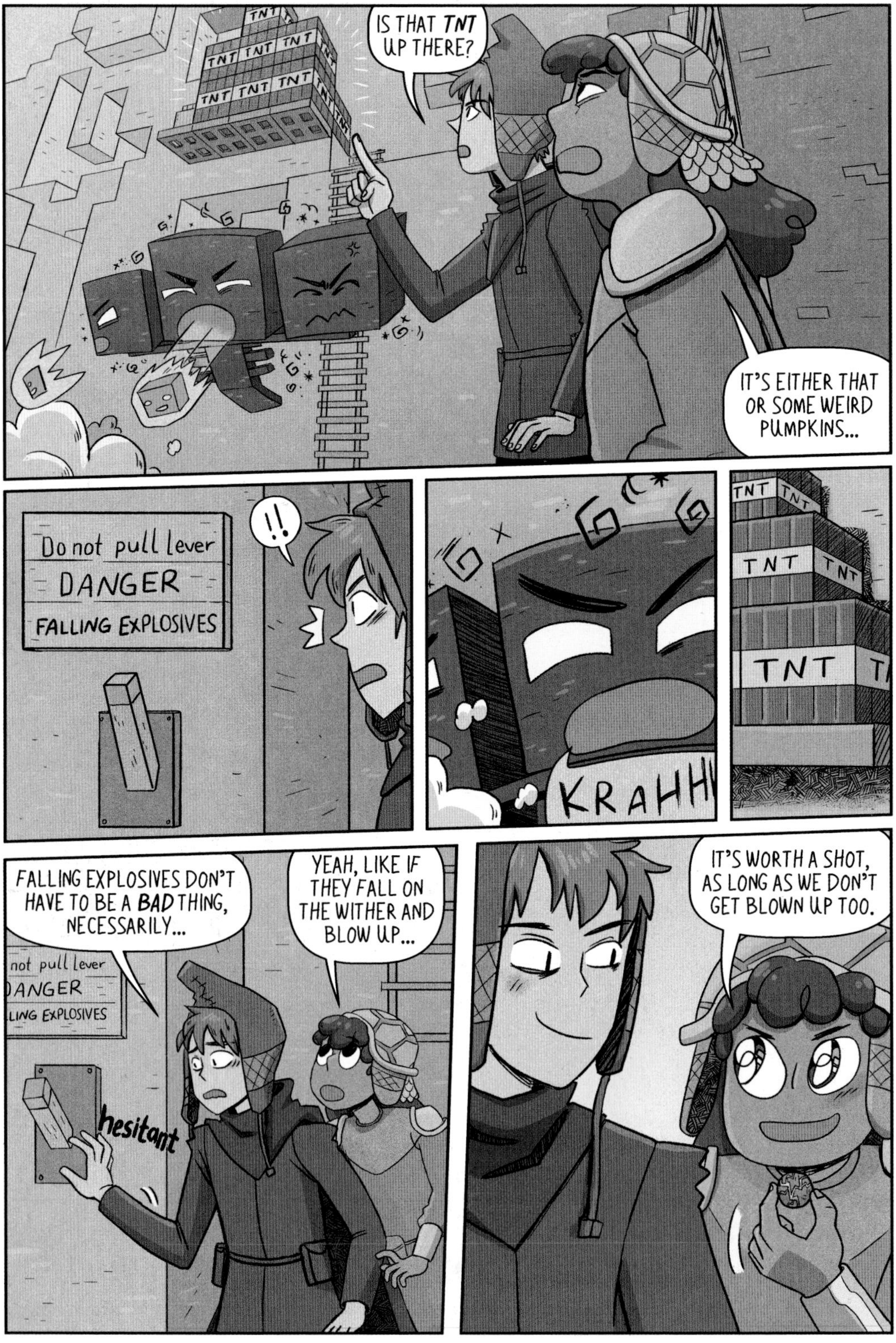

IS THAT TNT UP THERE?
IT'S EITHER THAT OR SOME WEIRD PUMPKINS...
Do not pull lever
DANGER
FALLING EXPLOSIVES
!!
KRAHH
TNT
FALLING EXPLOSIVES DON'T HAVE TO BE A BAD THING, NECESSARILY...
YEAH, LIKE IF THEY FALL ON THE WITHER AND BLOW UP...
hesitant
IT'S WORTH A SHOT, AS LONG AS WE DON'T GET BLOWN UP TOO.

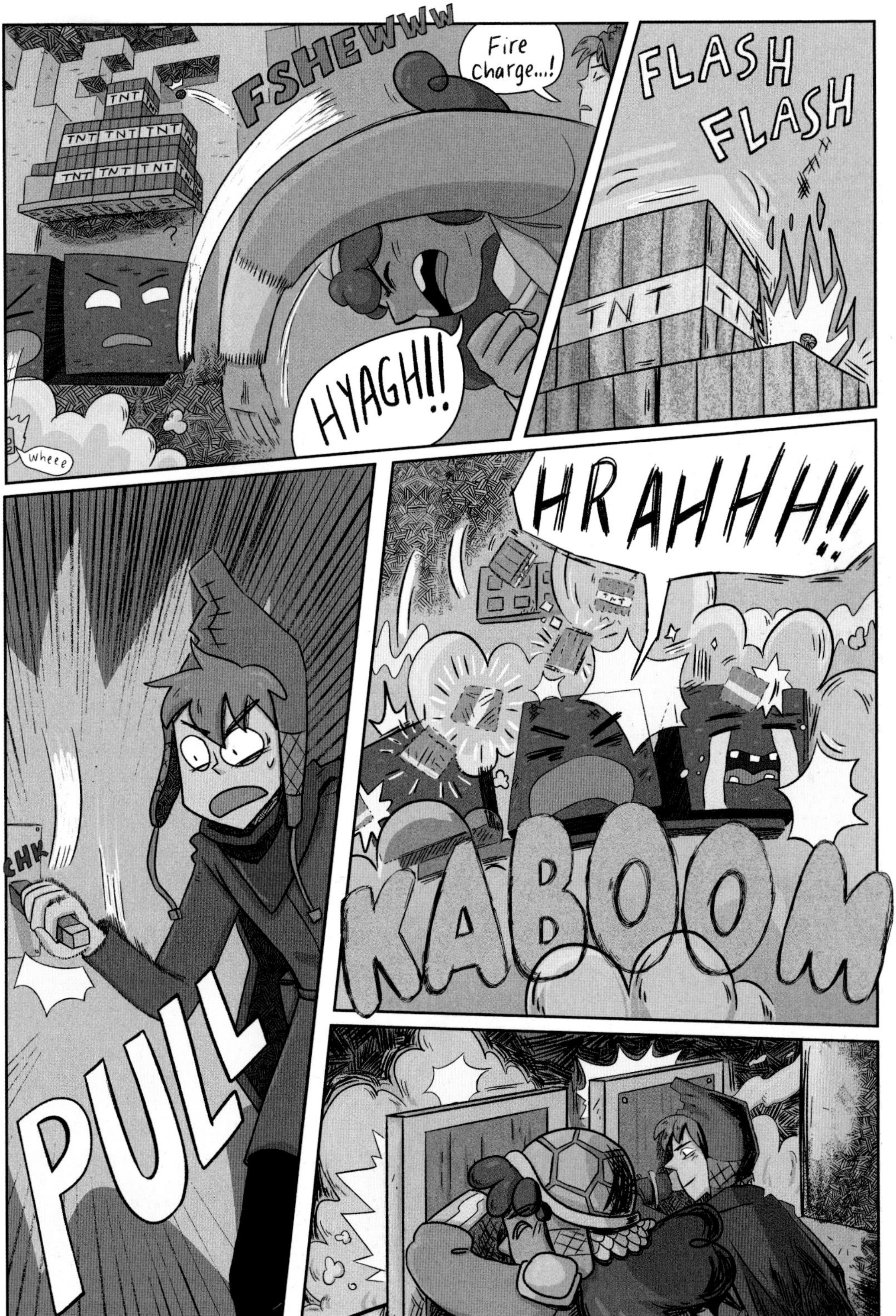
FSHEWWW
Fire charge...!
TNT
HYAGH!!
wheee
FLASH
FLASH
TNT
CHK
PULL
HRAHHH!!
KABOOM

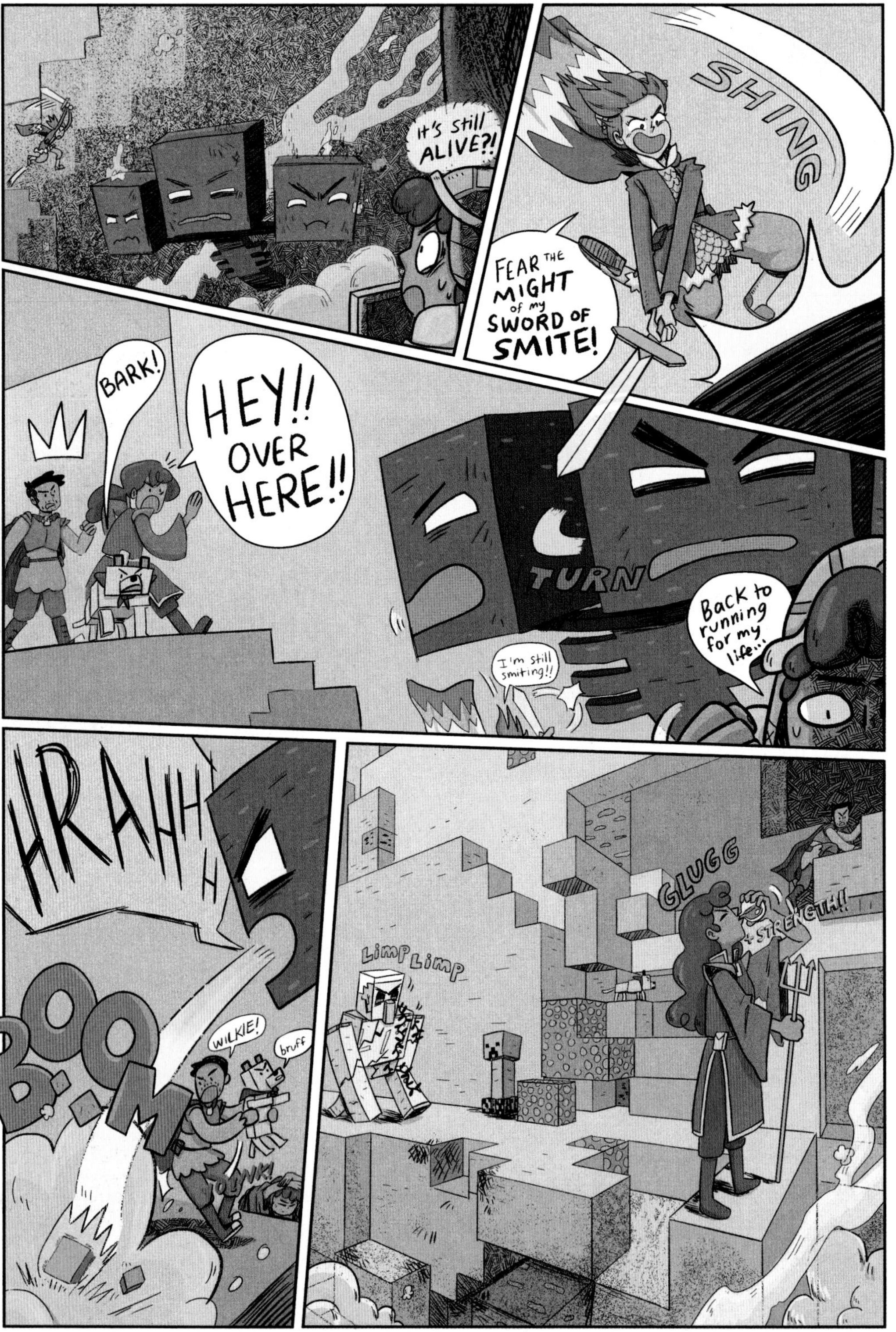

It's still ALIVE?!
SHING
FEAR THE MIGHT of my SWORD OF SMITE!
BARK!
HEY!! OVER HERE!!
TURN
I'm still smiting!!
Back to running for my life...
HRAHHH
BOOM
WILKIE!
bruff
LIMP LIMP
GLUGG
+STRENGTH!!

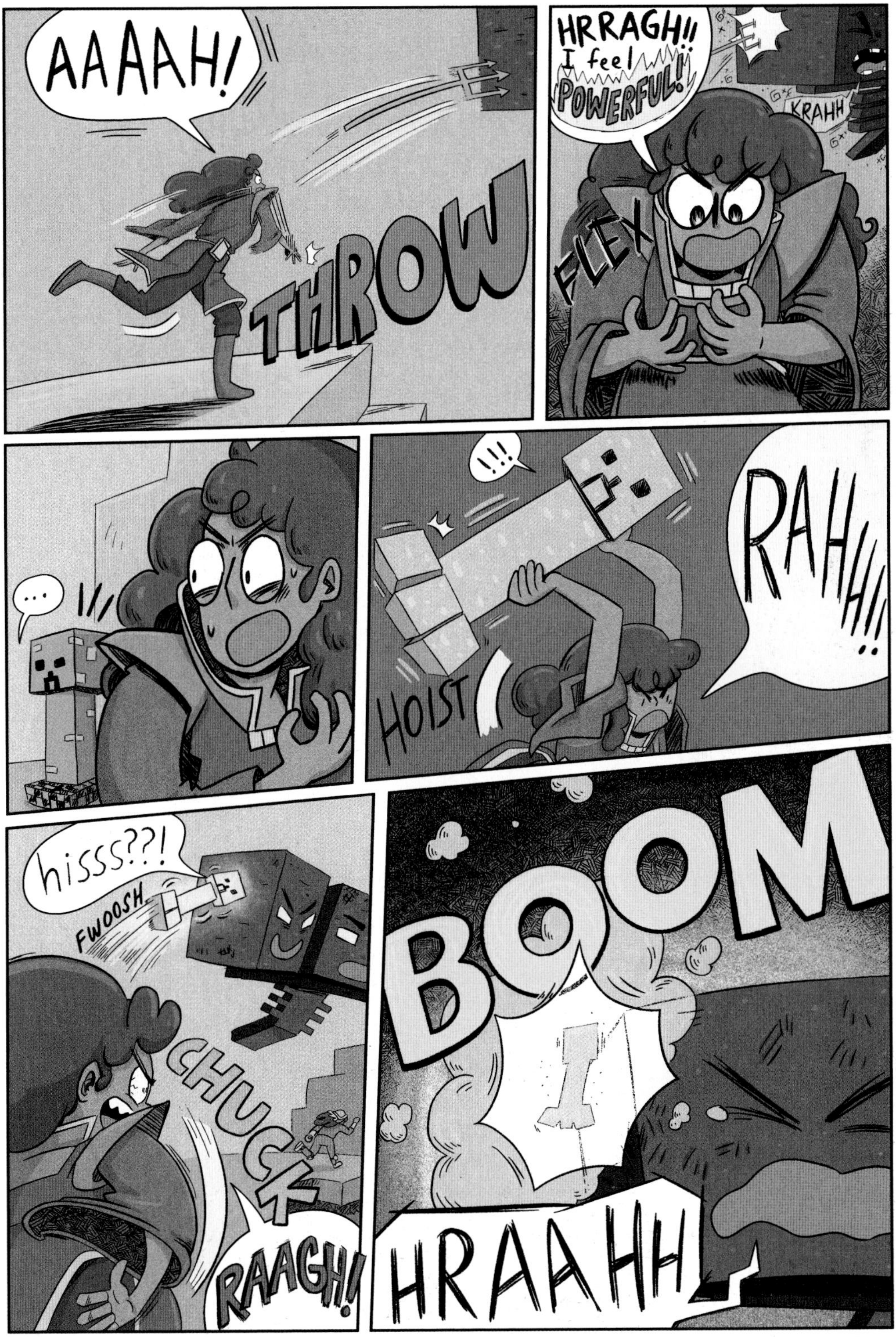
AAAAH!
THROW
HRRAGH!! I feel POWERFUL!
KRAHH
FLEX
...
!!!
RAHHH!!
HOIST
hisss??!
FWOOSH
CHUCK
RAAGH!
BOOM
HRAAHH

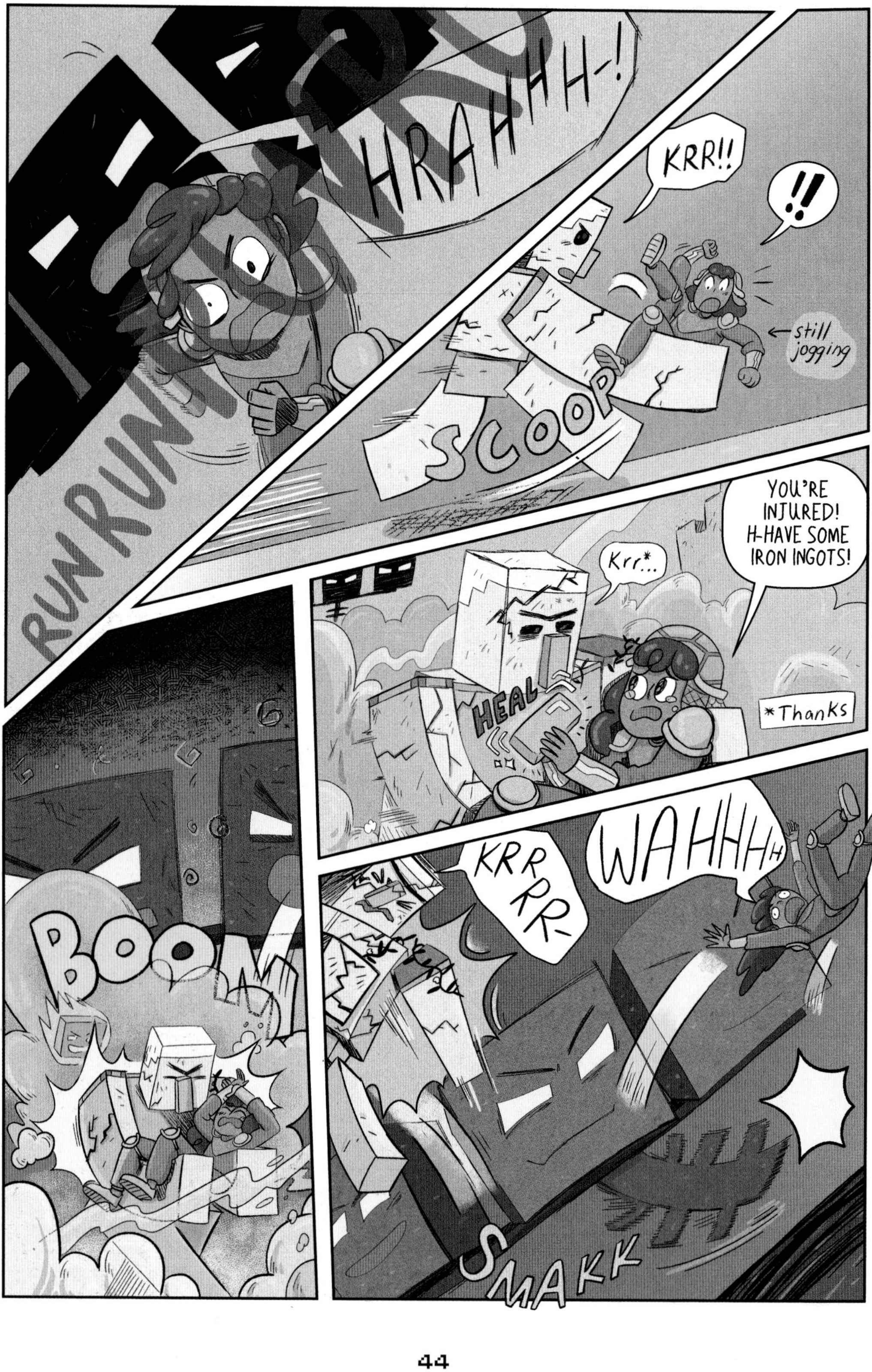
HRAHHH-!
RUN RUN
KRR!!
!!
still jogging
SCOOP
YOU'RE INJURED! H-HAVE SOME IRON INGOTS!
Krr*...
HEAL
*Thanks
BOOM
KRR RR-
WAHHHH
SMAKK

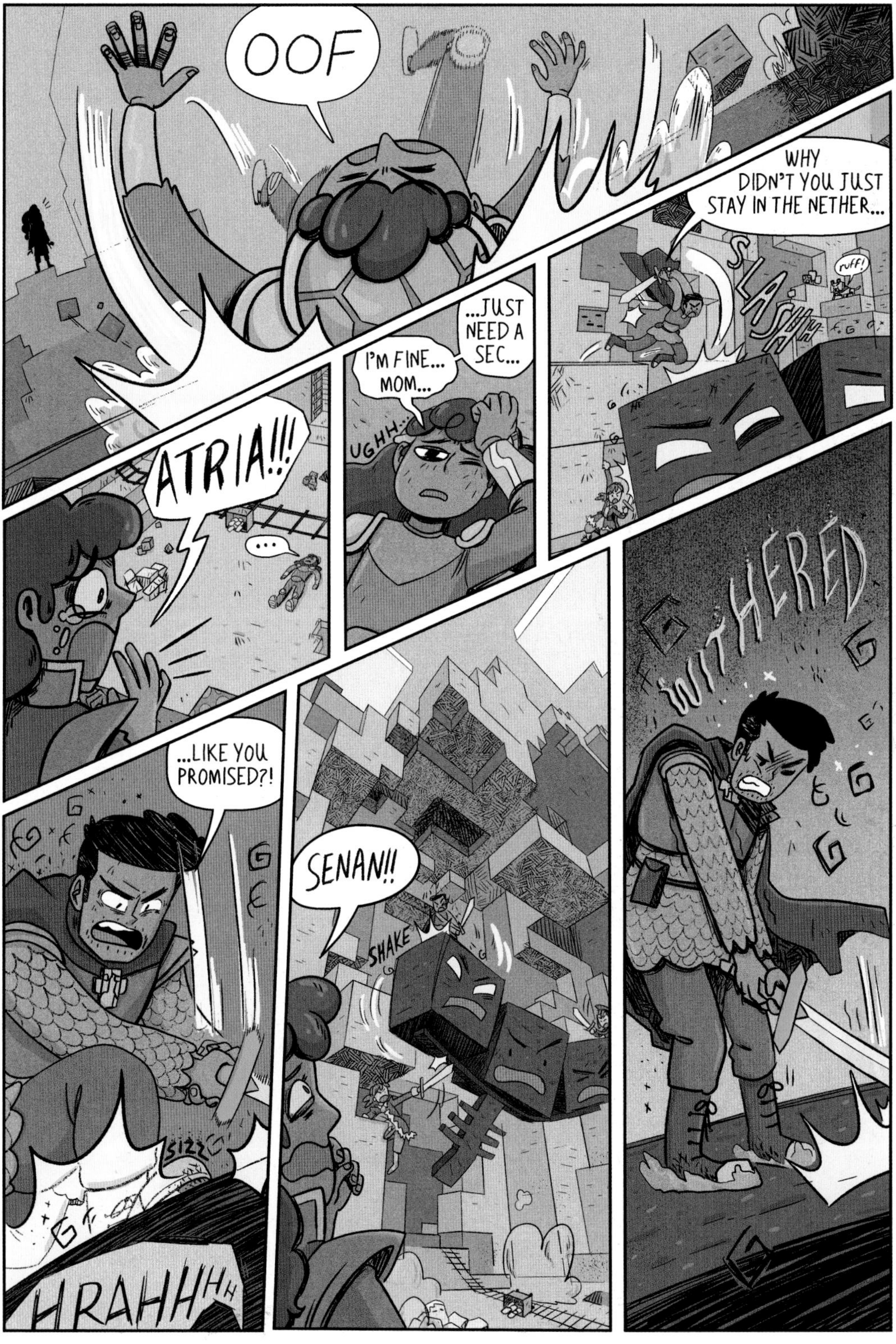
OOF
WHY DIDN'T YOU JUST STAY IN THE NETHER...
SLASHH
RUFF!
I'M FINE... MOM...
...JUST NEED A SEC...
UGHH
ATRIA!!!
...
...LIKE YOU PROMISED?!
SENAN!!
SHAKE
WITHERED
SIZZ
HRAHHHH

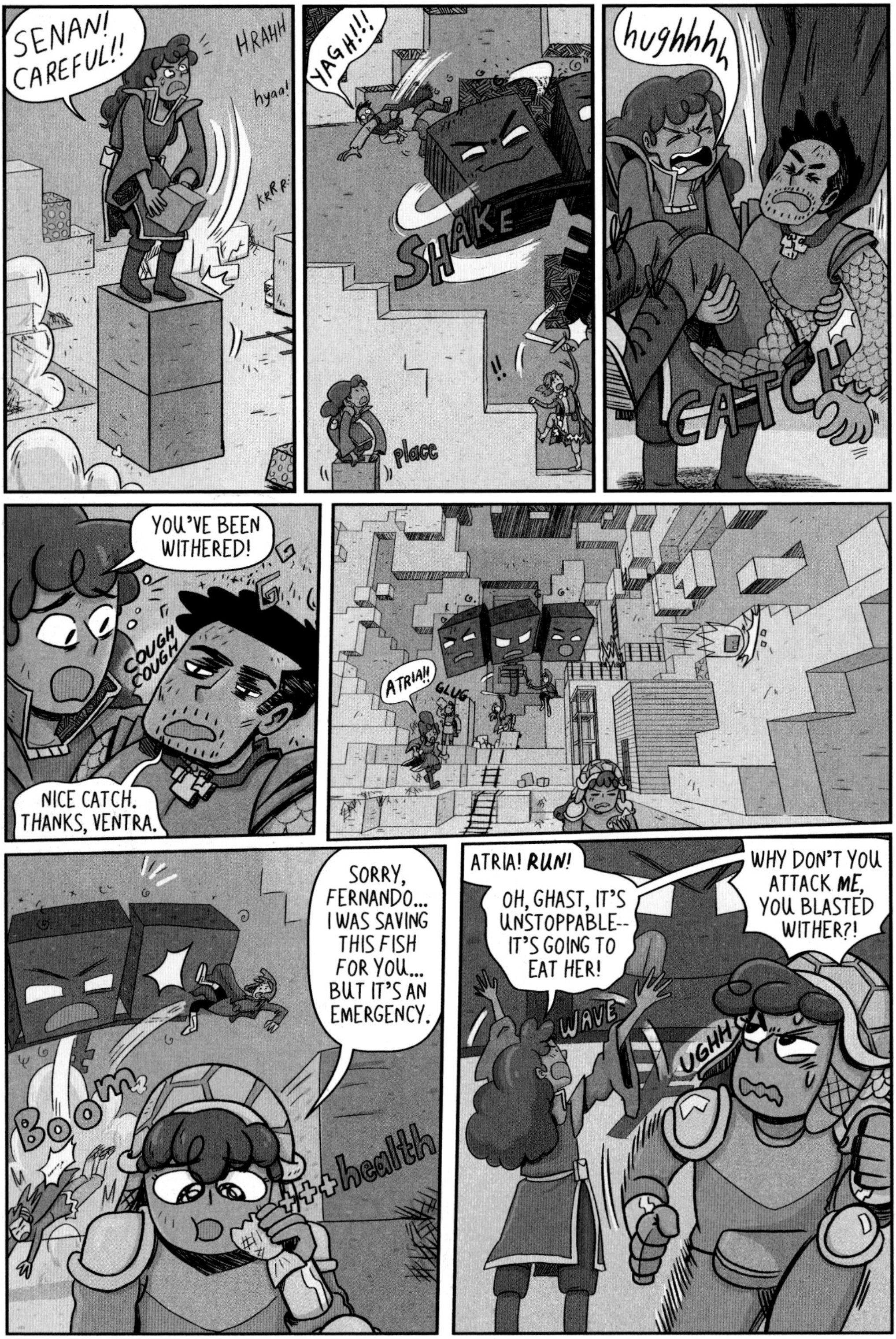
SENAN! CAREFUL!!
HRAHH
hyaa!
KRRR
YAGH!!!
SHAKE
!!
place
hughhhh
CATCH
YOU'VE BEEN WITHERED!
COUGH COUGH
NICE CATCH. THANKS, VENTRA.
ATRIA!!
GLUG
SORRY, FERNANDO... I WAS SAVING THIS FISH FOR YOU... BUT IT'S AN EMERGENCY.
Boom
+++health
ATRIA! RUN!
OH, GHAST, IT'S UNSTOPPABLE-- IT'S GOING TO EAT HER!
WHY DON'T YOU ATTACK ME, YOU BLASTED WITHER?!
WAVE
UGHH

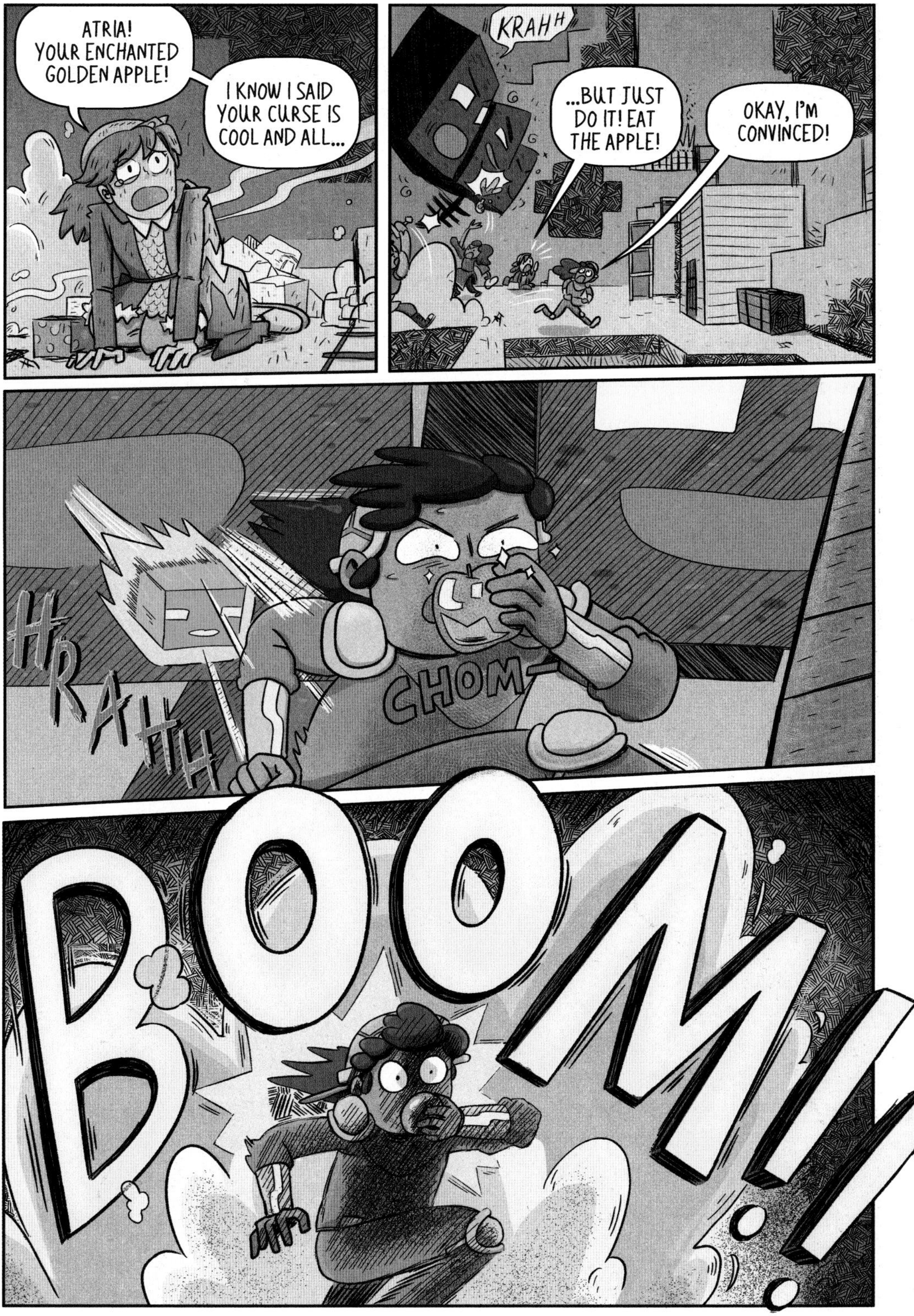
ATRIA! YOUR ENCHANTED GOLDEN APPLE!
I KNOW I SAID YOUR CURSE IS COOL AND ALL...
KRAHH
...BUT JUST DO IT! EAT THE APPLE!
OKAY, I'M CONVINCED!
HRAHH
CHOM-
BOOM!!

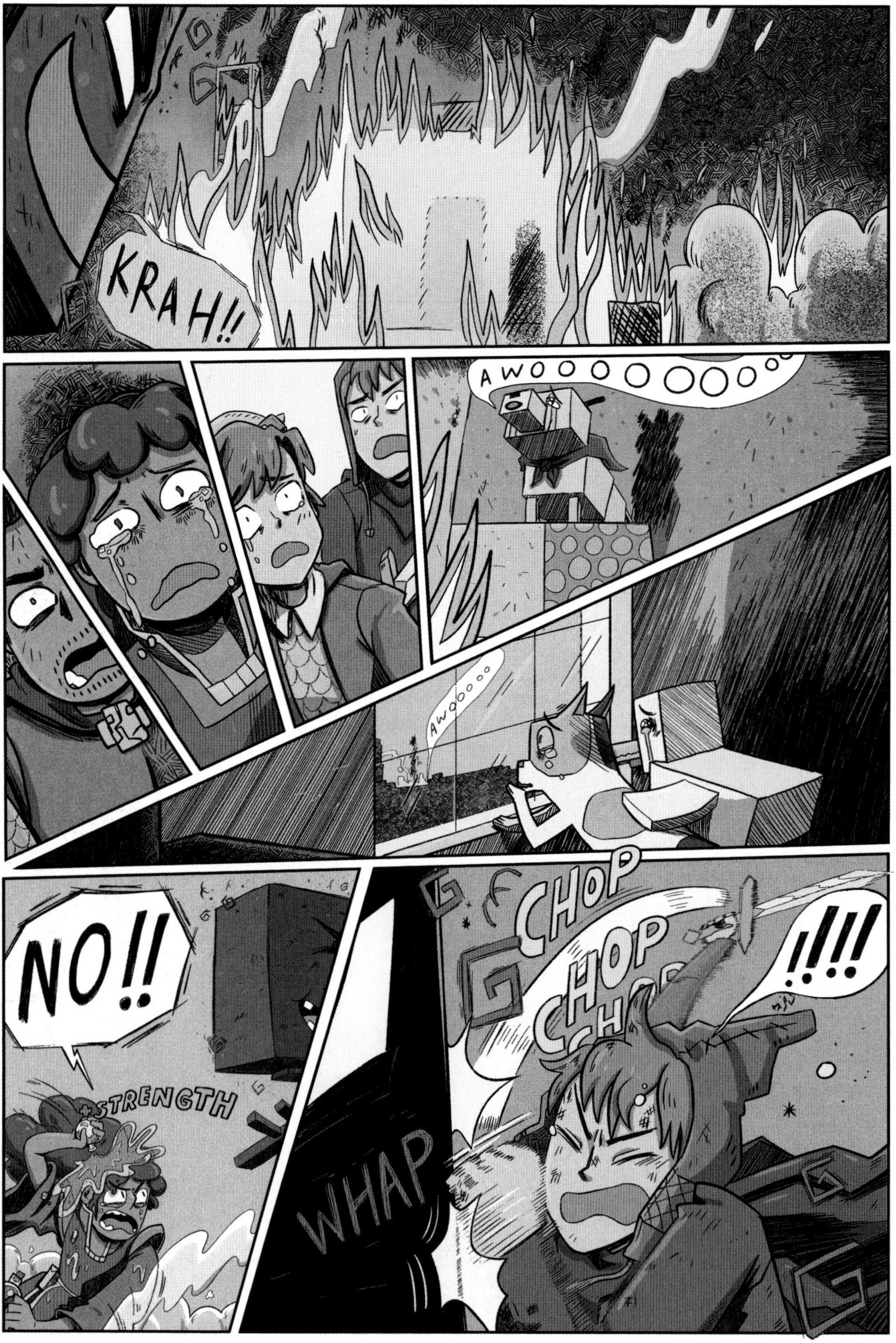
KRAH!!
AWOOOOOOOOOOo
AWOOOOO
NO!!
+STRENGTH
WHAP
CHOP
CHOP
!!!!

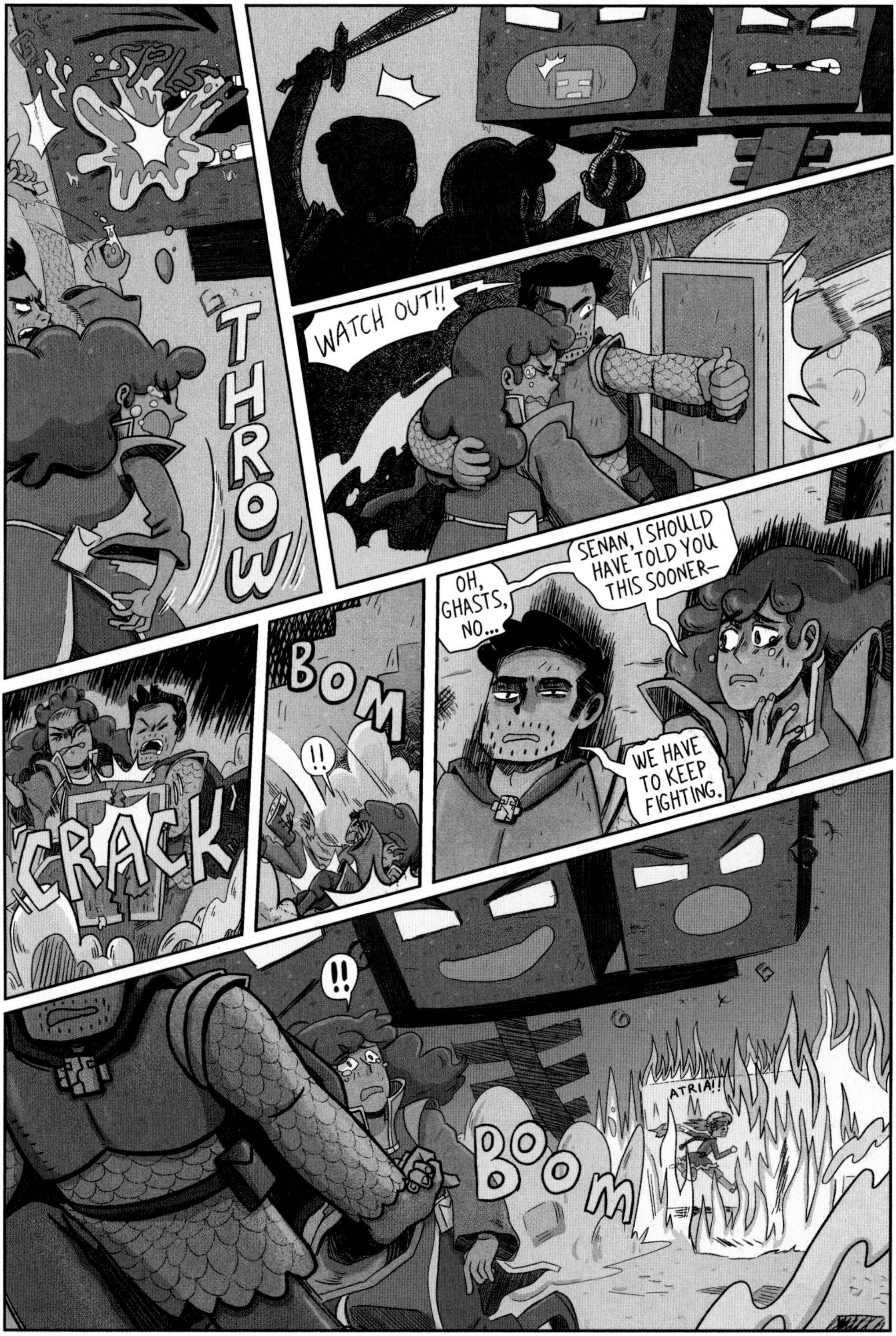
SPLSH
THROW
WATCH OUT!!
CRACK
BOM
!!
OH, GHASTS, NO...
SENAN, I SHOULD HAVE TOLD YOU THIS SOONER—
WE HAVE TO KEEP FIGHTING.
!!
ATRIA!!
BOOOM

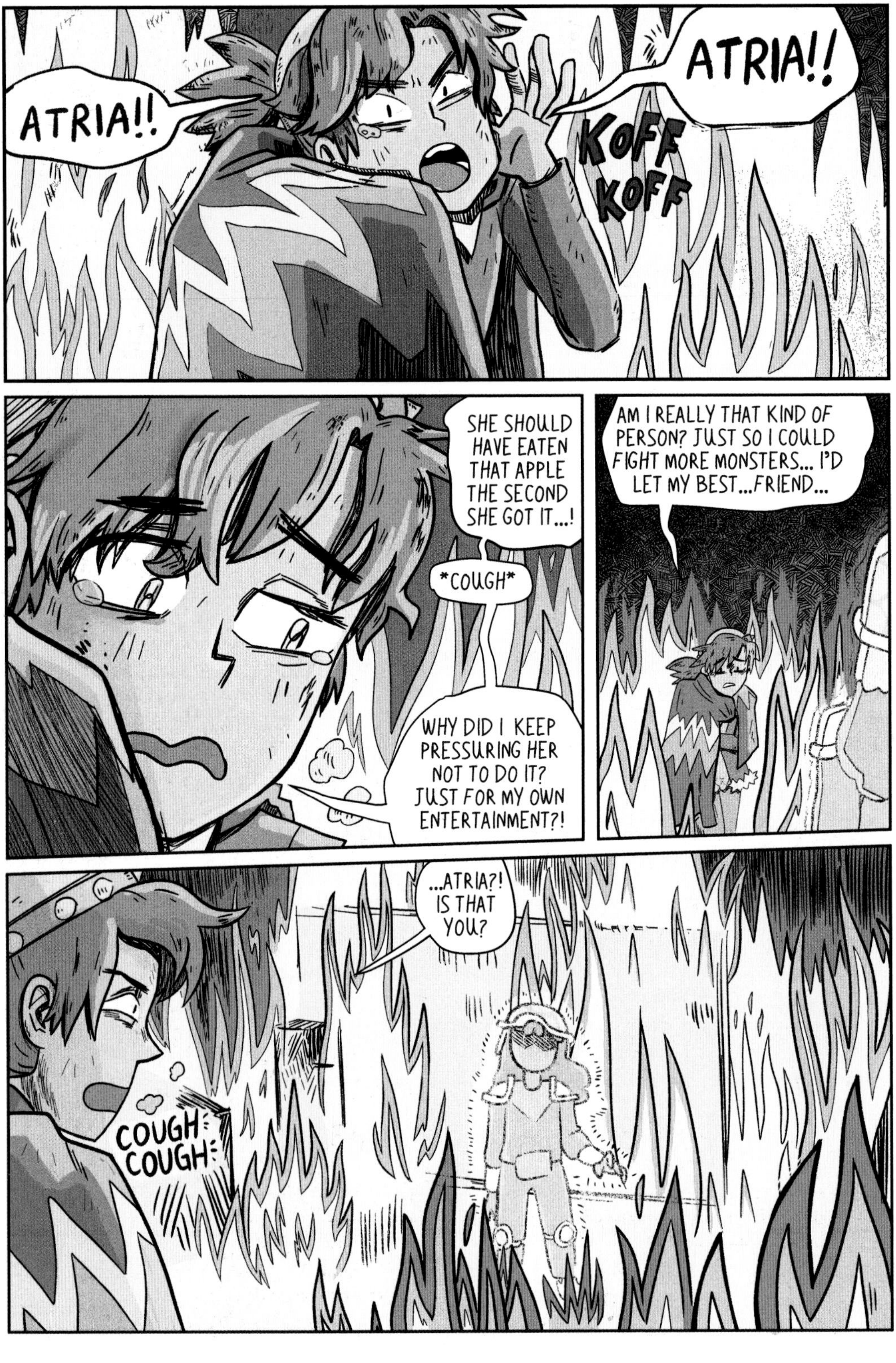
ATRIA!!
ATRIA!!
KOFF KOFF
SHE SHOULD HAVE EATEN THAT APPLE THE SECOND SHE GOT IT...!
COUGH
WHY DID I KEEP PRESSURING HER NOT TO DO IT? JUST FOR MY OWN ENTERTAINMENT?!
AM I REALLY THAT KIND OF PERSON? JUST SO I COULD FIGHT MORE MONSTERS... I'D LET MY BEST...FRIEND...
...ATRIA?! IS THAT YOU?
COUGH COUGH

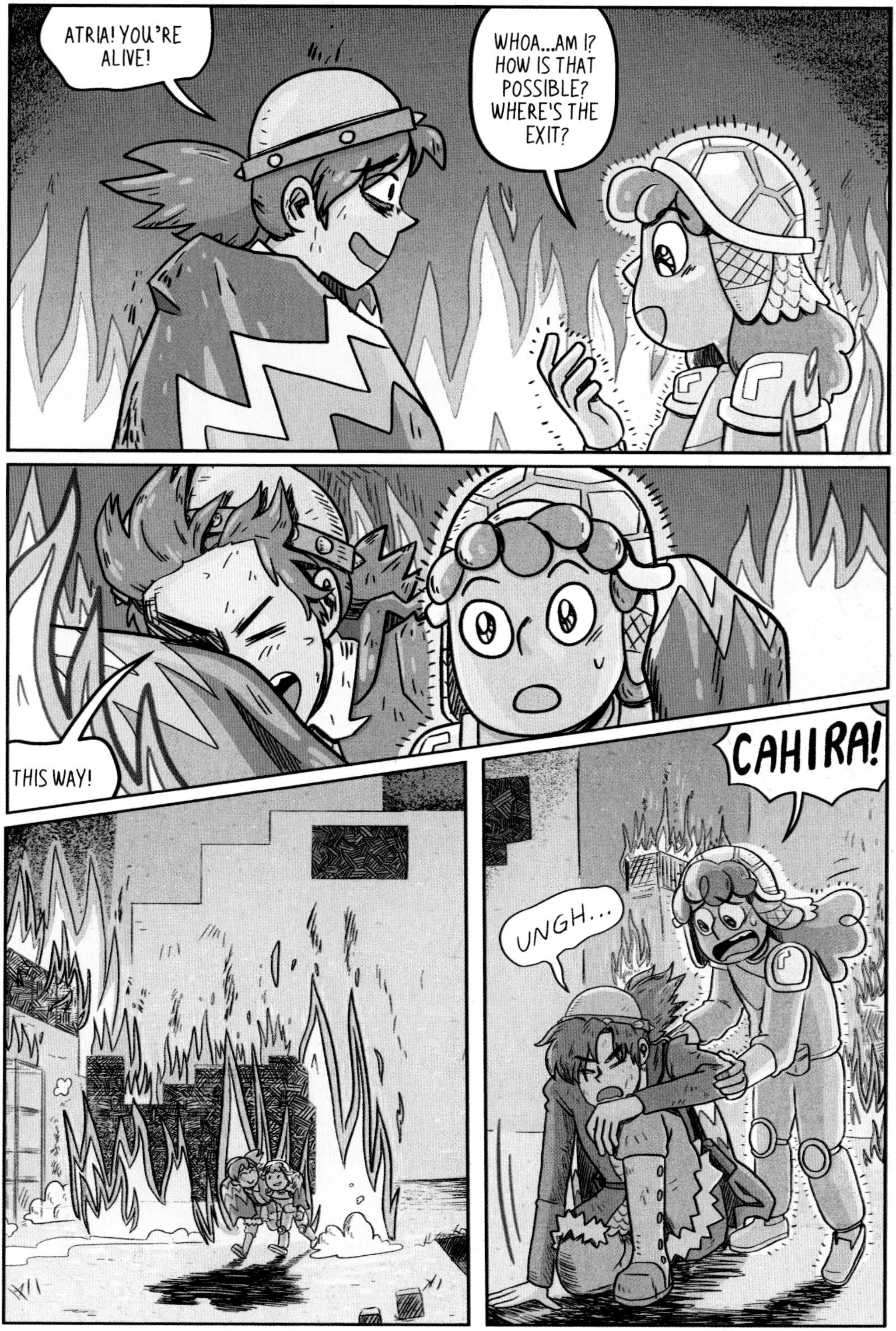
ATRIA! YOU'RE ALIVE!
WHOA...AM I? HOW IS THAT POSSIBLE? WHERE'S THE EXIT?
THIS WAY!
CAHIRA!
UNGH...

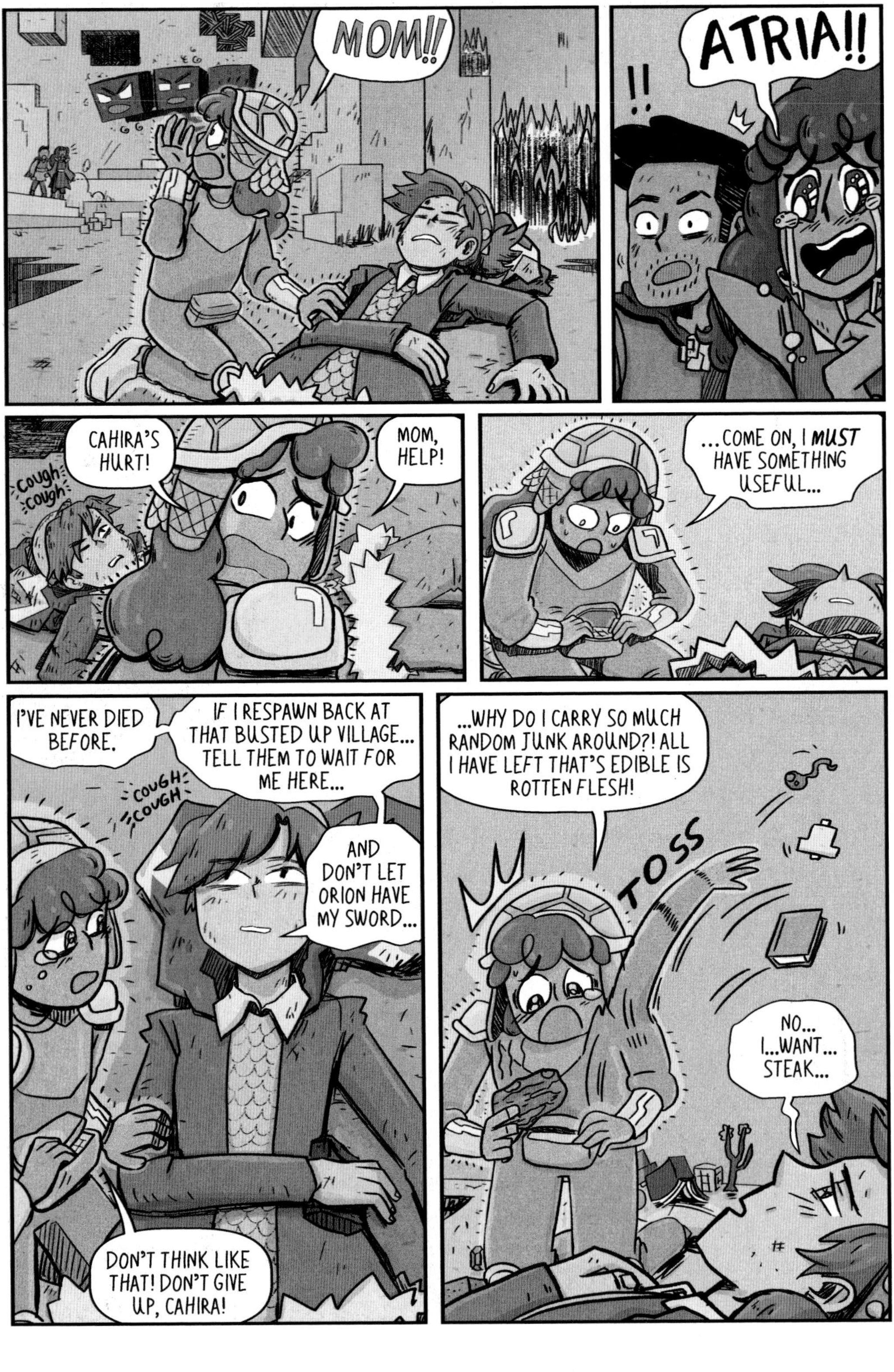

MOM!!
ATRIA!!
!!
CAHIRA'S HURT!
COUGH COUGH
MOM, HELP!
...COME ON, I MUST HAVE SOMETHING USEFUL...
I'VE NEVER DIED BEFORE.
IF I RESPAWN BACK AT THAT BUSTED UP VILLAGE... TELL THEM TO WAIT FOR ME HERE...
COUGH COUGH
AND DON'T LET ORION HAVE MY SWORD...
DON'T THINK LIKE THAT! DON'T GIVE UP, CAHIRA!
...WHY DO I CARRY SO MUCH RANDOM JUNK AROUND?! ALL I HAVE LEFT THAT'S EDIBLE IS ROTTEN FLESH!
TOSS
NO... I...WANT... STEAK...

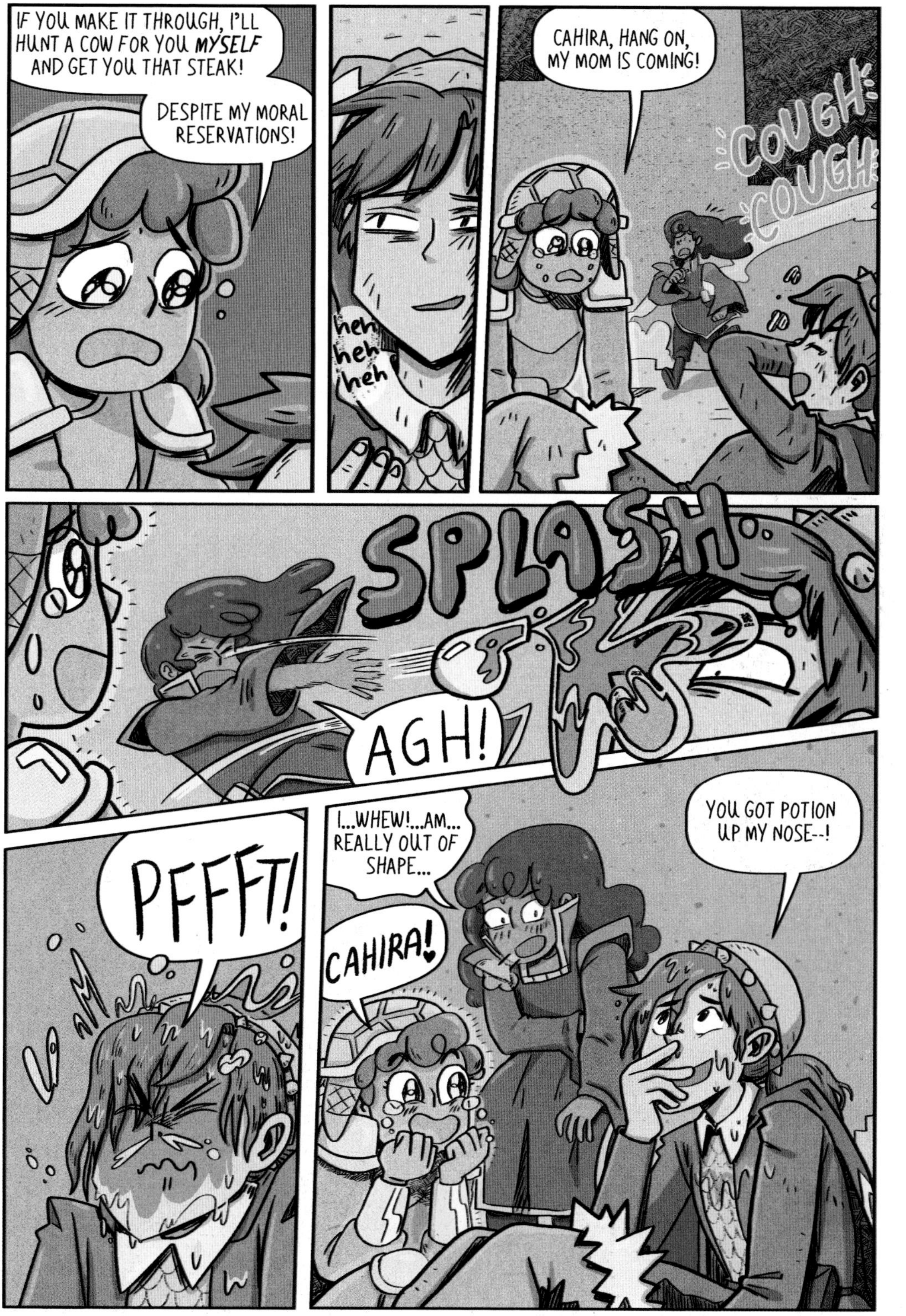

IF YOU MAKE IT THROUGH, I'LL HUNT A COW FOR YOU MYSELF AND GET YOU THAT STEAK!
DESPITE MY MORAL RESERVATIONS!
heh heh heh
CAHIRA, HANG ON, MY MOM IS COMING!
COUGH COUGH
SPLASH
AGH!
PFFFT!
I...WHEW!...AM... REALLY OUT OF SHAPE...
CAHIRA!
YOU GOT POTION UP MY NOSE--!

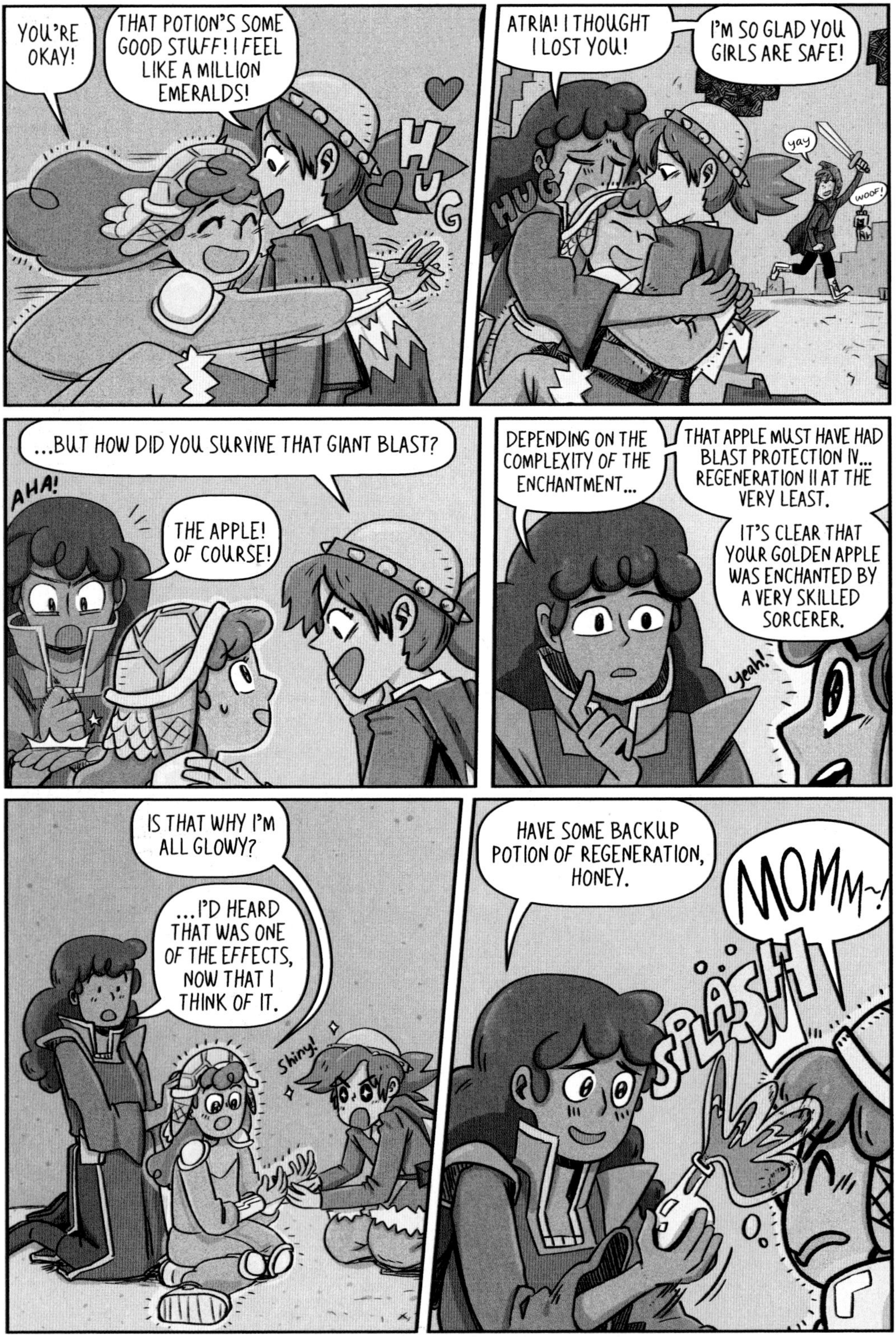
YOU'RE OKAY!
THAT POTION'S SOME GOOD STUFF! I FEEL LIKE A MILLION EMERALDS!
HUG
ATRIA! I THOUGHT I LOST YOU!
I'M SO GLAD YOU GIRLS ARE SAFE!
HUG
yay
WOOF!
...BUT HOW DID YOU SURVIVE THAT GIANT BLAST?
AHA!
THE APPLE! OF COURSE!
DEPENDING ON THE COMPLEXITY OF THE ENCHANTMENT...
THAT APPLE MUST HAVE HAD BLAST PROTECTION IV... REGENERATION II AT THE VERY LEAST.
IT'S CLEAR THAT YOUR GOLDEN APPLE WAS ENCHANTED BY A VERY SKILLED SORCERER.
yeah!
IS THAT WHY I'M ALL GLOWY?
...I'D HEARD THAT WAS ONE OF THE EFFECTS, NOW THAT I THINK OF IT.
Shiny!
HAVE SOME BACKUP POTION OF REGENERATION, HONEY.
MOMM~!
SPLASH

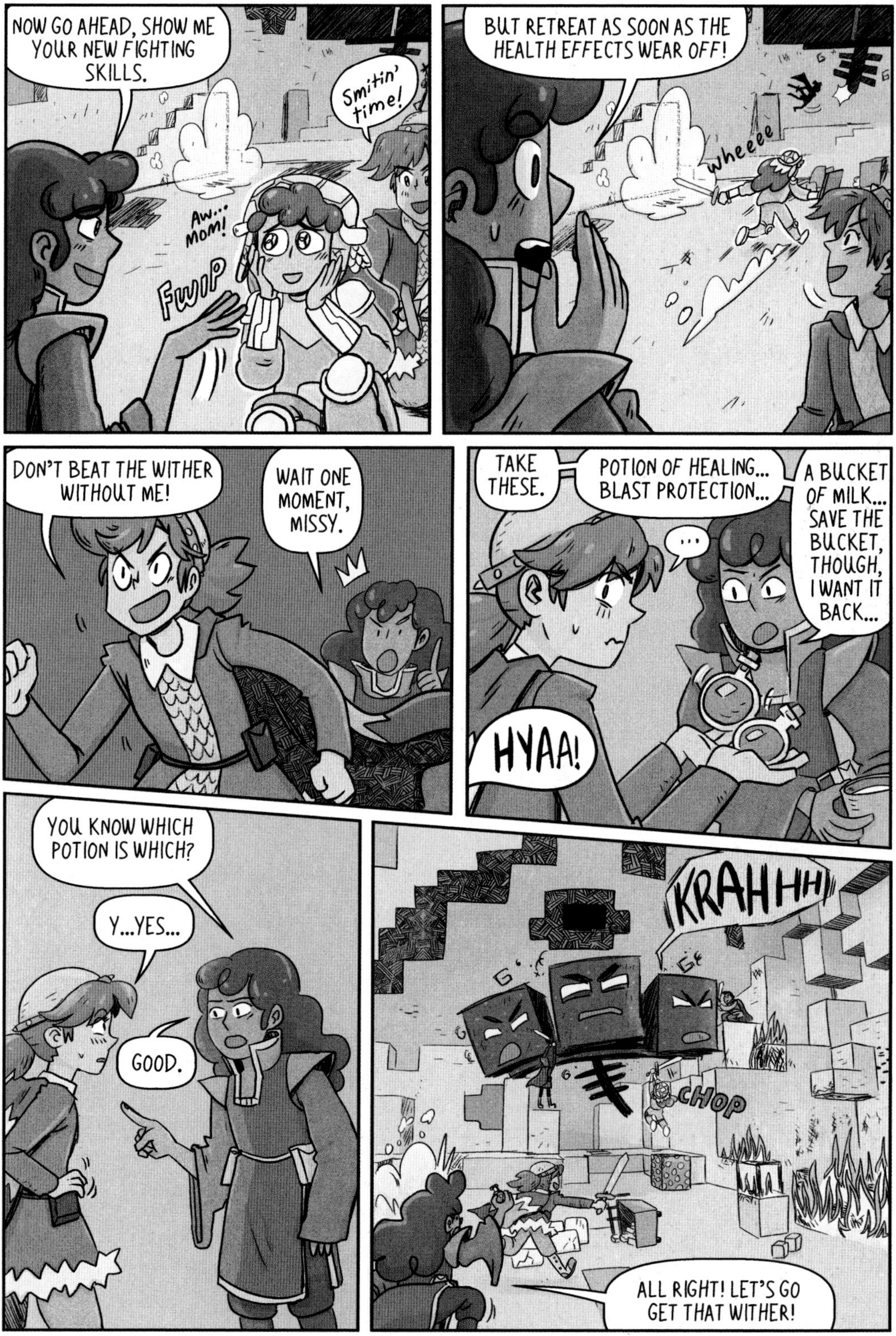
NOW GO AHEAD, SHOW ME YOUR NEW FIGHTING SKILLS.
Smitin' time!
AW... MOM!
FWIP
BUT RETREAT AS SOON AS THE HEALTH EFFECTS WEAR OFF!
wheeee
DON'T BEAT THE WITHER WITHOUT ME!
WAIT ONE MOMENT, MISSY.
TAKE THESE.
POTION OF HEALING... BLAST PROTECTION...
A BUCKET OF MILK... SAVE THE BUCKET, THOUGH, I WANT IT BACK...
...
HYAA!
YOU KNOW WHICH POTION IS WHICH?
Y...YES...
GOOD.
KRAHHH
CHOP
ALL RIGHT! LET'S GO GET THAT WITHER!

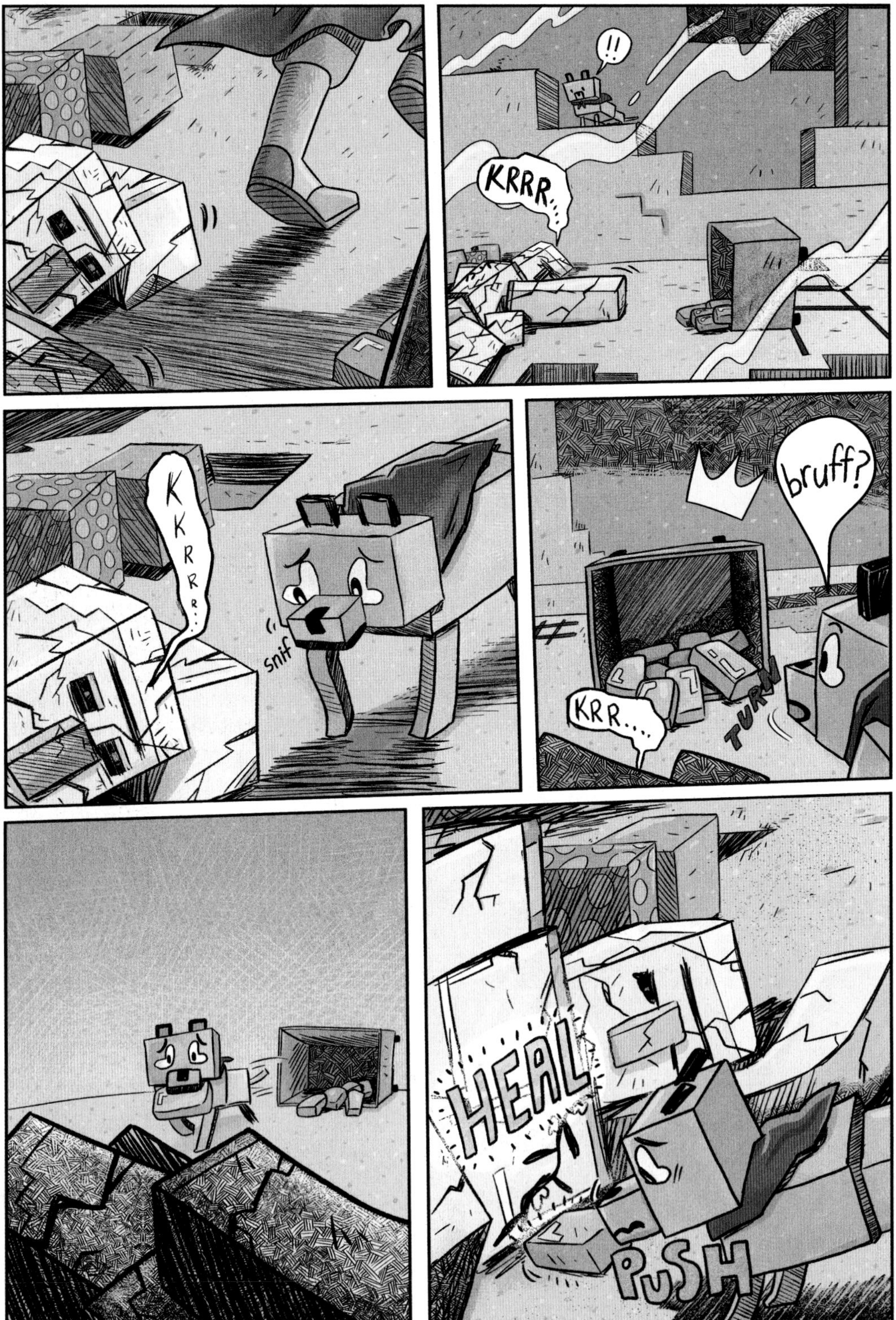

!!
KRRR...
KKRRr...
snif
bruff?
KRR....
TURN
HEAL
PUSH

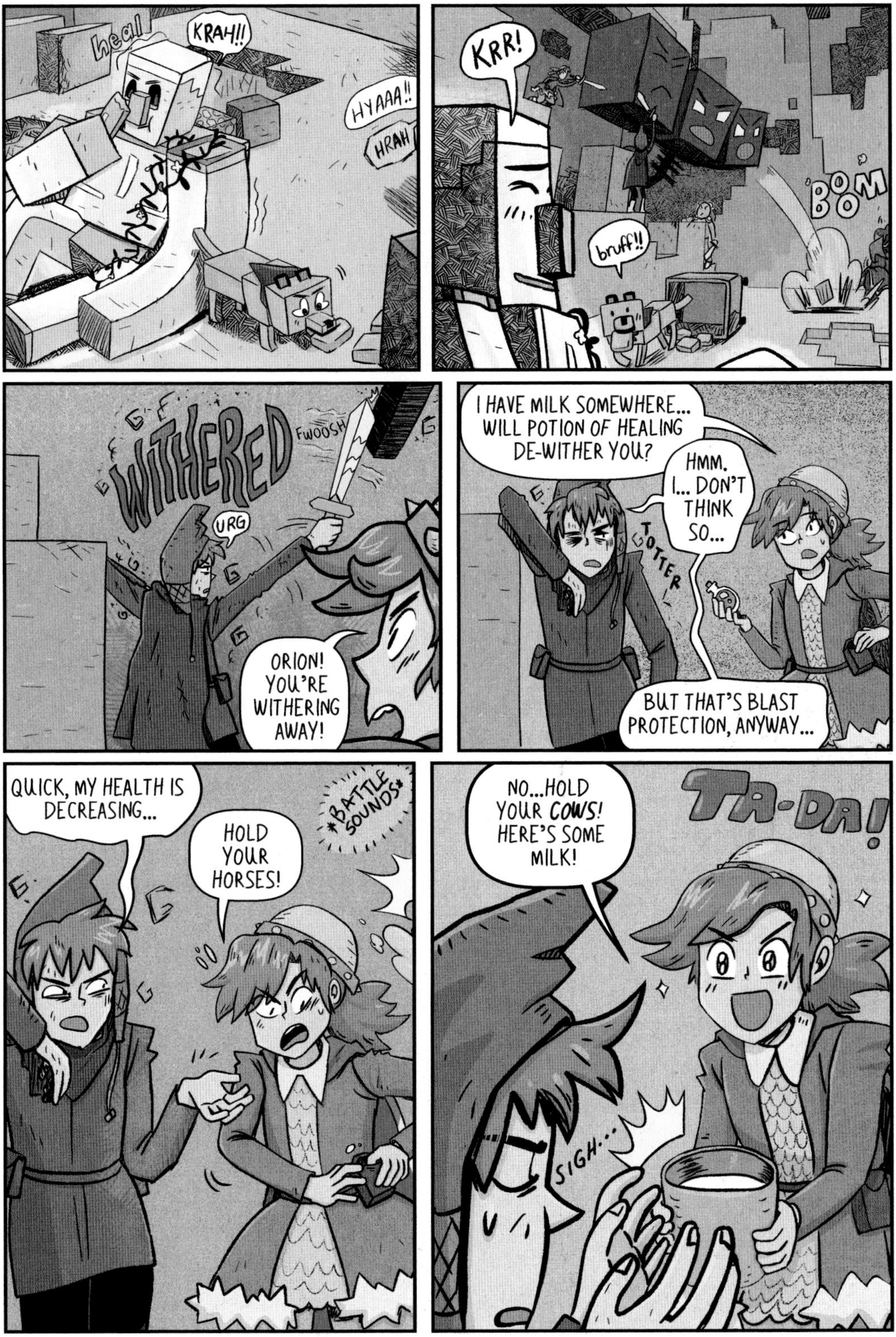
heal
KRAH!!
HYAAA!!
HRAH
KRR!
bruff!!
BOOM
WITHERED
FWOOSH
URG
ORION! YOU'RE WITHERING AWAY!
I HAVE MILK SOMEWHERE... WILL POTION OF HEALING DE-WITHER YOU?
HMM. I... DON'T THINK SO...
TOTTER
BUT THAT'S BLAST PROTECTION, ANYWAY...
QUICK, MY HEALTH IS DECREASING...
HOLD YOUR HORSES!
BATTLE SOUNDS
NO...HOLD YOUR COWS! HERE'S SOME MILK!
TA-DA!
SIGH...

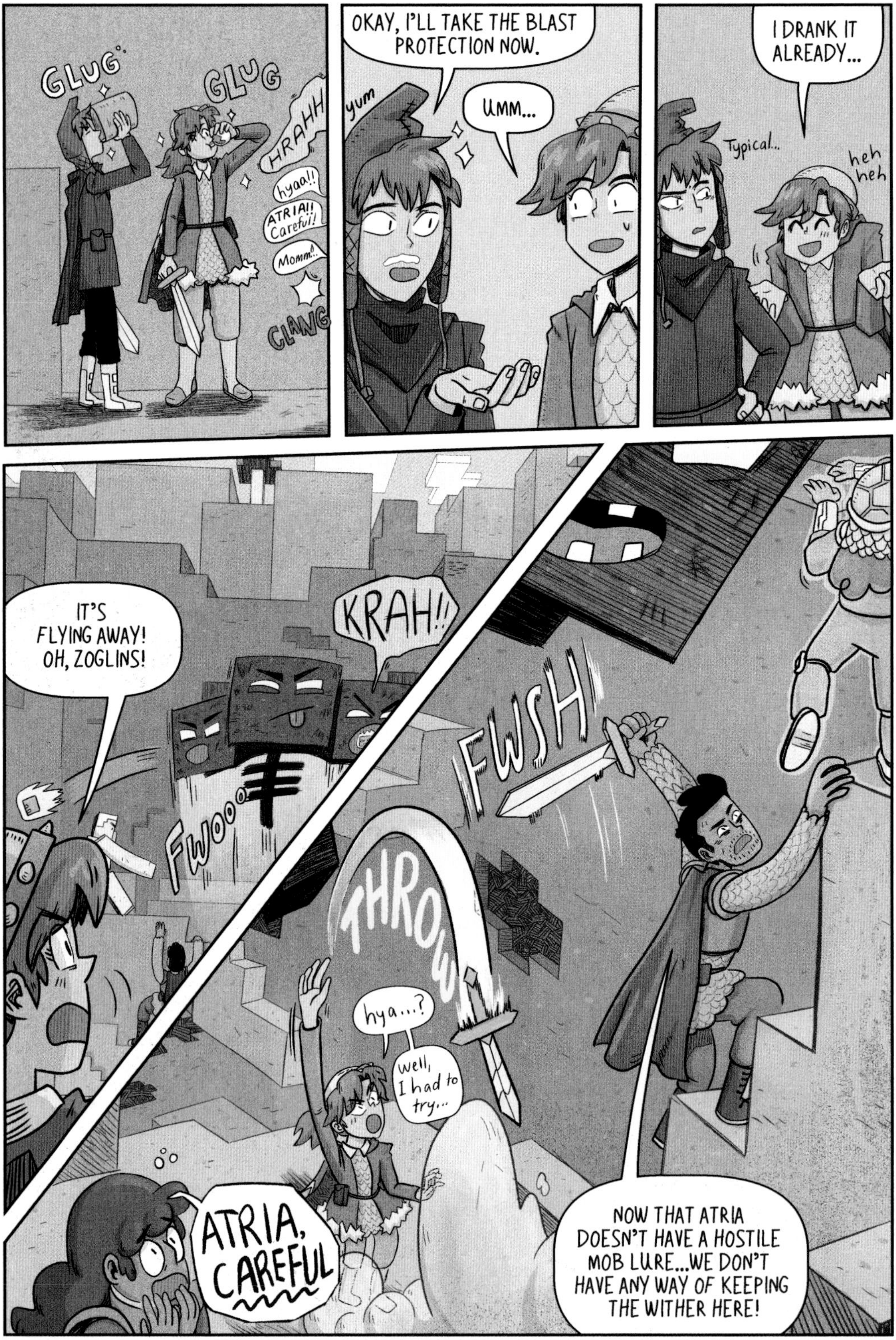
GLUG
GLUG
HRAHH
hyaa!!
ATRIA!! Careful!
Momm..
CLANG
OKAY, I'LL TAKE THE BLAST PROTECTION NOW.
yum
UMM...
I DRANK IT ALREADY...
Typical...
heh heh
IT'S FLYING AWAY! OH, ZOGLINS!
KRAH!!
FWOOO
FWSH
THROW
hya...?
well, I had to try...
ATRIA, CAREFUL
NOW THAT ATRIA DOESN'T HAVE A HOSTILE MOB LURE...WE DON'T HAVE ANY WAY OF KEEPING THE WITHER HERE!

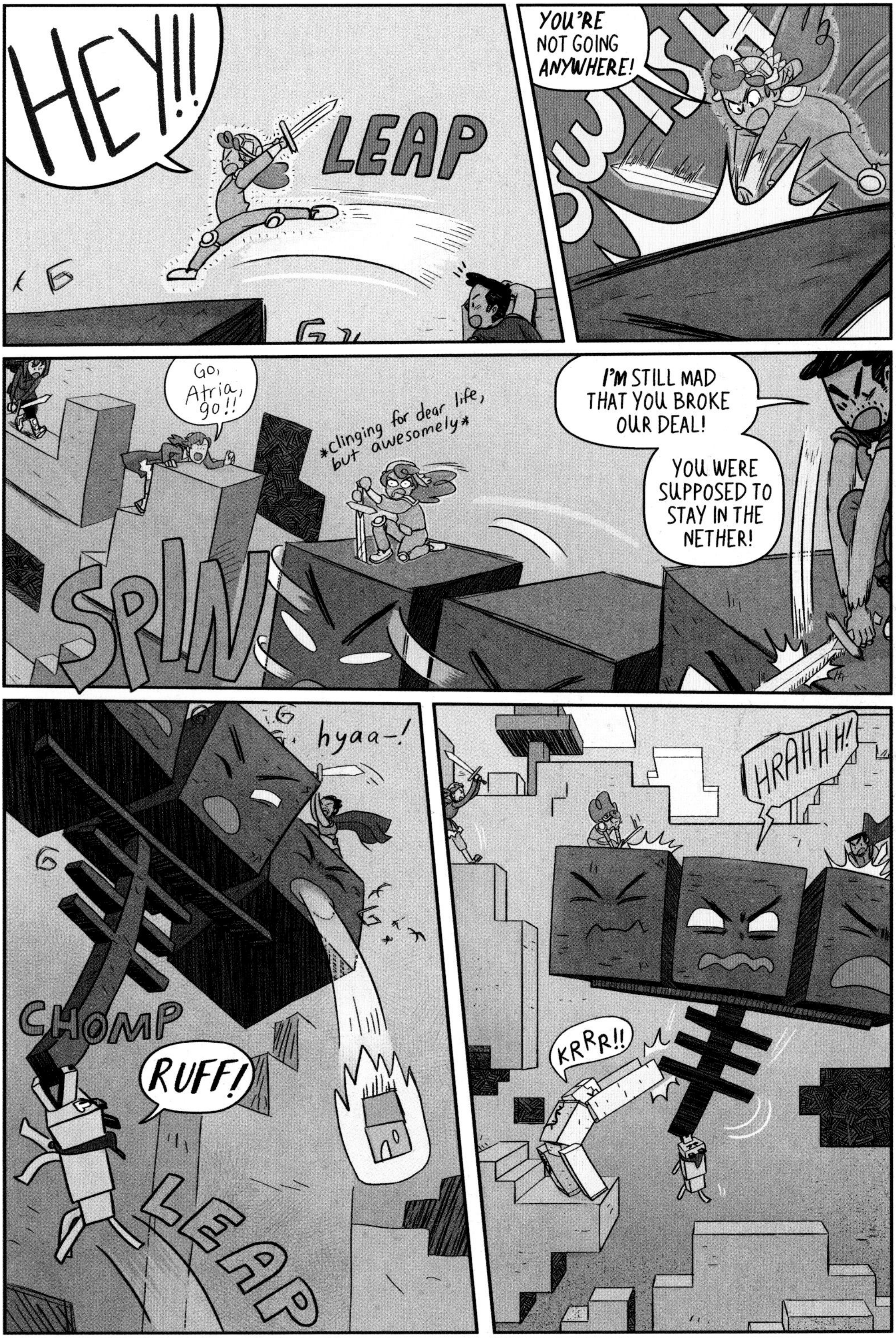
HEY!!
LEAP
YOU'RE NOT GOING ANYWHERE!
Go, Atria, go!!
clinging for dear life, but awesomely
I'M STILL MAD THAT YOU BROKE OUR DEAL!
YOU WERE SUPPOSED TO STAY IN THE NETHER!
SPIN
hyaa-!
CHOMP
RUFF!
LEAP
HRAHHH!
KRRR!!

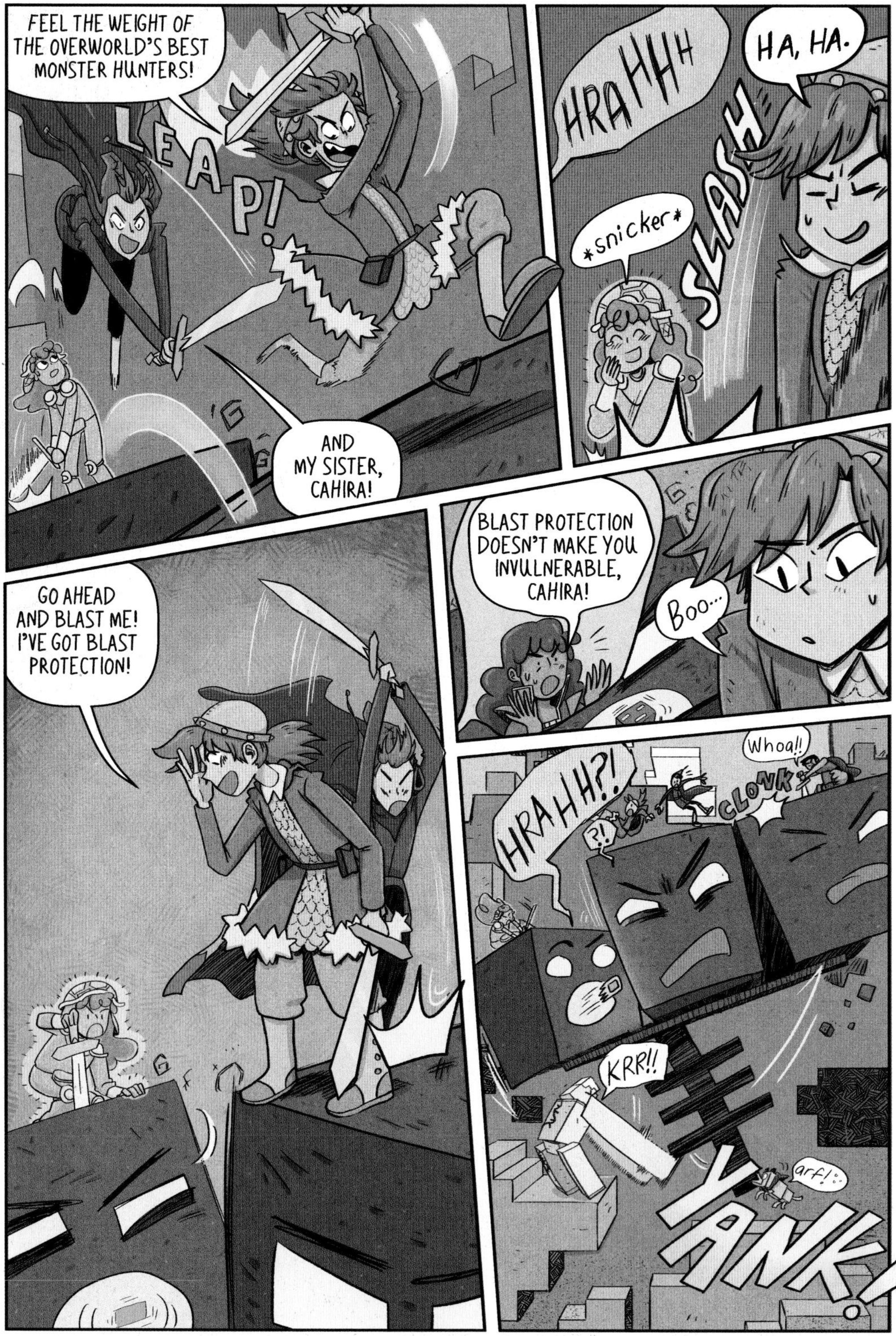

FEEL THE WEIGHT OF THE OVERWORLD'S BEST MONSTER HUNTERS!
LEAP!
AND MY SISTER, CAHIRA!
HRAHHH
HA, HA.
SLASH
snicker
GO AHEAD AND BLAST ME! I'VE GOT BLAST PROTECTION!
BLAST PROTECTION DOESN'T MAKE YOU INVULNERABLE, CAHIRA!
Boo...
Whoa!!
HRAHH?!
CLONK
KRR!!
arf!
YANK!

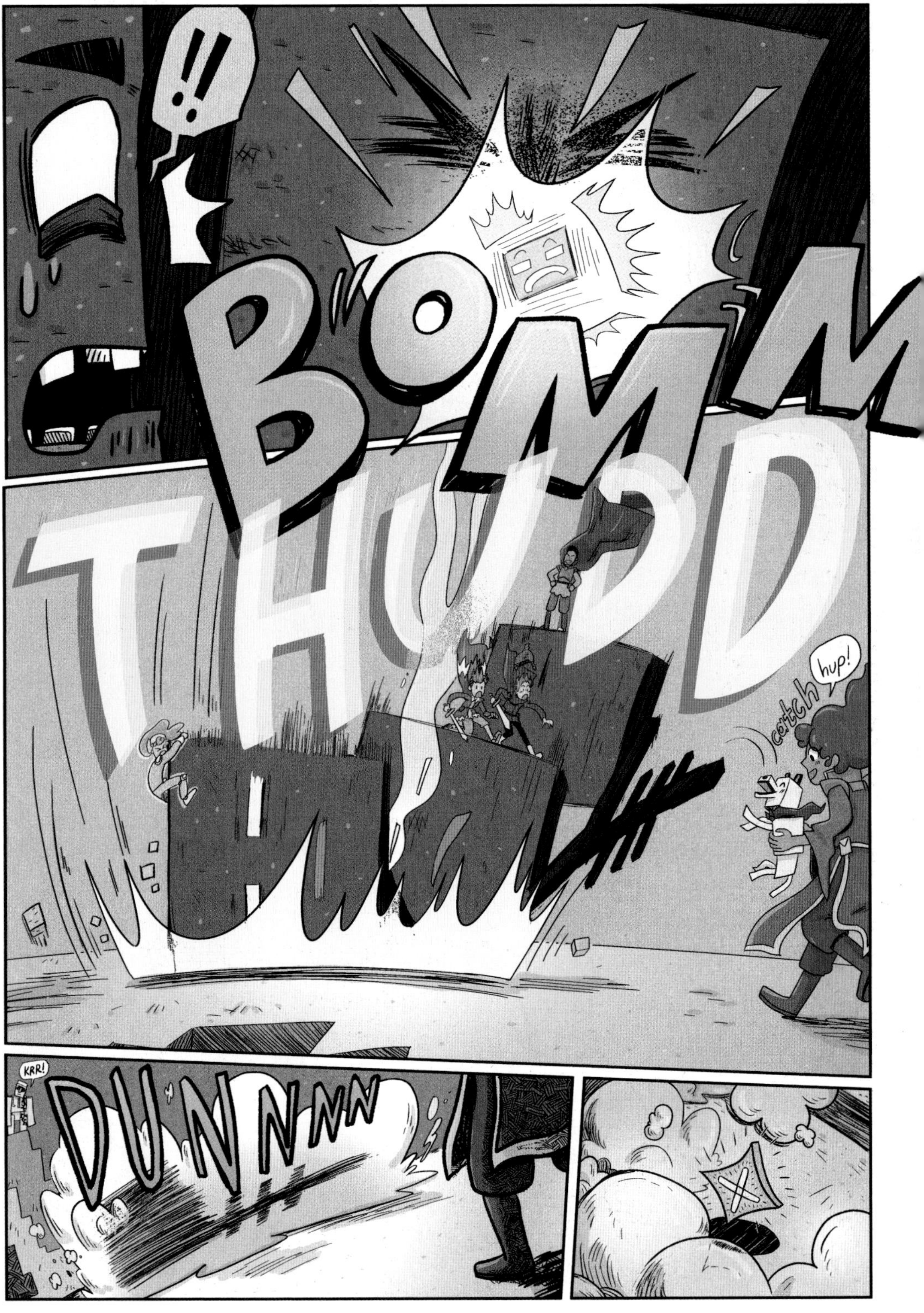
!!
BOMM
THUDD
catch
hup!
KRR!
DUNNNN

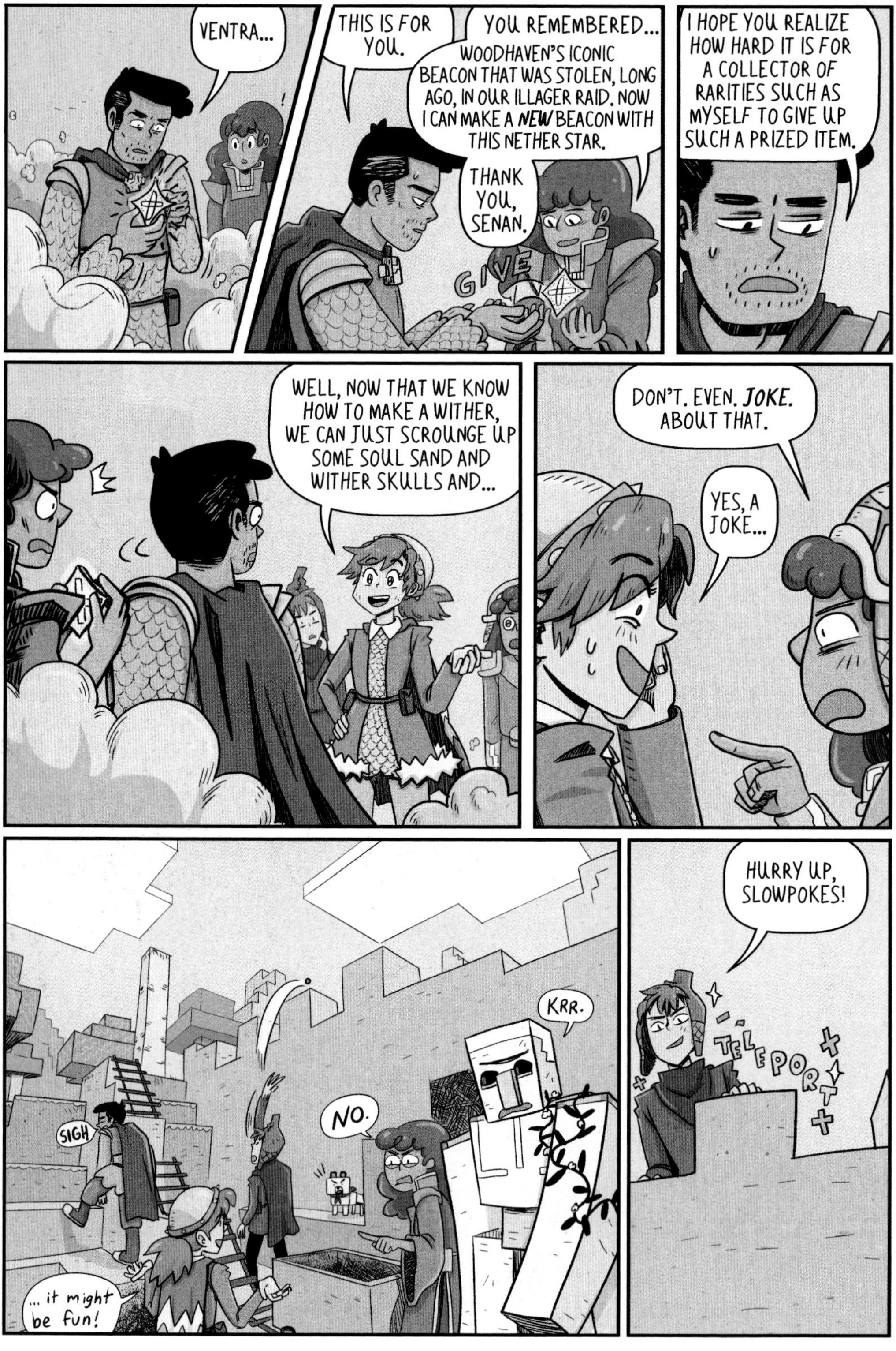
VENTRA...
THIS IS FOR YOU.
YOU REMEMBERED... WOODHAVEN'S ICONIC BEACON THAT WAS STOLEN, LONG AGO, IN OUR ILLAGER RAID. NOW I CAN MAKE A NEW BEACON WITH THIS NETHER STAR.
THANK YOU, SENAN.
GIVE
I HOPE YOU REALIZE HOW HARD IT IS FOR A COLLECTOR OF RARITIES SUCH AS MYSELF TO GIVE UP SUCH A PRIZED ITEM.
WELL, NOW THAT WE KNOW HOW TO MAKE A WITHER, WE CAN JUST SCROUNGE UP SOME SOUL SAND AND WITHER SKULLS AND...
DON'T. EVEN. JOKE. ABOUT THAT.
YES, A JOKE...
KRR.
NO.
SIGH
... it might be fun!
HURRY UP, SLOWPOKES!
TELEPORT

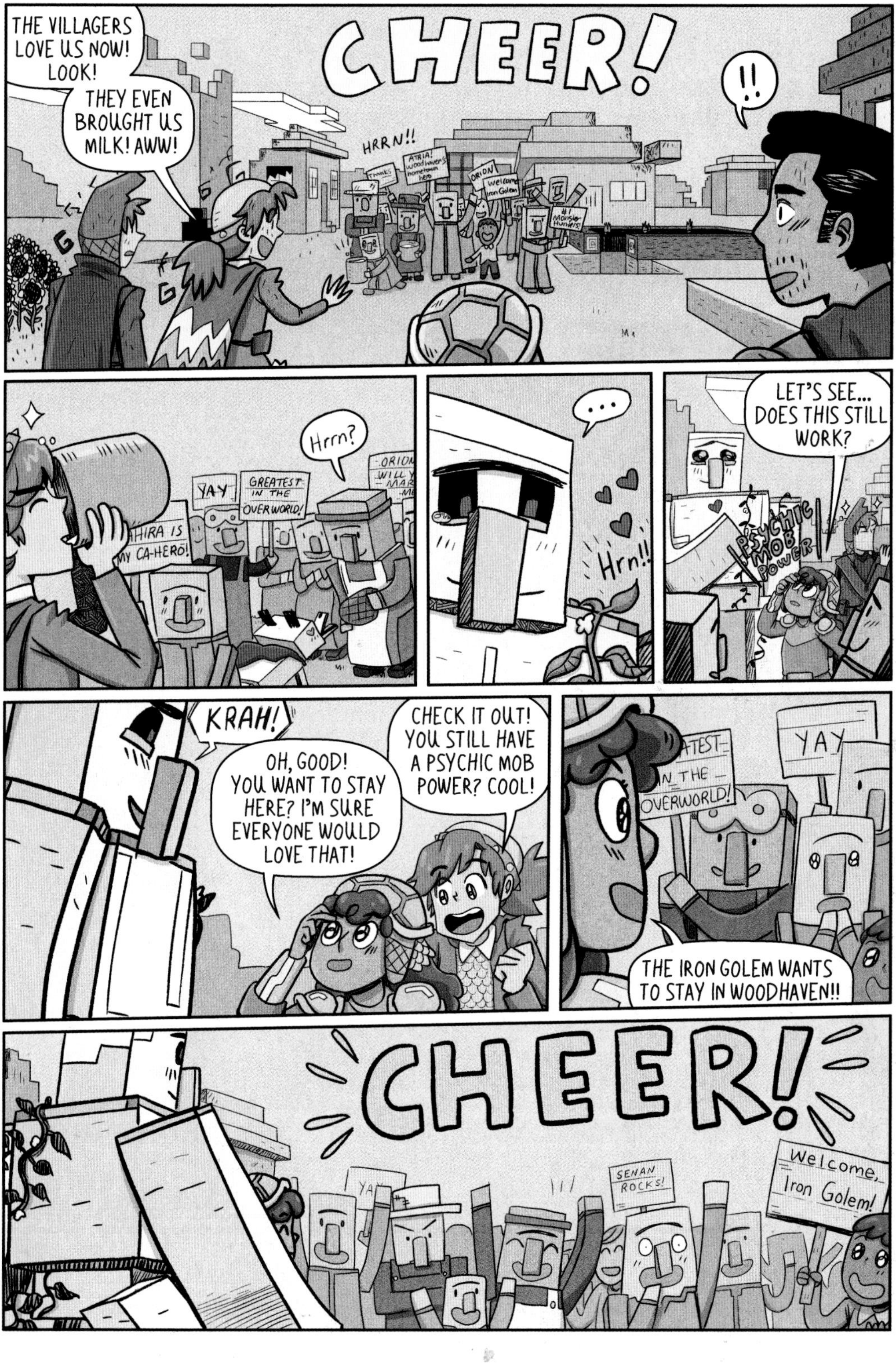
THE VILLAGERS LOVE US NOW! LOOK!
THEY EVEN BROUGHT US MILK! AWW!
CHEER!
!!
HRRN!!
Hrrn?
YAY
GREATEST IN THE OVERWORLD!
...
Hrn!!
LET'S SEE... DOES THIS STILL WORK?
PSYCHIC MOB POWER
KRAH!
OH, GOOD! YOU WANT TO STAY HERE? I'M SURE EVERYONE WOULD LOVE THAT!
CHECK IT OUT! YOU STILL HAVE A PSYCHIC MOB POWER? COOL!
THE IRON GOLEM WANTS TO STAY IN WOODHAVEN!!
CHEER!
SENAN ROCKS!
Welcome, Iron Golem!

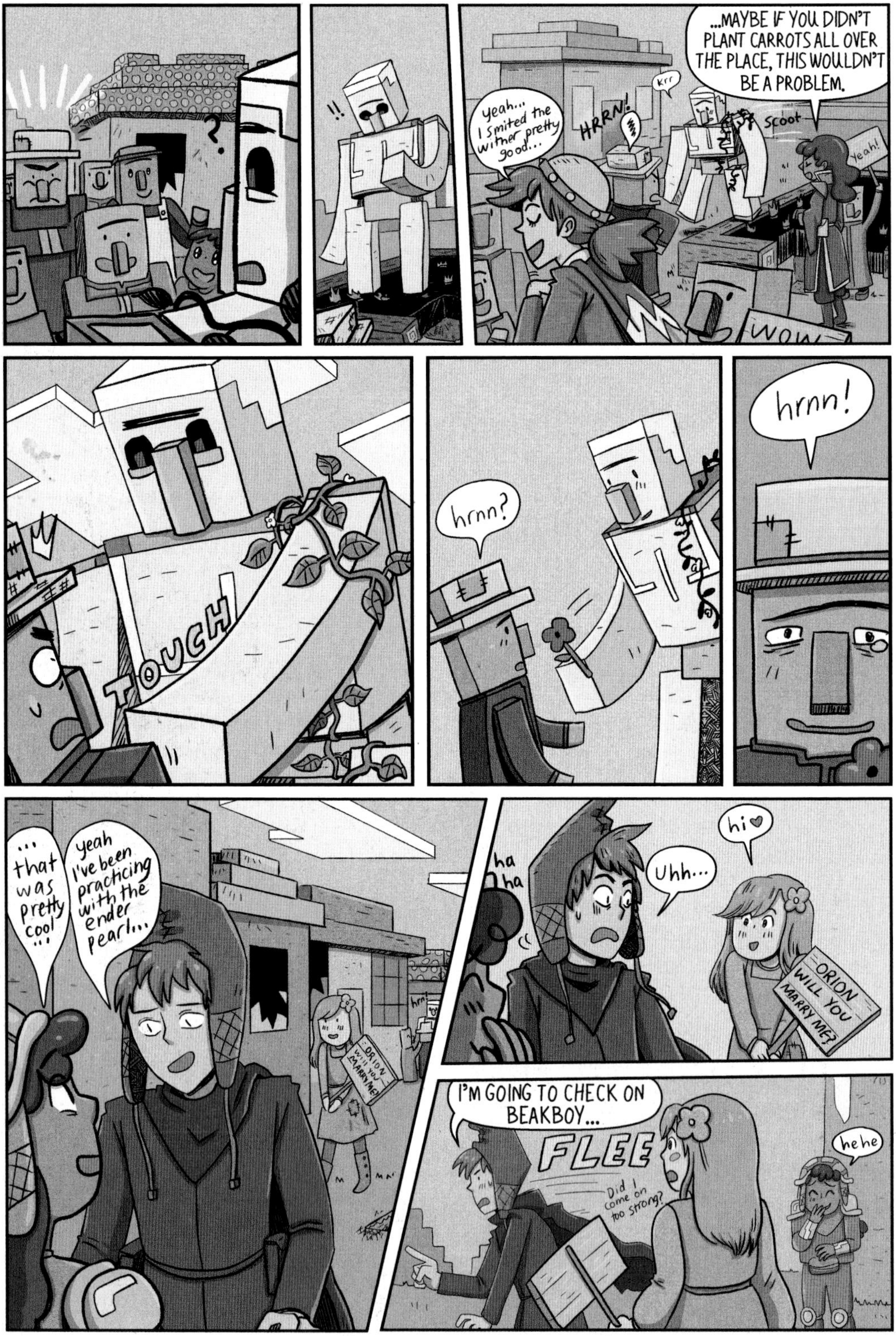
?
!!
yeah... I smited the wither pretty good...
HRRN!
Krr
...MAYBE IF YOU DIDN'T PLANT CARROTS ALL OVER THE PLACE, THIS WOULDN'T BE A PROBLEM.
scoot
Yeah!
WOW
TOUCH
hrnn?
hrnn!
...that was pretty cool...
yeah I've been practicing with the ender pearl...
ORION WILL YOU MARRY ME?
ha ha
Uhh...
hi♥
ORION WILL YOU MARRY ME?
I'M GOING TO CHECK ON BEAKBOY...
FLEE
Did I come on too strong?
hehe

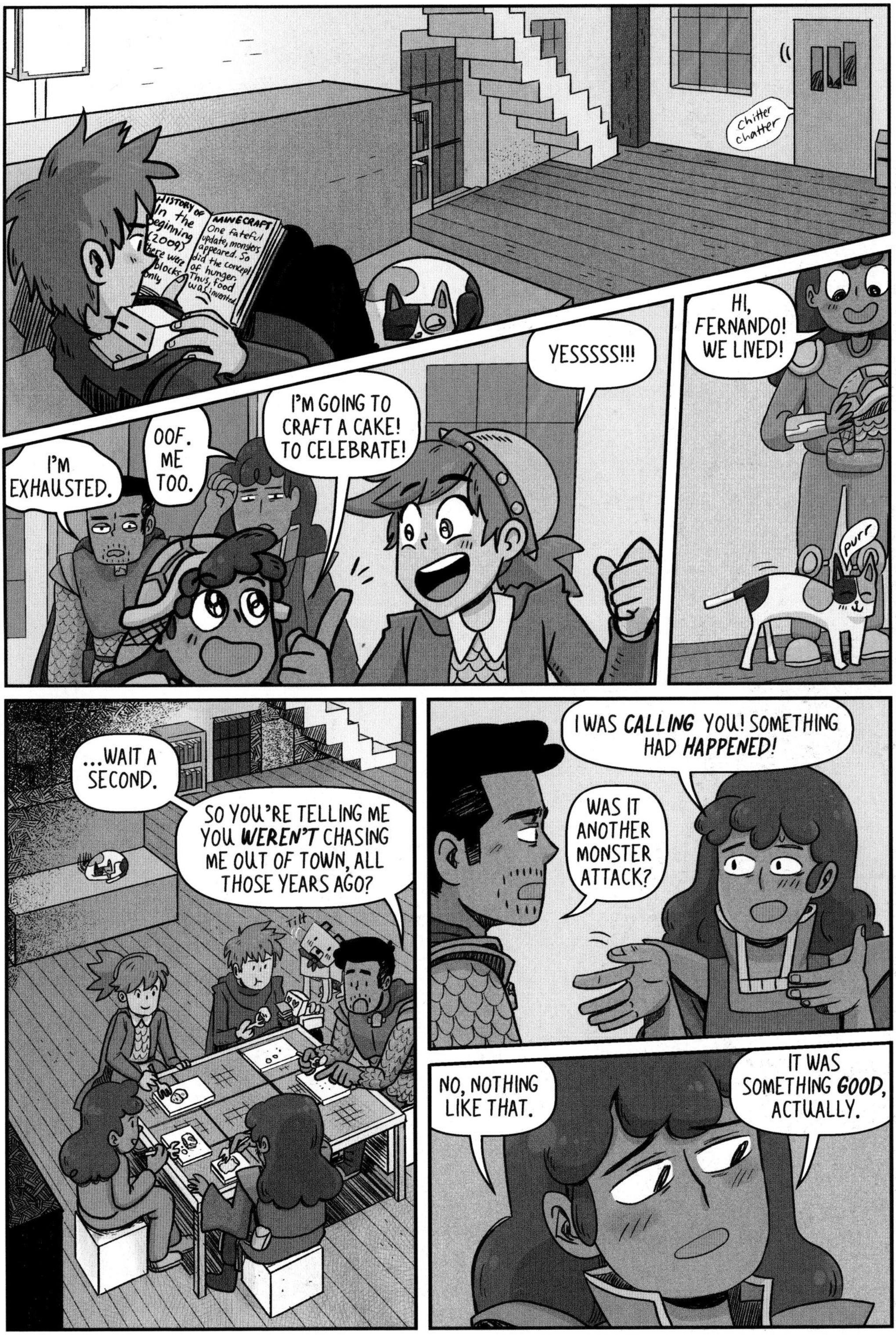
HISTORY OF MINECRAFT
In the beginning (2009) there were only blocks.
One fateful update, monsters appeared. So did the concept of hunger. Thus, food was invented.
Chitter chatter
HI, FERNANDO! WE LIVED!
purr
YESSSSS!!!
I'M GOING TO CRAFT A CAKE! TO CELEBRATE!
OOF. ME TOO.
I'M EXHAUSTED.
...WAIT A SECOND.
SO YOU'RE TELLING ME YOU **WEREN'T** CHASING ME OUT OF TOWN, ALL THOSE YEARS AGO?
TILT
I WAS **CALLING** YOU! SOMETHING HAD **HAPPENED!**
WAS IT ANOTHER MONSTER ATTACK?
NO, NOTHING LIKE THAT.
IT WAS SOMETHING **GOOD**, ACTUALLY.

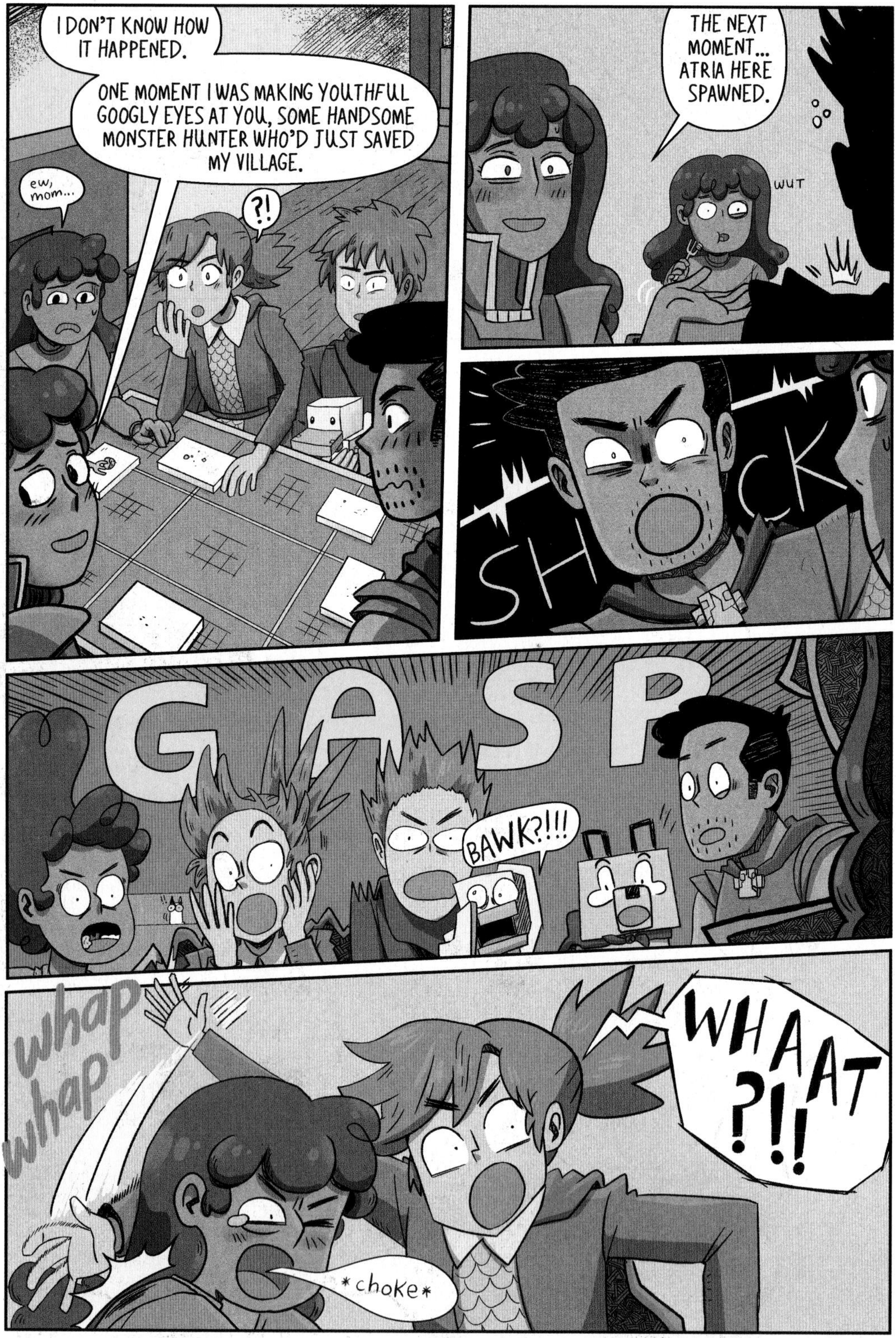
I DON'T KNOW HOW IT HAPPENED.
ONE MOMENT I WAS MAKING YOUTHFUL GOOGLY EYES AT YOU, SOME HANDSOME MONSTER HUNTER WHO'D JUST SAVED MY VILLAGE.
ew, mom...
?!
THE NEXT MOMENT... ATRIA HERE SPAWNED.
WUT
SHOCK
GASP
BAWK?!!!
whap whap
WHAAT?!!
choke

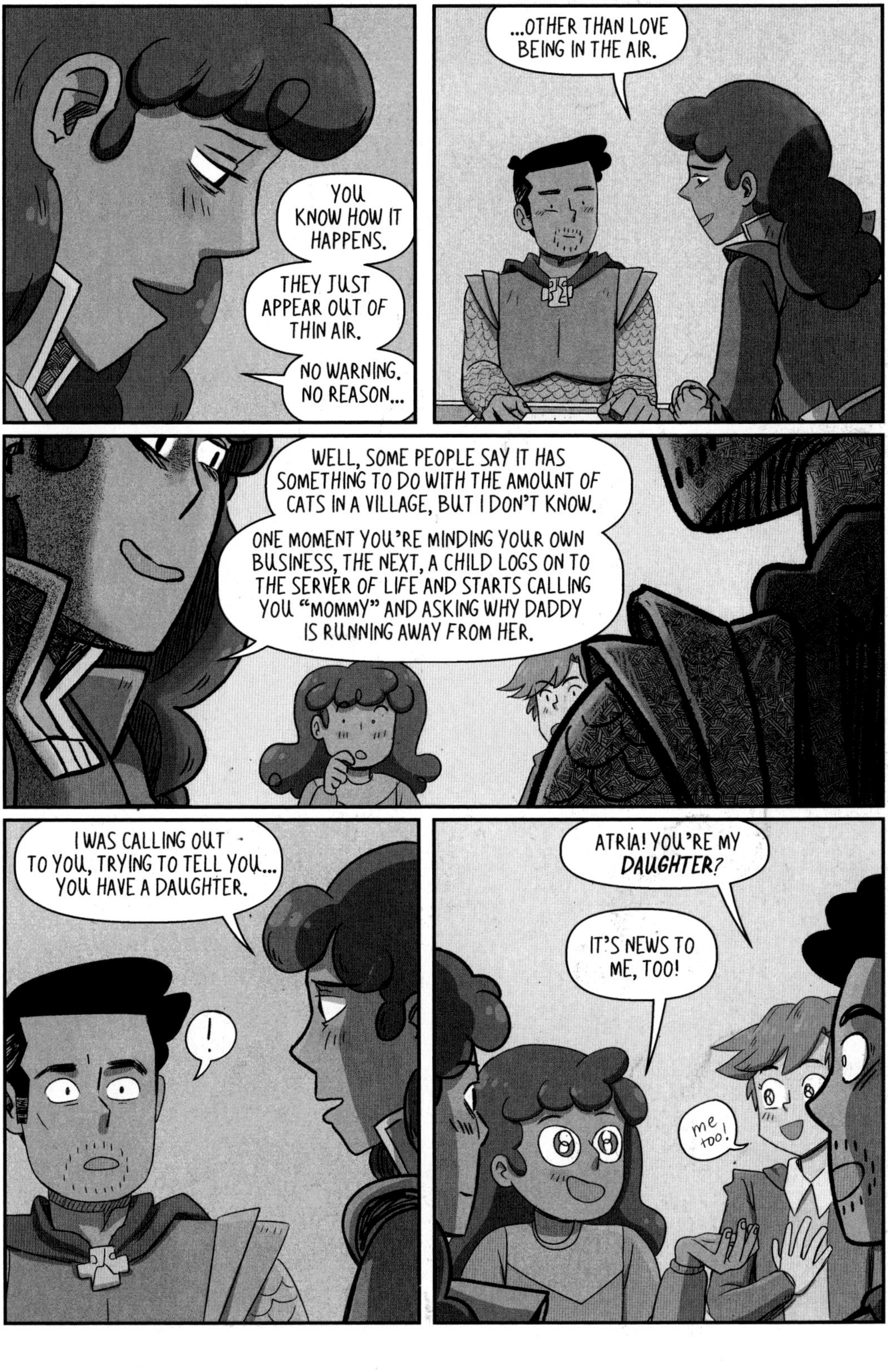
YOU KNOW HOW IT HAPPENS.
THEY JUST APPEAR OUT OF THIN AIR.
NO WARNING. NO REASON...
...OTHER THAN LOVE BEING IN THE AIR.
WELL, SOME PEOPLE SAY IT HAS SOMETHING TO DO WITH THE AMOUNT OF CATS IN A VILLAGE, BUT I DON'T KNOW.
ONE MOMENT YOU'RE MINDING YOUR OWN BUSINESS, THE NEXT, A CHILD LOGS ON TO THE SERVER OF LIFE AND STARTS CALLING YOU "MOMMY" AND ASKING WHY DADDY IS RUNNING AWAY FROM HER.
I WAS CALLING OUT TO YOU, TRYING TO TELL YOU... YOU HAVE A DAUGHTER.
!
ATRIA! YOU'RE MY ***DAUGHTER?***
IT'S NEWS TO ME, TOO!
me too!

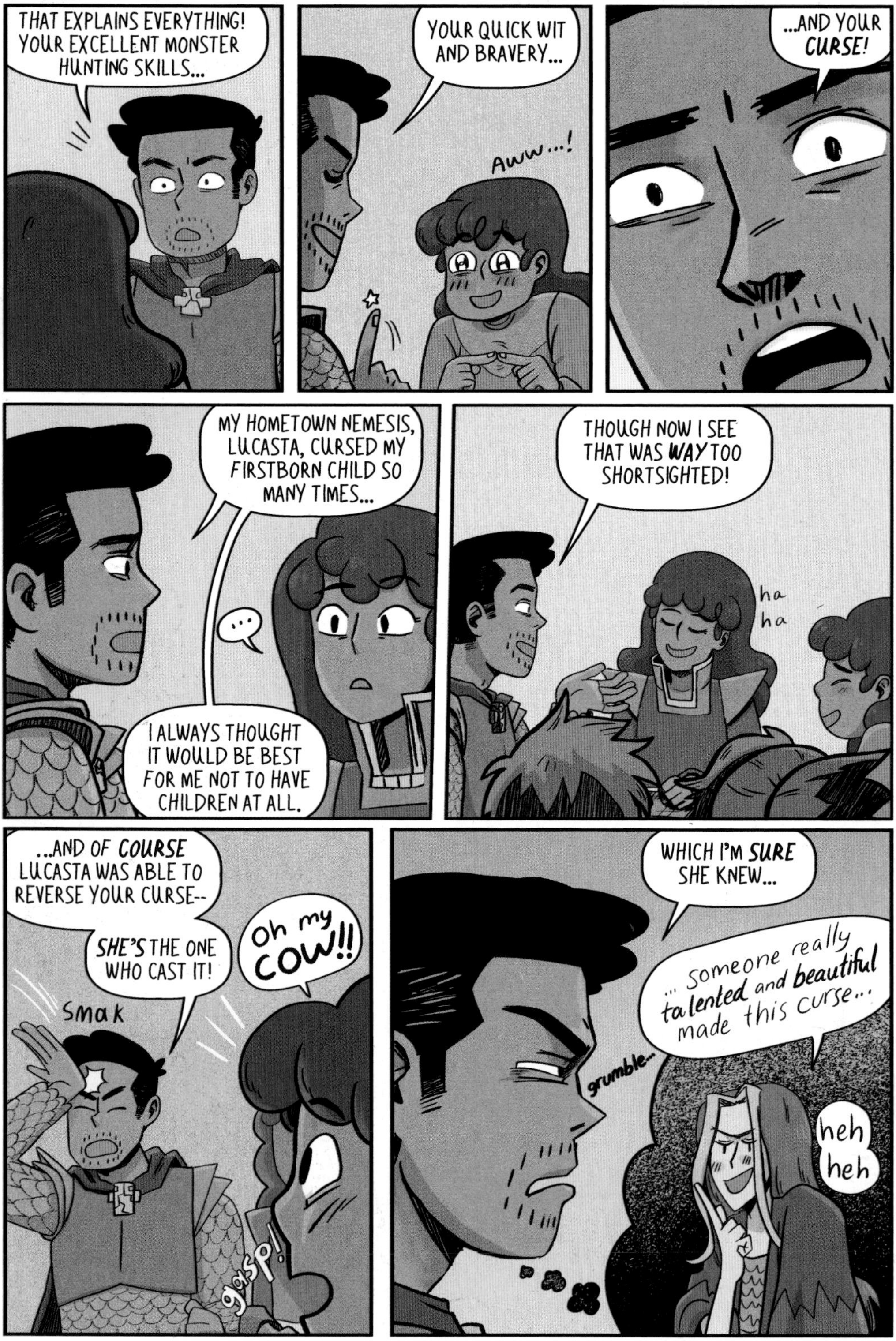
THAT EXPLAINS EVERYTHING! YOUR EXCELLENT MONSTER HUNTING SKILLS...
YOUR QUICK WIT AND BRAVERY...
AWW...!
...AND YOUR CURSE!
MY HOMETOWN NEMESIS, LUCASTA, CURSED MY FIRSTBORN CHILD SO MANY TIMES...
...
I ALWAYS THOUGHT IT WOULD BE BEST FOR ME NOT TO HAVE CHILDREN AT ALL.
THOUGH NOW I SEE THAT WAS WAY TOO SHORTSIGHTED!
ha ha
...AND OF COURSE LUCASTA WAS ABLE TO REVERSE YOUR CURSE--
SHE'S THE ONE WHO CAST IT!
Oh my COW!!
SMAK
GASP!
WHICH I'M SURE SHE KNEW...
... Someone really talented and beautiful made this curse...
grumble...
heh heh

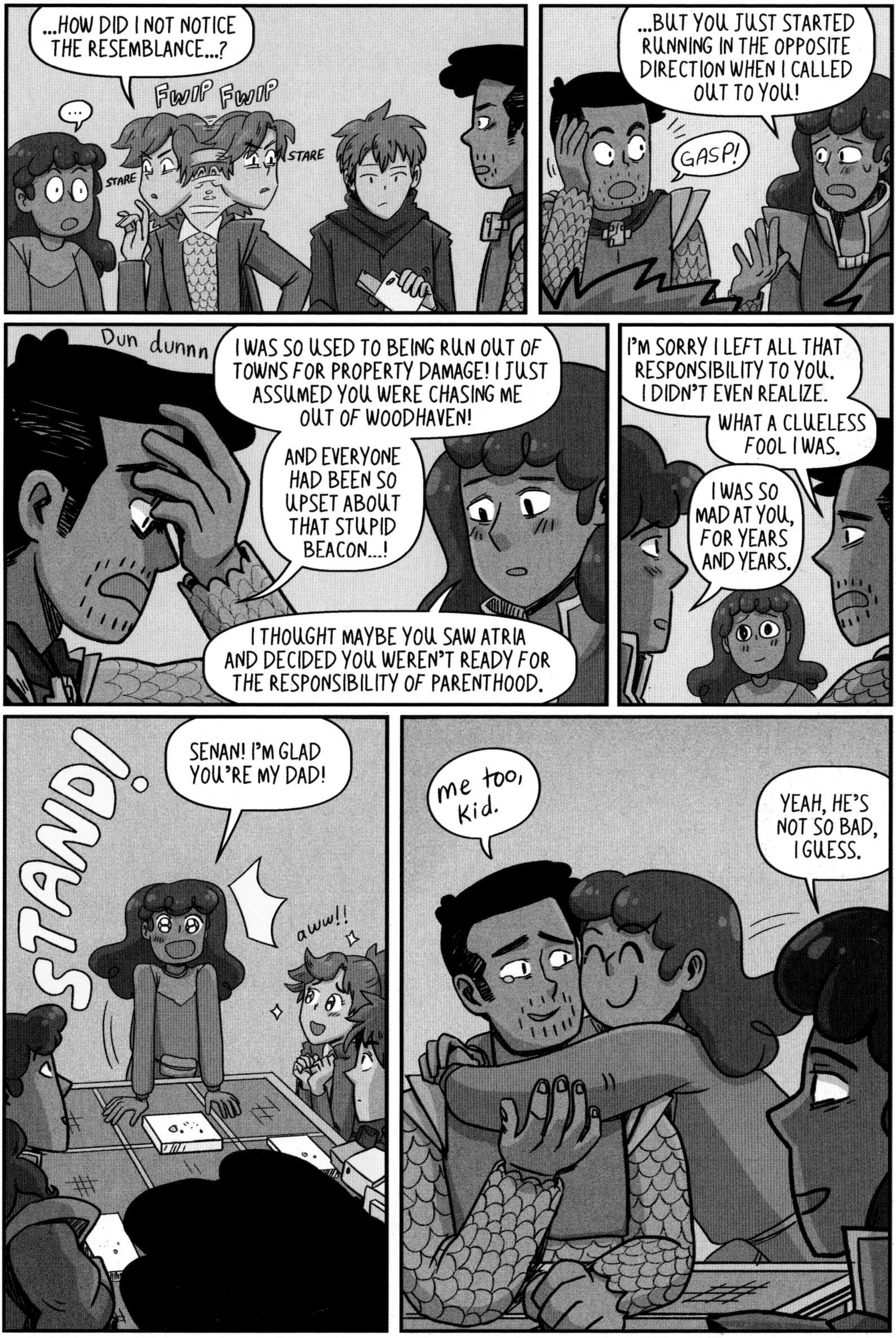
...HOW DID I NOT NOTICE THE RESEMBLANCE...?
...
FWIP FWIP
STARE
STARE
...BUT YOU JUST STARTED RUNNING IN THE OPPOSITE DIRECTION WHEN I CALLED OUT TO YOU!
GASP!
Dun dunnn
I WAS SO USED TO BEING RUN OUT OF TOWNS FOR PROPERTY DAMAGE! I JUST ASSUMED YOU WERE CHASING ME OUT OF WOODHAVEN!
AND EVERYONE HAD BEEN SO UPSET ABOUT THAT STUPID BEACON...!
I THOUGHT MAYBE YOU SAW ATRIA AND DECIDED YOU WEREN'T READY FOR THE RESPONSIBILITY OF PARENTHOOD.
I'M SORRY I LEFT ALL THAT RESPONSIBILITY TO YOU. I DIDN'T EVEN REALIZE.
WHAT A CLUELESS FOOL I WAS.
I WAS SO MAD AT YOU, FOR YEARS AND YEARS.
STAND!
SENAN! I'M GLAD YOU'RE MY DAD!
aww!!
me too, kid.
YEAH, HE'S NOT SO BAD, I GUESS.

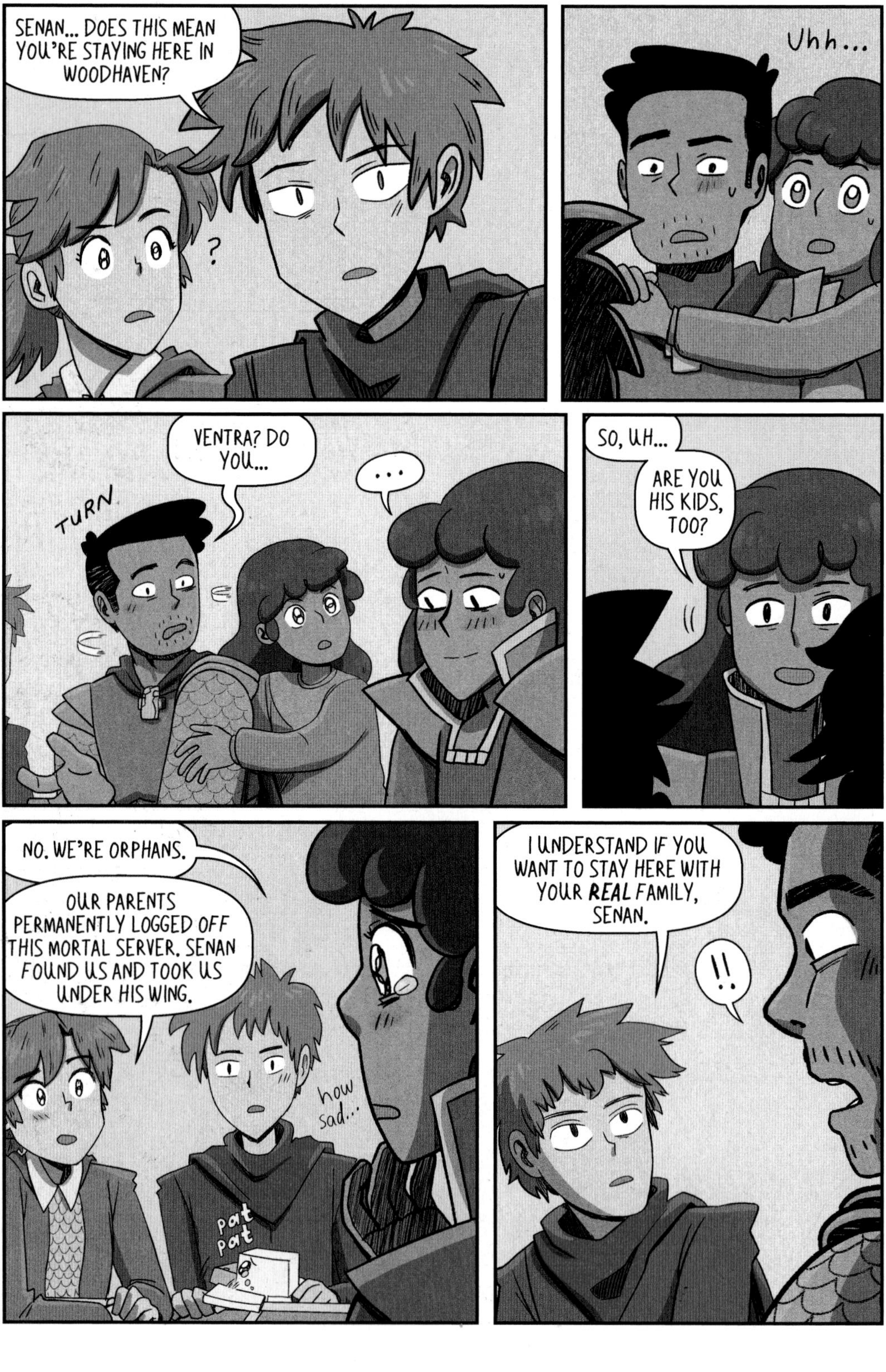
SENAN... DOES THIS MEAN YOU'RE STAYING HERE IN WOODHAVEN?
?
Uhh...
TURN
VENTRA? DO YOU...
...
SO, UH...
ARE YOU HIS KIDS, TOO?
NO. WE'RE ORPHANS.
OUR PARENTS PERMANENTLY LOGGED OFF THIS MORTAL SERVER. SENAN FOUND US AND TOOK US UNDER HIS WING.
how sad...
pat pat
I UNDERSTAND IF YOU WANT TO STAY HERE WITH YOUR REAL FAMILY, SENAN.
!!

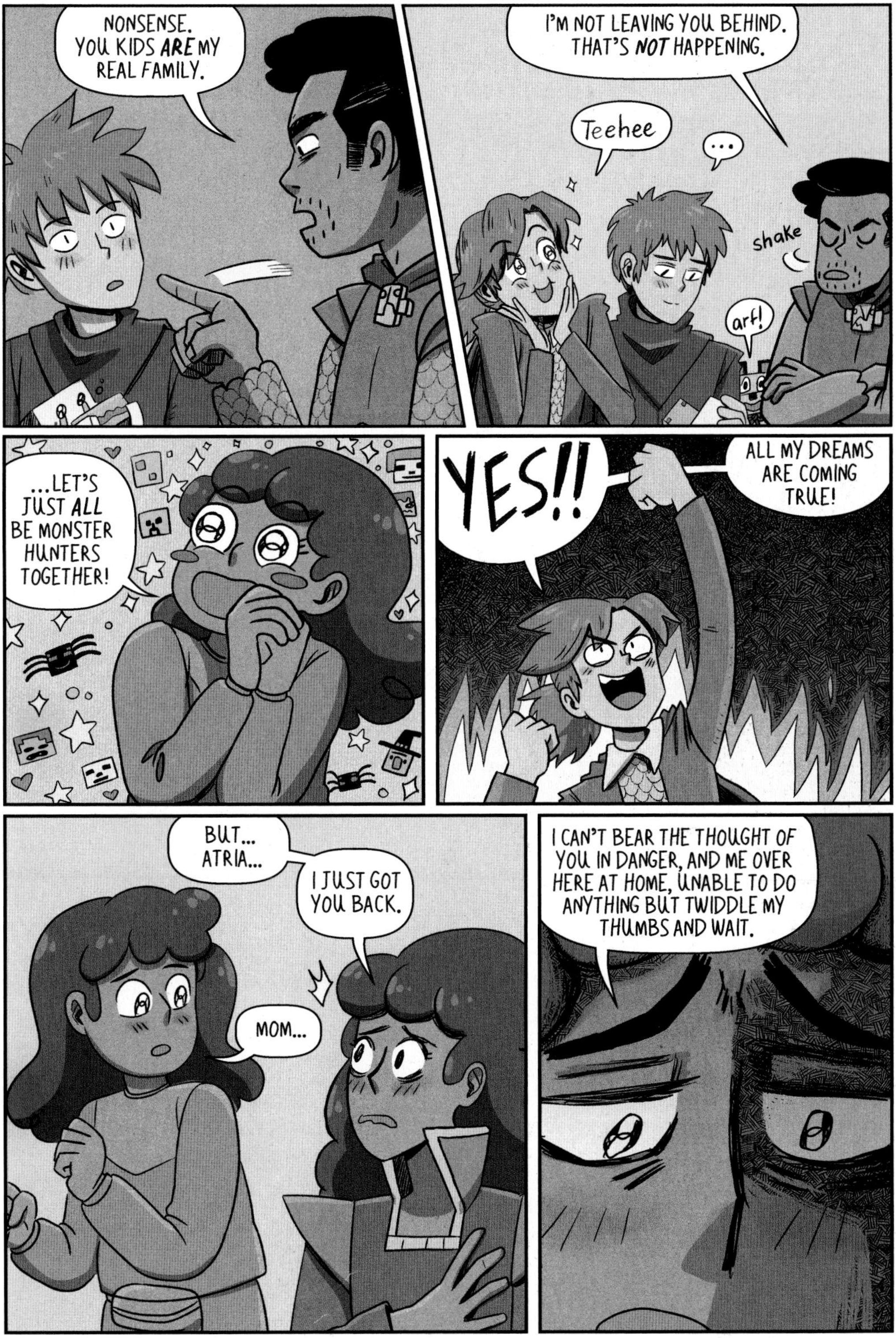
NONSENSE. YOU KIDS **ARE** MY REAL FAMILY.
I'M NOT LEAVING YOU BEHIND. THAT'S **NOT** HAPPENING.
Teehee
...
shake
arf!
...LET'S JUST **ALL** BE MONSTER HUNTERS TOGETHER!
YES!!
ALL MY DREAMS ARE COMING TRUE!
BUT... ATRIA...
I JUST GOT YOU BACK.
MOM...
I CAN'T BEAR THE THOUGHT OF YOU IN DANGER, AND ME OVER HERE AT HOME, UNABLE TO DO ANYTHING BUT TWIDDLE MY THUMBS AND WAIT.

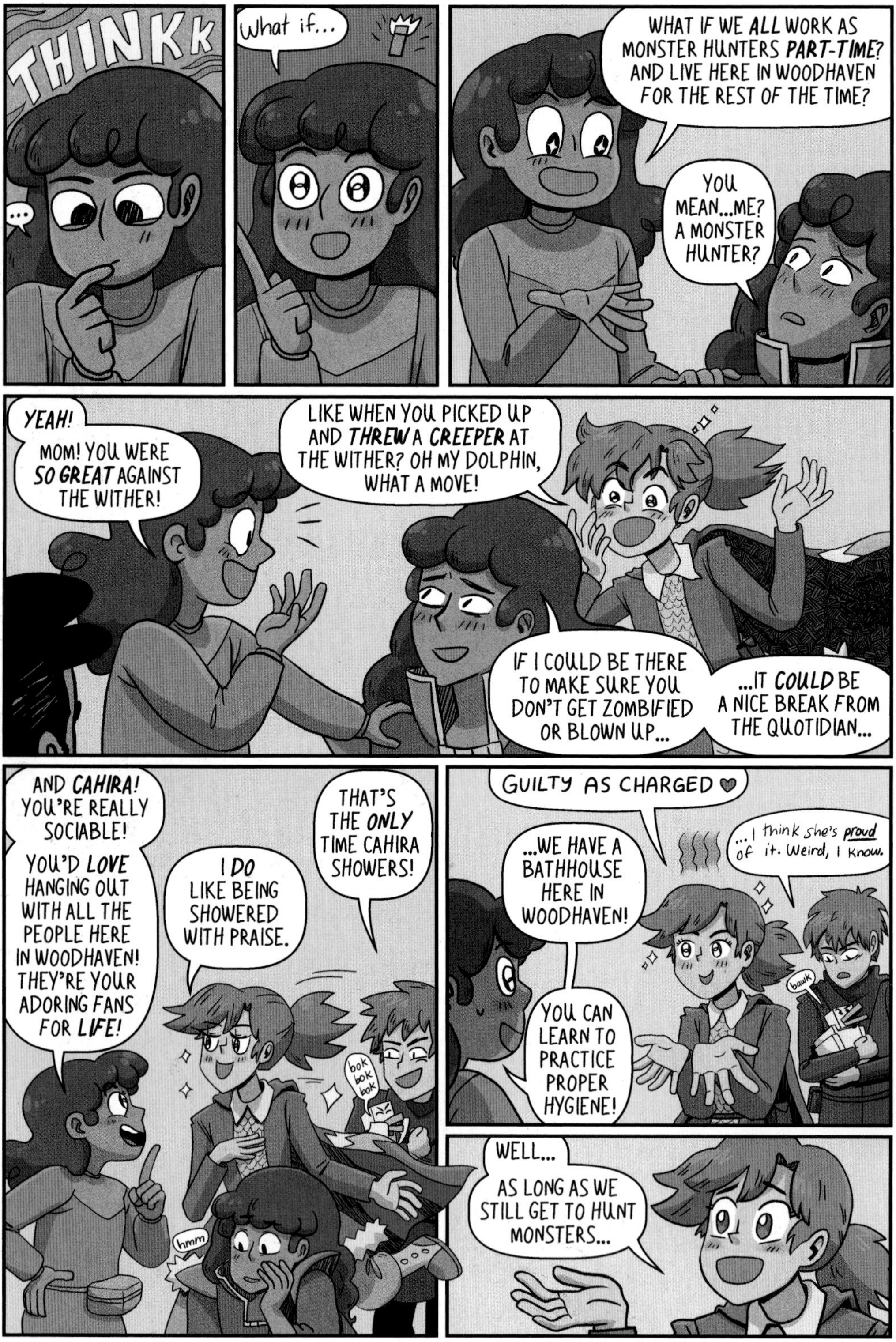
THINKk
...
What if...
WHAT IF WE ALL WORK AS MONSTER HUNTERS PART-TIME? AND LIVE HERE IN WOODHAVEN FOR THE REST OF THE TIME?
YOU MEAN...ME? A MONSTER HUNTER?
YEAH!
MOM! YOU WERE SO GREAT AGAINST THE WITHER!
LIKE WHEN YOU PICKED UP AND THREW A CREEPER AT THE WITHER? OH MY DOLPHIN, WHAT A MOVE!
IF I COULD BE THERE TO MAKE SURE YOU DON'T GET ZOMBIFIED OR BLOWN UP...
...IT COULD BE A NICE BREAK FROM THE QUOTIDIAN...
AND CAHIRA! YOU'RE REALLY SOCIABLE!
YOU'D LOVE HANGING OUT WITH ALL THE PEOPLE HERE IN WOODHAVEN! THEY'RE YOUR ADORING FANS FOR LIFE!
I DO LIKE BEING SHOWERED WITH PRAISE.
THAT'S THE ONLY TIME CAHIRA SHOWERS!
bok bok bok
hmm
GUILTY AS CHARGED
...WE HAVE A BATHHOUSE HERE IN WOODHAVEN!
...I think she's proud of it. Weird, I know.
bawk
YOU CAN LEARN TO PRACTICE PROPER HYGIENE!
WELL...
AS LONG AS WE STILL GET TO HUNT MONSTERS...

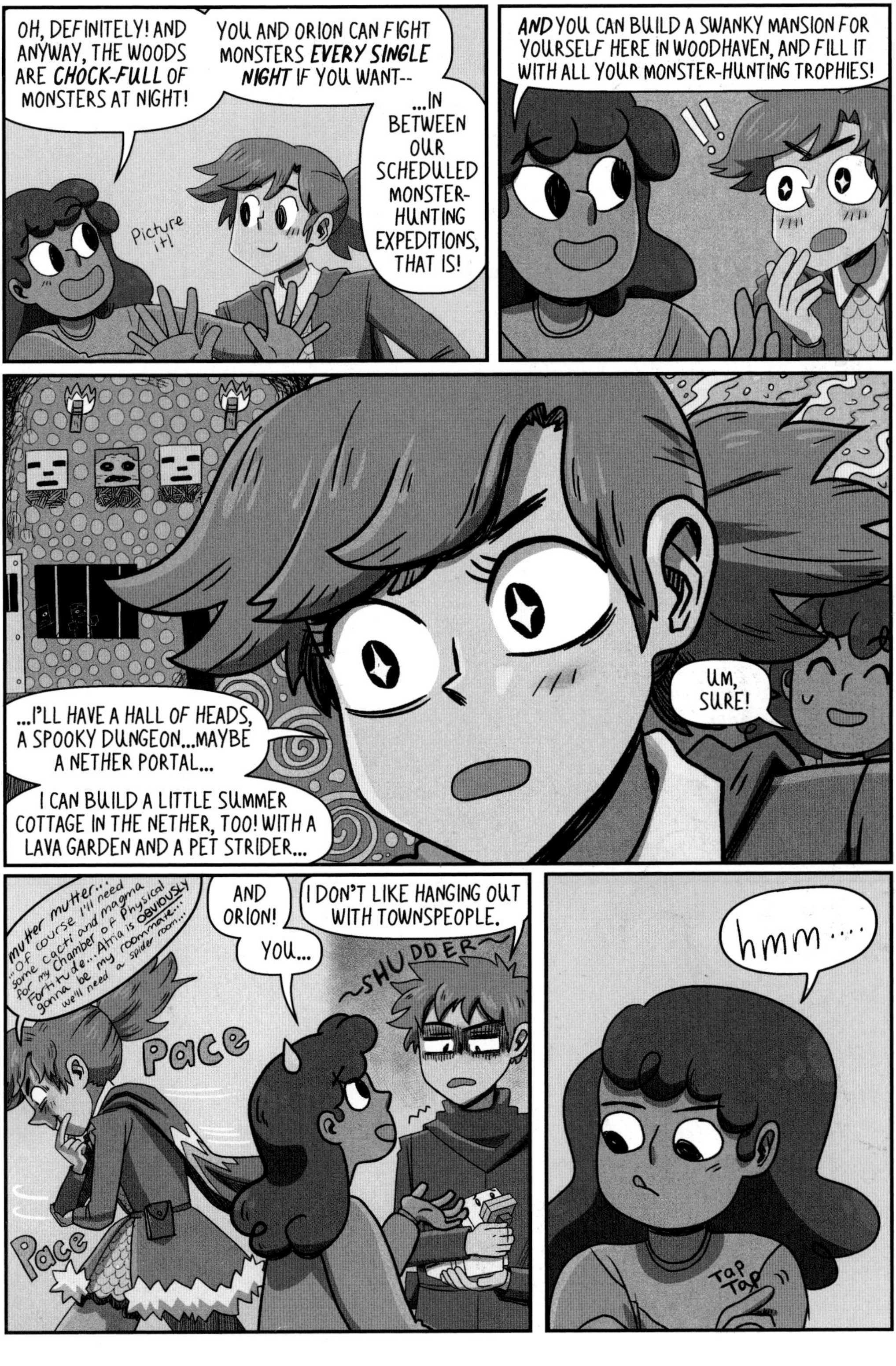
OH, DEFINITELY! AND ANYWAY, THE WOODS ARE CHOCK-FULL OF MONSTERS AT NIGHT!
Picture it!
YOU AND ORION CAN FIGHT MONSTERS EVERY SINGLE NIGHT IF YOU WANT--
...IN BETWEEN OUR SCHEDULED MONSTER-HUNTING EXPEDITIONS, THAT IS!
AND YOU CAN BUILD A SWANKY MANSION FOR YOURSELF HERE IN WOODHAVEN, AND FILL IT WITH ALL YOUR MONSTER-HUNTING TROPHIES!
!!
...I'LL HAVE A HALL OF HEADS, A SPOOKY DUNGEON...MAYBE A NETHER PORTAL...
I CAN BUILD A LITTLE SUMMER COTTAGE IN THE NETHER, TOO! WITH A LAVA GARDEN AND A PET STRIDER...
UM, SURE!
mutter mutter... ...Of course I'll need some cacti and magma for my Chamber of Physical Fortitude... Atria is OBVIOUSLY gonna be my roommate... we'll need a spider room...
Pace
Pace
AND ORION!
YOU...
I DON'T LIKE HANGING OUT WITH TOWNSPEOPLE.
~SHUDDER~
hmm....
Tap Tap

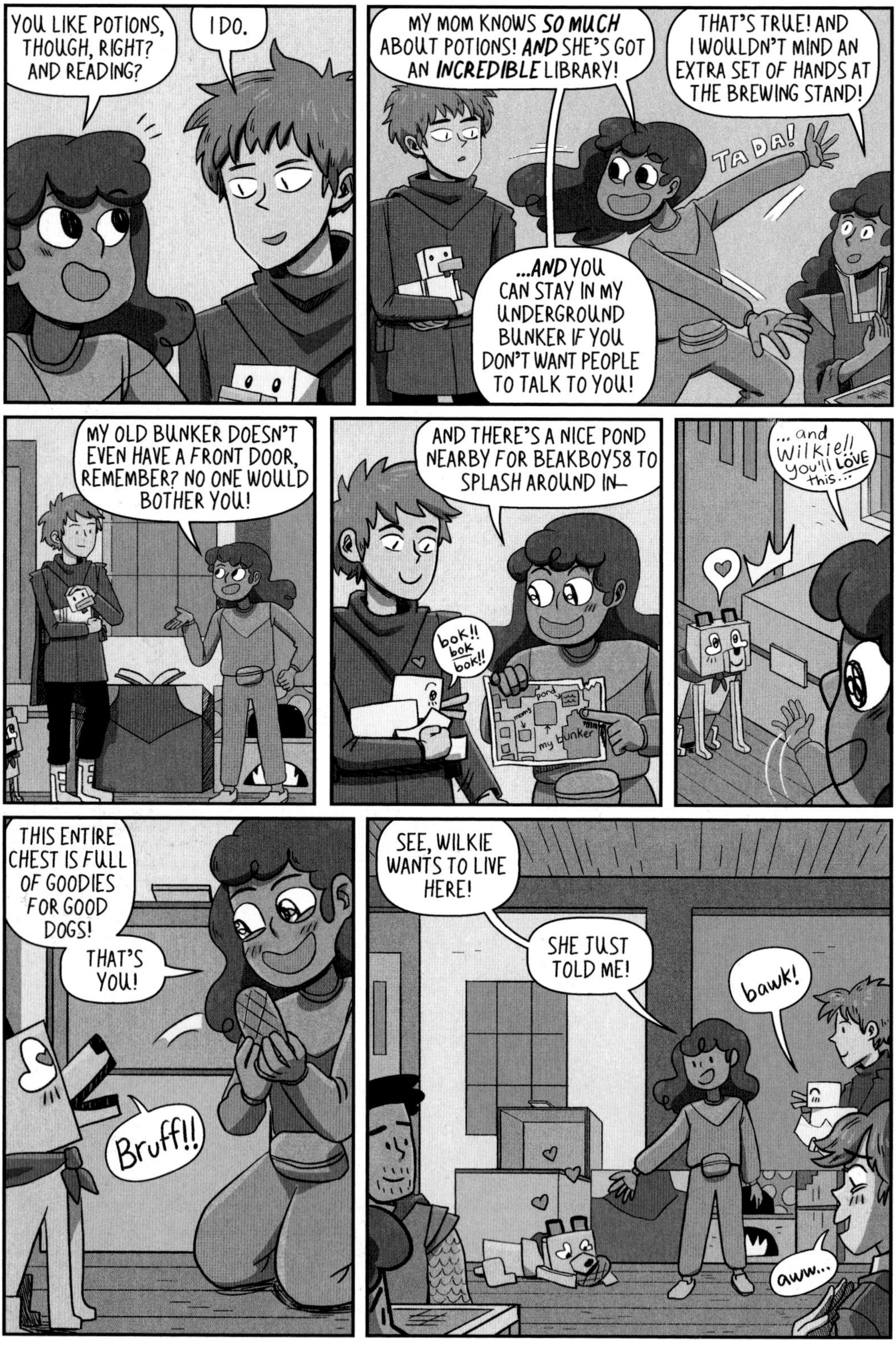
YOU LIKE POTIONS, THOUGH, RIGHT? AND READING?
I DO.
MY MOM KNOWS SO MUCH ABOUT POTIONS! AND SHE'S GOT AN INCREDIBLE LIBRARY!
THAT'S TRUE! AND I WOULDN'T MIND AN EXTRA SET OF HANDS AT THE BREWING STAND!
TA DA!
...AND YOU CAN STAY IN MY UNDERGROUND BUNKER IF YOU DON'T WANT PEOPLE TO TALK TO YOU!
MY OLD BUNKER DOESN'T EVEN HAVE A FRONT DOOR, REMEMBER? NO ONE WOULD BOTHER YOU!
AND THERE'S A NICE POND NEARBY FOR BEAKBOY58 TO SPLASH AROUND IN—
bok!! bok bok!!
pond
moms
my bunker
...and Wilkie!! you'll LOVE this...
THIS ENTIRE CHEST IS FULL OF GOODIES FOR GOOD DOGS!
THAT'S YOU!
Bruff!!
SEE, WILKIE WANTS TO LIVE HERE!
SHE JUST TOLD ME!
bawk!
aww...

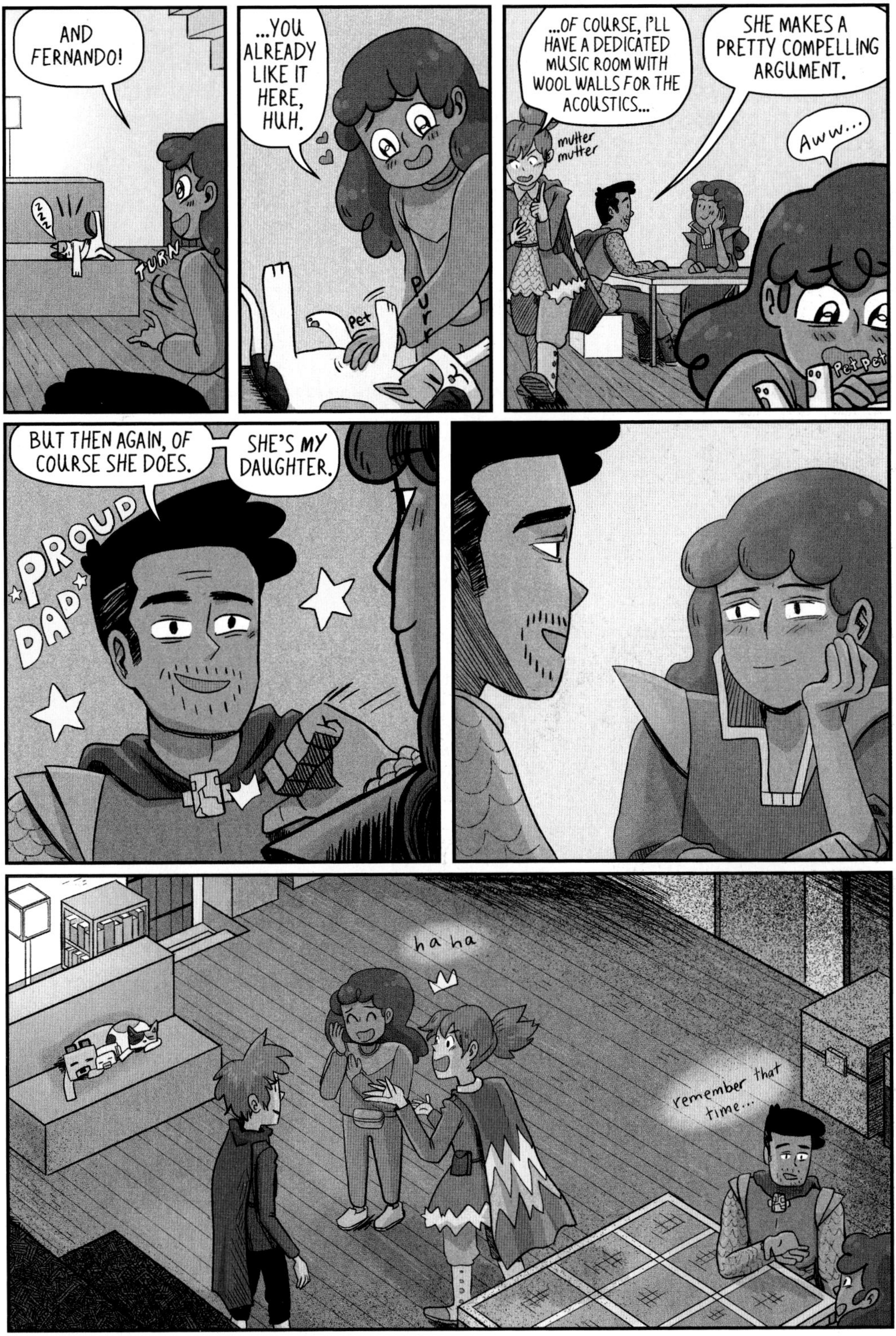
AND FERNANDO!
zzz
TURN
...YOU ALREADY LIKE IT HERE, HUH.
Pet
Purr
...OF COURSE, I'LL HAVE A DEDICATED MUSIC ROOM WITH WOOL WALLS FOR THE ACOUSTICS...
mutter mutter
SHE MAKES A PRETTY COMPELLING ARGUMENT.
Aww...
Pet pet
BUT THEN AGAIN, OF COURSE SHE DOES.
SHE'S MY DAUGHTER.
PROUD DAD
ha ha
remember that time...

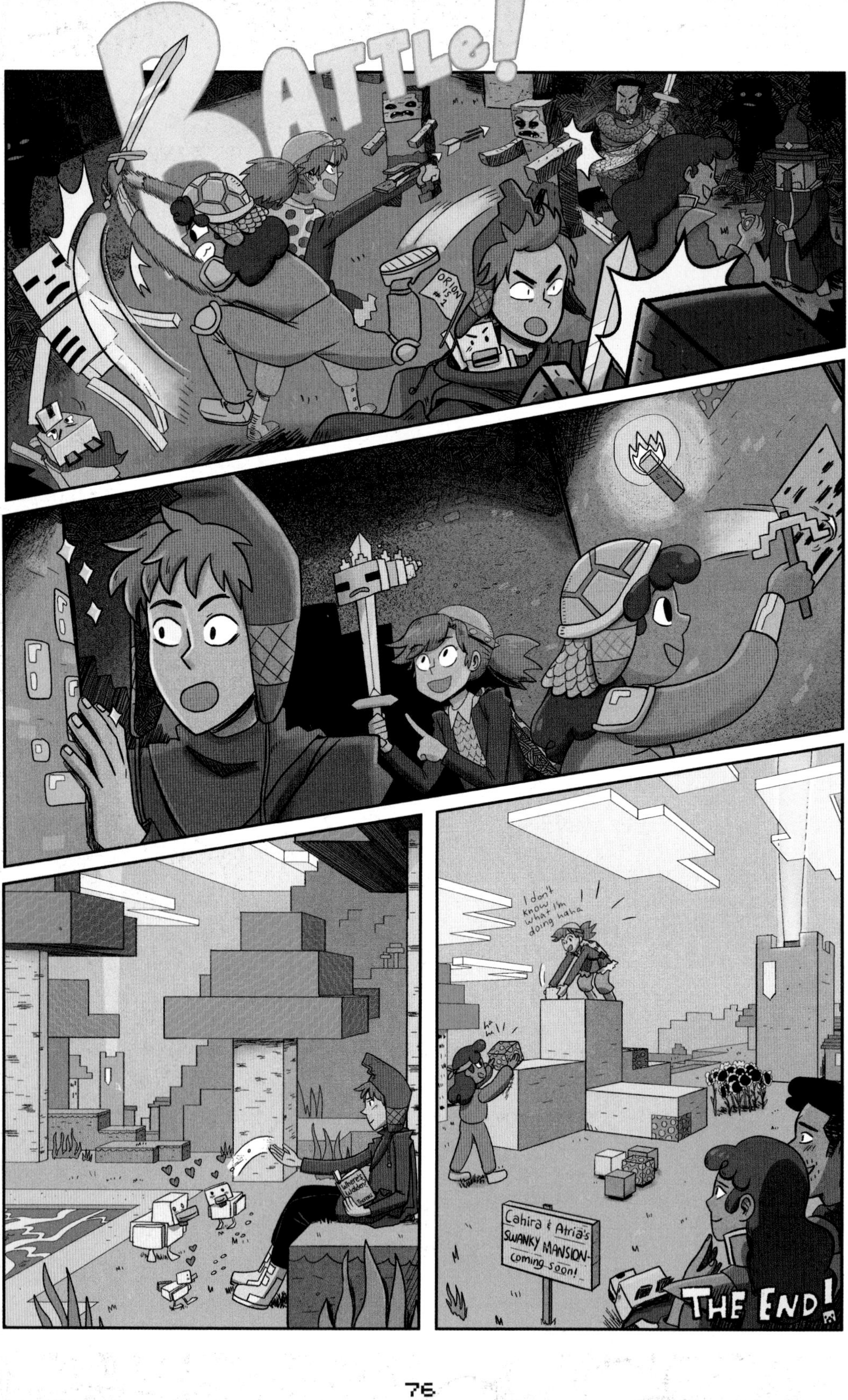
BATTLE!
ORION IS #1
Where's Waldo?
I don't know what I'm doing haha
ha ha
Cahira & Atria's SWANKY MANSION coming soon!
THE END!

PAINTING MADE EASY

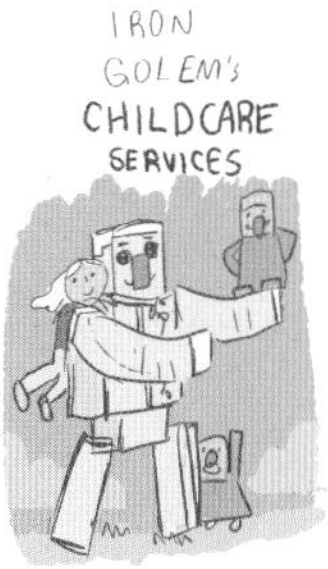

IRON GOLEM's
CHILDCARE SERVICES

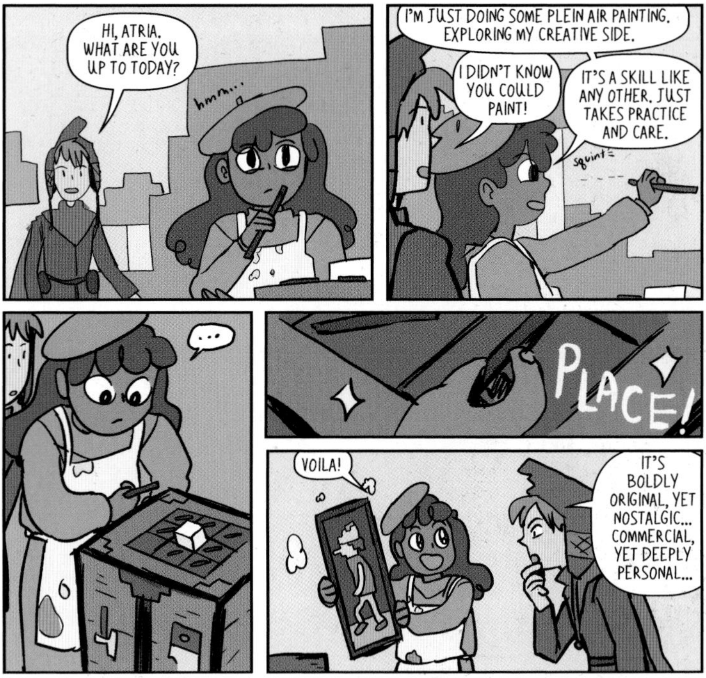

HI, ATRIA. WHAT ARE YOU UP TO TODAY?
hmm...
I'M JUST DOING SOME PLEIN AIR PAINTING. EXPLORING MY CREATIVE SIDE.
I DIDN'T KNOW YOU COULD PAINT!
IT'S A SKILL LIKE ANY OTHER. JUST TAKES PRACTICE AND CARE.
squint
...
PLACE!
VOILA!
IT'S BOLDLY ORIGINAL, YET NOSTALGIC... COMMERCIAL, YET DEEPLY PERSONAL...

STRIDERS ON THE STORM

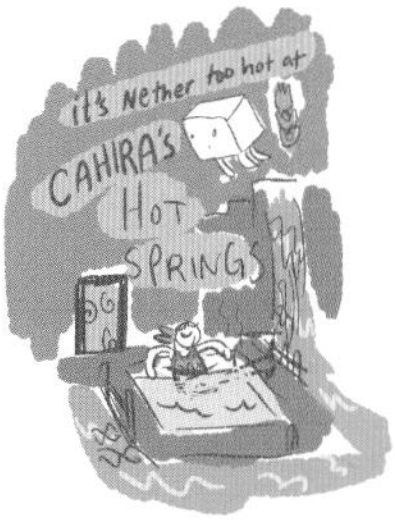

it's Nether too hot at
CAHIRA'S
HOT
SPRINGS

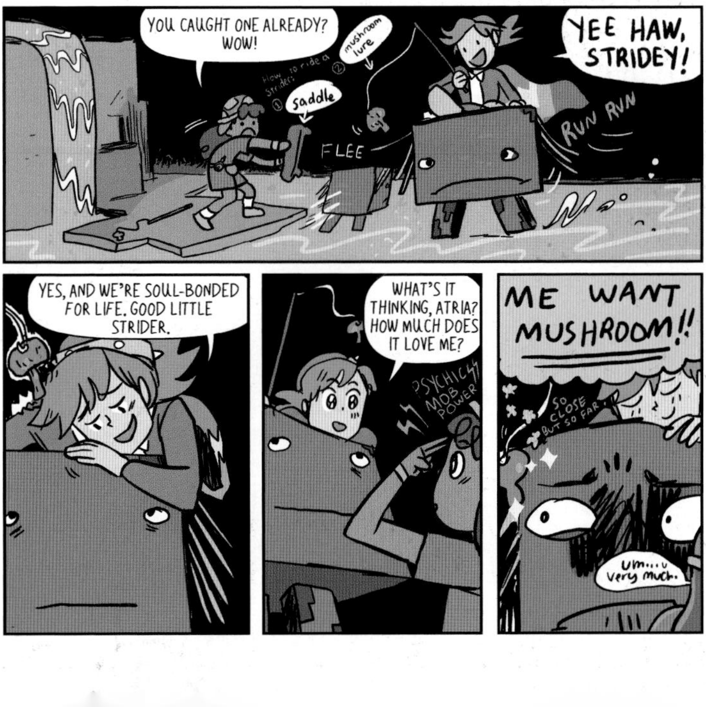

YOU CAUGHT ONE ALREADY? WOW!
How to ride a Strider:
① saddle
② mushroom lure
FLEE
YEE HAW, STRIDEY!
RUN RUN
YES, AND WE'RE SOUL-BONDED FOR LIFE. GOOD LITTLE STRIDER.
WHAT'S IT THINKING, ATRIA? HOW MUCH DOES IT LOVE ME?
PSYCHIC MOB POWER
ME WANT MUSHROOM!!
SO CLOSE BUT SO FAR
um... very much.

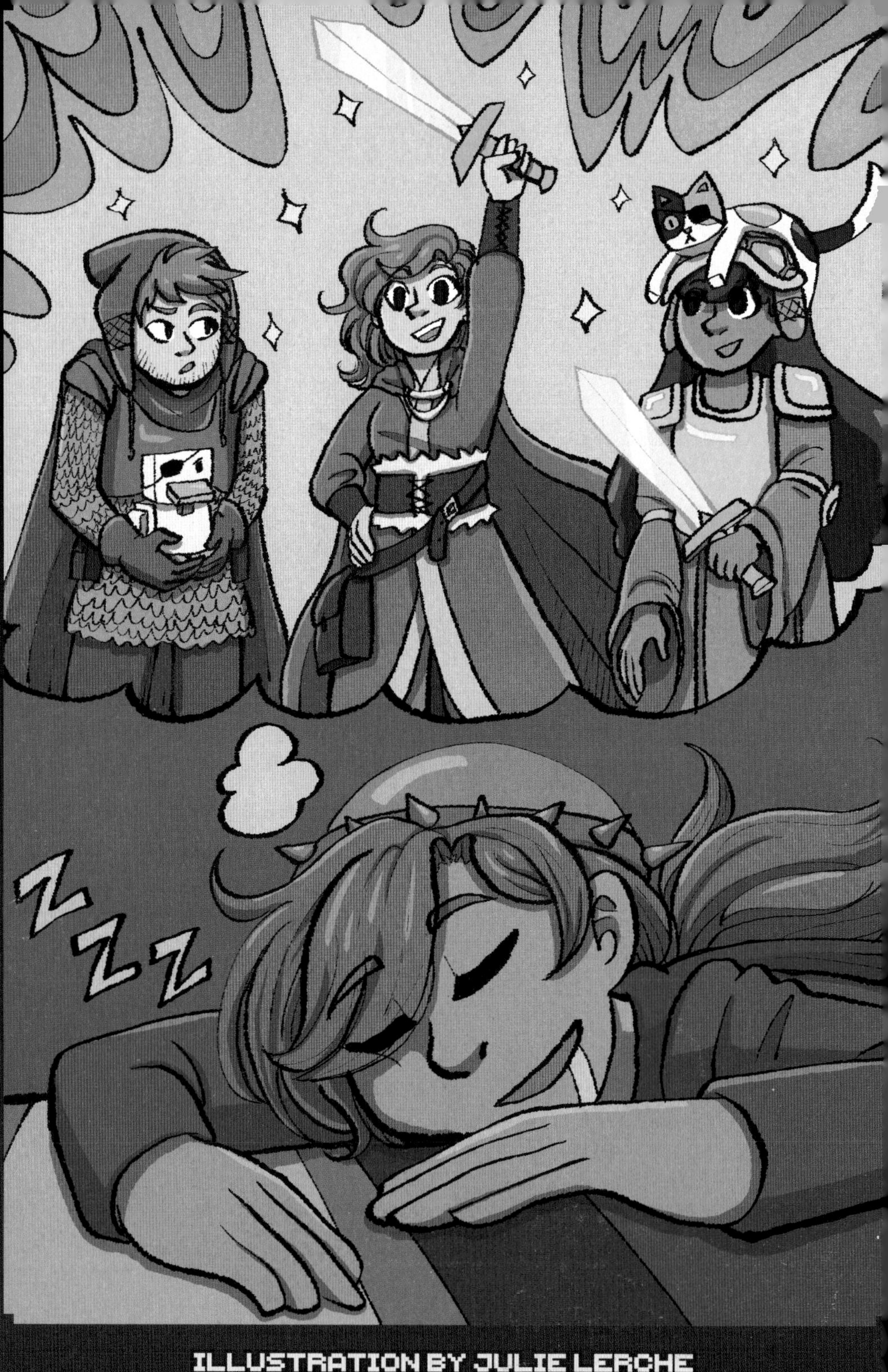
ZZZ

ILLUSTRATION BY JULIE LERCHE

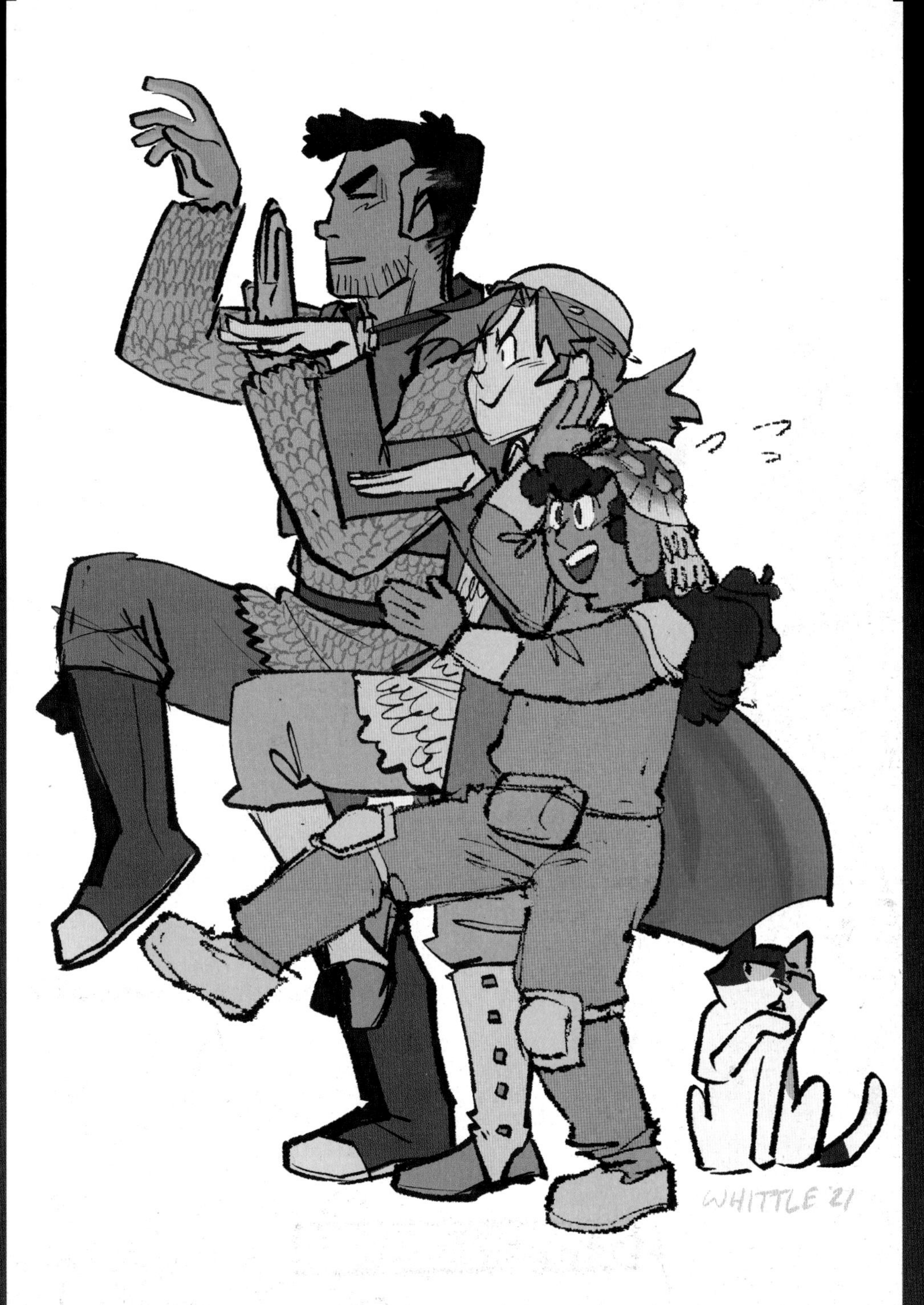
WHITTLE '21

ILLUSTRATION BY KNACK WHITTLE

MINECRAFT
OPEN WORLD

EXPLORE THE OVERWORLD IN THIS NEW TALE FROM THE WORLD'S BEST-SELLING VIDEOGAME, MINECRAFT!

Sarah is new to the world of Minecraft, and without much knowledge on the world or how to play, she finds herself looking to veteran player Hector for help. Hector isn't used to exploring the Minecraft world with anyone other than his parents, so he's reluctant at first. However, Sarah's enthusiasm and all-around energy bring Hector around, and the two become partners—but more importantly, friends!

Join Sarah and Hector on a brand-new adventure that takes them from the Overworld to the Nether, encountering numerous fan-favorite dangers and treasures along the way!

INTO THE NETHER

AVAILABLE OCTOBER 2022!